A GENTLEMAN'S PROMISE

Lesley,

All best wishes,

Perry

A Gentleman's Promise

PENNY HAMPSON

ISBN: 978-1-9160245-4-0 print copy
ISBN: 978-1-9160245-5-7 ebook

PP&M Publishing

Also by Penny Hampson:
The Gentlemen Series
(Regency Historical Mystery/Romances)
An Officer's Vow
A Bachelor's Pledge

The Unquiet Spirit
(A Contemporary Spooky Mystery/Romance)

Acknowledgements and Author Note

I DECIDED TO BRING out this second edition of *A Gentleman's Promise* when I got the rights back from my publisher. The plot is essentially the same, but I hope readers will find that this is a much improved version of the tale I originally told back in 2018. My grateful thanks go to my editor, Jenny Papworth of The History Quill and to Design For Writers who came up with a lovely revamped cover. Most of all, my thanks go to my husband, Mike, who has supported and encouraged my writing career every step of the way.

Chapter 1

THERE WAS NO GETTING away from it – someone wanted him dead. The trigger had surely been the notice of his recently acquired title in the *Gazette*. Richard Lacey's mouth twisted. Who begrudged him the title of viscount enough to try and kill him?

Richard eyed the decaying façade of Easterby Hall as he brought his curricle to a halt before the front door. Well, he was here now. With luck, he would find the answer. His gaze raked over pointed gables and large chimney stacks. No doubt at one time it had been an inviting house. Today there was a definite air of neglect. The disappearing sun glinted off stone-mullioned windows, and a lone curl of smoke ascended from one of the chimneys. Richard sighed. A closer inspection would be required before he could come to any firm decision about whether to keep the property, but at least it seemed habitable.

The impatient snorting and pawing of the horses drew Richard's attention back to his immediate problems. He handed the reins to his groom and climbed down, giving a reassuring pat to the nearside horse's flank.

'Steady, boys. Soon have you rubbed down and watered.'

'Shall I take them round to the stables, sir?' asked his groom.

'Yes, see what you can find.'

The front door at the top of the steps remained closed. *Fool.* Obviously, he wasn't expected. What was he thinking? If the interior was in too poor a state, he'd return to the inn at Minster Lovell. Not something he wanted to do. Like his horses, he'd had enough of travelling for the day.

Flexing his shoulders to ease aching muscles, Richard's hopes for a hot bath, a decent meal, and a warm bed began to fade as he eyed the closed door.

He smiled to himself and shook his head. *Must be getting set in my ways if all I'm anticipating is a bath and an early night.* His boots thudded on the steps as he marched to the door and gave the bell pull a vicious tug. Chimes resonated through the house. What seemed like minutes later, footsteps could be heard clattering over a tiled floor. A key grated in the lock. Through the now partly opened door, a grey-haired gentleman of advanced years peered out, the expression on his face far from welcoming.

'Yes, yes, may I help you? I'm afraid the family are not at home to visitors at present.'

The old man's querulous tone indicated that he'd been disturbed from a far more pleasant activity than opening the front door to passing strangers. Controlling his temper – this was now his property, after all – Richard replied with his own question.

'And you are…?'

The old chap pulled himself up to his full height and announced, 'I am Wrighton, butler to the late Lord Easterby. Who might you be, sir?'

'Richard Lacey, Viscount Easterby. Your new employer.'

Richard enjoyed the momentary look of shock on the

butler's face before the old retainer remembered his duty and opened the door to its full extent.

With a shaky bow, the butler greeted him. 'Welcome, my lord. I humbly apologise. We had no notice of your arrival.'

Wrighton gestured to a door to the left of the entrance hall. 'If you would care to come into the library for now, my lord, I'll arrange for some refreshments.' The old man cleared his throat, clearly still nervous. 'However, I'm afraid Mrs Henning hasn't got a fully stocked pantry at the moment, what with there only being a few of us kept on here.'

Richard, tired and hungry and guessing the reason for the butler's anxiety, decided to cut to the essentials.

'Never mind, I don't require anything fancy. Something nourishing will suffice. My groom has taken the curricle round to the stables. Will he be able to find everything he needs there, or will it be necessary to return to Minster Lovell for stabling?'

To Richard's surprise, the butler now looked affronted.

'No need for that, sir. Joe Henning will see to everything. He'll be right glad to have some quality cattle to tend to again. Joe's been head groom here for many a year. He'll show your man where all the tackle and fodder are kept and where he can bed down for the night.'

Richard made his way towards the door that the butler had indicated, taking in with approval the gleaming linenfold panelling lining the walls and the glossy polished finish on the wooden furniture. The smell of beeswax hung in the air. It was clear that someone loved this old place.

'I'll have a bedroom made ready and hot water sent up as soon as possible, my lord. Barker, the family's solicitor, notified us that your claim to the title had been approved, but I'm afraid he omitted to let us know when you would arrive, so you find us sadly unprepared.'

'Well, never mind, Wrighton. I'm here now. There's a valise in my curricle with my night things. My valet and my man of business will also be coming within the next day or so. I intend to go over the account books and see how matters stand since Lord Easterby's demise. I daresay there are some things that need putting to rights.'

Wrighton's head bobbed up and down.

'Oh indeed. Yes, my lord. Things have been sadly neglected, especially outside, as you will see.' The old man wrung his hands. 'No disrespect to our bailiff, but the courts wouldn't allow him the funds to make necessary improvements. The house staff and tenants are relieved that matters are now sorted.'

Richard sent the old chap a reassuring smile.

'I've no intention of permitting any more neglect to the estate or its people. I'll be assessing what needs to be done, and all will be treated fairly in return for loyalty and hard work.'

Richard stepped into the library, which turned out to be a room of pleasing proportions, he noted gratefully, as he surveyed the bookcases. He always enjoyed spending time in a room filled with books. Holland covers shrouded the chairs, and a large fireplace – laid for a fire as yet unlit – dominated one side of the room. Despite the chill in the air, the room exuded a sense of peace and comfort.

Richard turned to Wrighton, who'd remained at the door.

'What staff are there here at present?'

'Not many, my lord. Apart from myself and Mrs Wrighton, who is the housekeeper, there's Mrs Henning the cook, one scullery maid, and a maid of all work. A couple of the village girls come in once a month to help clean and air all the rooms.' He sent Richard a meaningful look. 'Mrs Wrighton can't abide the house being empty and unloved. She's worked here since she was a girl and loves the place.'

Richard smiled. So that explained the cared-for feel.

'Mrs Henning has worked here nearly as long,' Wrighton continued. 'Joe, her son, is head groom, though we only have a few horses left. And there's Mr Finch the gardener...' Wrighton frowned.

'Go on,' prompted Richard.

'Well... He's getting on in years, but he manages to keep the formal gardens tidy. The park is too much for him on his own, sir. You see, the rest of the staff were let go after the old viscount's death and the dowager moved to London.' He shook his head. 'A sad business.'

Yes, a sad business, indeed. There'd been quite a to-do over the situation. Richard had discovered that the family to which he was linked had been extraordinarily unlucky. First, the son and heir, the Honourable Frederick Smythe – unmarried and a lifelong wastrel by all accounts – had died in a hunting accident five years previously. He'd been found with his neck broken after being thrown by his horse.

Around the same time, the younger son – an avid antiquarian – together with his wife and children had disappeared without trace somewhere in the Ottoman Empire. The aged viscount, rocked by these disasters, had died within a year of his eldest son's demise.

The courts, however, in their wisdom, had in fact only recently ruled that the younger son and his heir were certainly dead, notwithstanding that the normal period of seven years for such a declaration had not yet expired. The title was on the point of extinction and the estate was to be broken up and sold when, through the diligence of his solicitor, Richard's claim to it had been established. Something that had been as much a surprise to Richard as to everyone else.

Richard watched approvingly as Wrighton swept the covers off the furniture, located a spill on the mantelpiece, and set light to the fire with a small tinderbox he took from his pocket. Soon, plumes of smoke issued from the kindling at the base of the piled firewood in the grate.

'Tell Mrs Wrighton to hire any extra hands she needs for the house. I don't envisage doing much entertaining, but I'm sure she could do with more help, in any case. I can see she has made a valiant effort and I commend her for it.' Richard cocked his head. 'Now, about that food?' His stomach was beginning to think his throat had been cut.

Wrighton's wrinkled face broke into a broad smile.

'Yes, my lord, right away. And thank you, my lord. Mrs Wrighton will be delighted to carry out your instructions.'

Settled at last in a large leather armchair in front of the fireplace with his booted feet on a footstool, Richard felt the tension of the previous few days finally depart. Strange days and deeply disturbing, if the truth be known. The number of unfortunate occurrences had stretched even his normally sanguine nerves.

First had been the attack by two footpads in St James's two evenings previously. Not an unusual occurrence in itself – unscrupulous sorts were known to lie in wait for tipsy gentlemen leaving their clubs. He'd been celebrating the unexpected acquisition of his title, published only that morning, with George, his brother-in-law. Neither of them were great drinkers, and they'd luckily only been a little bosky when they'd departed White's. What was unusual was the fact that the two scoundrels concentrated their efforts on Richard and ignored George. There'd been no attempt to snatch his watch or fob either, just a persistent pummelling of his body. Somehow, he'd known that if they got him on the ground, they'd ensure he never got up. It was solely down to George's prompt action in firing his pistol, which found its target in the leg of one of the assailants, that the two villains abandoned their attack. But for George's intervention, Richard knew that he'd probably not be breathing the air today.

Then the girth of Richard's saddle had unaccountably snapped during the course of his morning ride in Hyde Park the day before. Sharp inquiries made of his distressed head groom had elicited no satisfactory explanation for the incident. One of the stable lads claimed to have sighted a stranger loitering near the tack room in the early hours, a chap who'd run off when challenged. As nothing appeared to have been taken, no more was thought of it until Richard had returned from his ride in an uncharacteristic bad temper, leading his mount and sporting several bruises.

Finally, that very morning, Richard had almost been driven into a ditch by a passing rider who'd cracked his whip over Richard's greys just as he was approaching a sharp bend. Top sawyer that he was, it had still taken some minutes to regain control of the highly strung pair, by which time the other rider was well out of sight.

Now that he was safely at Easterby Hall, surely there would be no further mishaps… at least for now? He'd taken a risk coming on his own, not wanting to admit that he truly might be in danger and telling himself that coincidences happened. But after a day's reflection, he wasn't quite so sure.

An hour or so later, having roused himself sufficiently to wash in the chilly dressing room attached to his bedchamber, Richard was beginning to feel human again. His supper, served in the hastily prepared dining room, had been a hearty meal of mutton broth well supplied with vegetables. It was accompanied by freshly baked bread, a game pie, a rather nice cheese, and some quince jelly, all washed down with a tankard or two of the local ale. Feeling replete, Richard returned to the library and settled again in the armchair near the now-blazing fire, a decanter of brandy at his elbow. He'd every intention of making a start on the estate papers. However, the warmth of the fire, the flickering candlelight, and the comfort of the chair all conspired against him. Feeling decidedly sleepy, he was on the point of retiring for the night to his hopefully less frigid bedroom – it contained a temptingly soft and capacious bed, after all – when all hell broke loose.

Chapter 2

It was almost dark as the Honourable Emma Smythe and her brother James reached Minster Lovell. Their pace had slowed with the passing of the hours, and Emma was growing anxious that they might have to spend another evening under the stars – not a pleasant prospect. The cloudless evening sky was giving a clear indication that a frost was in store.

It was only when they'd passed through the village that she'd at last begun to recognise some landmarks.

'I'm sure the gates to Easterby Hall are only a short distance up this road. Somewhere on the right, if I'm not mistaken.'

'I hope so. I don't know how much further I can walk.'

Emma smiled and gave her brother an encouraging tug on the sleeve.

'Not far now, Jamie. I'm sure of it, love.'

Don't stop. Got to get there. Get Jamie home safe. The words repeated in her head. She'd ignore the agony in her feet and the exhaustion of her body until she'd seen her brother safely home. It was her duty as his sister. Despite the pain slicing through her at every step, she knew she couldn't give up.

Emma's worn spirits lifted briefly as the vaguely remembered gates came into view, but as she drew closer a shiver of foreboding ran down her spine. The gates were propped up, leaning drunkenly off their hinges and the once-pristine gravel drive was now peppered with clumps of grass, the bordering shrubs overgrown and unkempt. Emma's apprehension grew. Grandfather had been proud of his demesne. Woe betide the gardener if a weed had been spied amongst the flowerbeds. But ground elder and brambles now trespassed freely across the driveway. This wasn't right.

In the meantime, Jamie, oblivious to these signs of neglect, had quickened his pace and was peering eagerly through the gloom at the surrounding parkland.

'Look, lights over there,' he shouted. 'It can't be far now and someone is at home. Come on, Emm!'

'Yes, I see. Please wait for me. I can't go any faster.'

Jamie slowed his steps momentarily but was unable to contain his excitement.

'Oh goodness. We're here at last. But...'

Jamie halted so suddenly that Emma almost bumped into him. 'Will Grandfather remember me? I was little more than a babe in leading strings when we left.' Jamie turned a worried face to his sister. 'Emma, do you think Grandfather will even *want* to see us?'

Emma inwardly recoiled at his question, the very one she'd been asking herself. Ever since they'd set off on their long journey back to England, she'd been harbouring similar doubts about the welcome in store for them.

'Of course he will. The very idea!'

Behind her back, Emma crossed her fingers and hoped her words would prove true. In fact, there'd been no news from home for years. Despite all her father's assurances to the contrary, Emma couldn't help thinking that Grandfather had deliberately cut off connections with his younger son and his family.

'Of course he'll see us. We're his grandchildren.' It was said as much to convince herself as well as her brother.

Jamie helped Emma up the broad steps towards the front door. Almost overcome with exhaustion and fighting to remain upright, Emma closed her eyes and leaned against the wall while Jamie pulled on the bell. The stone felt cold and unwelcoming against her skin.

Footsteps sounded, a key turned, then the creaking door opened, throwing a shaft of light on her brother.

'Yes? Who's calling at this time of night?' It was a man's voice. He sounded elderly. Emma tensed in anticipation. Was he someone who would remember them?

'We're James and Emma Smythe, grandchildren of Viscount Easterby. P-please let him know we are here.' Jamie's quavering voice betrayed his nerves.

The door opened wider, illuminating her brother's dishevelled and disreputable appearance.

'Nonsense. Away with you, or I'll call the magistrate. The Honourable Charles and his family are dead. How dare you come here pretending to be someone you're not? Away with you, I say.'

Emma's insides coiled in fear. This wasn't good; the man was angry. Had her doubts been justified?

To his credit, Jamie stood his ground and persisted.

'No, no, it's true. Please let us in. Please let me speak to Grandfather.'

Those were the last words Emma heard as she slid down the wall towards the ground, not even feeling the impact as her head struck the doorstep.

Seeing the lad turn away, Wrighton opened the door wider to ensure he could watch him return down the drive. Instead, there were further horrors in the shape of another urchin lying on the ground. Even by the meagre light afforded by his flickering lamp, it was evident to the old chap that this youngster was ill. Not an unkindly man, Wrighton decided that a wiser mind than his was required.

'Mrs Wrighton, Mrs Wrighton, do come at once. Mrs Wrighton, hurry!'

'What's amiss, Wrighton? What's all the noise?' a deep male voice boomed out behind him, causing the old butler to freeze.

Richard strode across the tiled hallway. With one glimpse, he took in the butler's shocked countenance and the two small figures on the top front step, one of whom appeared to be unconscious. The other was crouched over his prone companion, alternately urging him to get up, then darting looks of fear at the still-immobilised Wrighton. Richard came to a swift decision. He had to take control before things got out of hand.

'For goodness' sake, pull yourself together, man. We need to bring them in,' he said, relieving his transfixed butler of the lamp and placing it on the floor. Then Richard gently but decisively pulled the crouching boy away from his unconscious companion and shoved him into Wrighton's arms before scooping up the remaining child.

Wrighton came to his senses at last.

'My lord, may I suggest the drawing room? There is a sofa in there. The covers are still on, so the upholstery will not suffer, and I can soon light the fire.'

The lad, passive in the butler's grasp, followed Richard's every move with startled blue eyes as Wrighton endeavoured to guide him in the direction of the drawing room. At that moment, the door from the staff quarters banged open.

'Well, Mr Wrighton, I'm here. What do you mean by shouting like that? Oh, my goodness...'

Better equipped than her husband to deal with domestic emergencies, the housekeeper bustled across to open the drawing-room door.

'Over here, my lord. I'll get some lights and start the fire. The sofa here is larger than the one in the library and nearer the fireplace.'

Richard gratefully followed the housekeeper, who he'd decided had more wits than her husband. Having placed his still-unconscious burden down, Richard reached out with careful fingers to remove the lad's battered hat, his eyes widening at the boy's pale, translucent skin, rosebud mouth, and long, dark eyelashes, all framed by thick chestnut hair. Richard frowned, briefly pondering the lad's identity, before a trickle of blood oozing down one ashen cheek sent all thoughts about the origins of his unexpected visitor fleeing.

'Bring some cloths and clean water, Mrs Wrighton. I think the lad caught his head against the flagstone as he collapsed. He'll have a bruise to boast about come tomorrow.'

Filled with a gut-wrenching fear that the lad might die, Richard kept a grip on his nerves by focussing on a closer examination of the lad's clothes. They were threadbare and somewhat grubby but had been well made. He started to remove the worn and dirty boots encasing the lad's feet. The first one came off easily enough, so Richard proceeded to peel off the threadbare stocking, gasping at the sight of the dried blood caking the skin and the angry blisters adorning the raw ankle. It took a great effort not to cast up his accounts.

'Oh my goodness, the poor love,' exclaimed Mrs Wrighton over Richard's shoulder. 'Let me do that, sir, while you speak to the other lad,' she ordered, elbowing him out of the way.

'Yes, of course,' he answered, feeling guiltily relieved. The sight of blood always unnerved him, bringing as it did too many memories. Richard turned to the other urchin, still trembling near the door, the butler's firm hand on his shoulder.

'Who are you, my lad, and why are you here at this time of night?'

The stripling, eyes entirely fixed on his companion, remained silent. Richard wondered if he'd even heard. In a raised voice he repeated his questions.

The lad blinked as if coming to his senses.

'I… I'm James Smythe, son of Charles Smythe and grandson of Viscount Easterby. I want to see my grandfather. He lives here.' At Richard's look of disbelief, the lad started to fumble beneath his tattered jacket. 'See, this belonged to my father.' The boy drew a cord from around his neck, from which dangled an ornate seal, and held it out for Richard to take.

Cold against the skin of his palm, from the weight and colour, Richard knew it could only be gold. He'd been inclined to think the lad was spinning him a line, but looking at the object, his doubts receded. The seal was indeed engraved with the Easterby crest. Richard recognised it immediately – a depiction of a bear leading a bull.

He passed it back to the lad, recalling the story of the missing family. Could the boy be telling the truth?

'Where have you been? How did you get here?' Richard gestured to the figure on the sofa. 'And who is that? Your younger brother?'

'We've been living in the Peloponnesus, in southern Greece, with our parents.' The lad sniffed and wiped a grubby hand across his eyes. 'But th-they drowned some months ago. Got to Patras with help from our housekeeper's family. Then on our own to Gibraltar... We got a ship there back to England.' Casting another lingering look at the figure on the sofa, he turned worried eyes to Richard. 'And that's not my brother. Emma is my sister. I wouldn't have got here at all without her.' With a hint of defiance in his voice, he added, 'If you still don't believe me, there is further proof. Emma has it sewn in the lining of her coat for safekeeping.'

Richard, his jaw slack, stared wordlessly at the unconscious girl for several moments before finding his voice.

'How old are you, young man, and how old is your sister?' He calculated that the lad was no more than fourteen years which might make his sister what? Twelve, thirteen, possibly sixteen years at most? She certainly didn't look any older.

'I've turned thirteen, sir, and Emma had her twenty-fourth birthday just before Christmas.'

Richard sucked in his breath. Good Lord, what was he supposed to do now? Things were getting decidedly complicated. It was a young woman lying on the sofa, not a girl – and a gently born one too. He was rapidly revising his opinion of the lad's truthfulness. Surely no-one would dare to come up with such a fantastical tale? It was so unbelievable it had to be true. Then there was the seal. That was genuine. But again, it could've been stolen. He'd instruct Mrs Wrighton to bring him the young woman's jacket once she'd been comfortably settled so that he could examine the hidden documents mentioned by the lad.

But questions remained. Why had nothing been heard from the family for several years? And why appear now? If all the boy had told him was true, it was nothing short of a miracle.

Richard looked anew at the white-faced and trembling lad, noticing how the bones of his wrists jutted through the grubby skin. He looked as if he hadn't eaten a good meal in some time. 'Wrighton, take the young man down to Mrs Henning and see that he's fed and watered.'

Wrighton started at the sound of his name. He'd been giving the lad strange looks, but now his face brightened.

'Master James, it is you… and so like your papa. Why didn't I see it straightaway? To think I nearly turned you away. And poor Miss Emma too. Whatever is the world coming to?' His voice became husky as he patted the lad's shoulder. 'Don't worry, Master James. You're home now.'

Well, if the old retainer recognised the lad and the documents supported his claims, there was even more reason for him to take care of the young pair, Richard decided. They were related, albeit distantly, and as the head of the family, it was his responsibility. But the first priority was to ensure the young lady survived.

'Mrs Wrighton, where is the nearest doctor to be found? I'll ride out and fetch him.'

'Don't worry, sir,' called Wrighton over his shoulder, as he tugged the dazed lad out of the room. 'I'll send Joe for Dr Chesney. He lives in Minster Lovell, so he should be able to get here without too much delay. He's young, but he seems to know what he is doing.'

Richard hoped so. The last thing he needed was a medical fool destroying the young woman's chance of recovery. She'd banged her head hard against the flagstones, by the looks of things, and he knew head injuries could be fatal. On top of that, she looked seriously undernourished. Richard struggled to quell the anxiety churning in his stomach. Not being in control always left him unsettled.

The housekeeper turned from her task of bathing the young woman's head.

'Poor Miss Emma, still as pretty as the day she left, despite all her bruises. I remember when her father came off his horse as a lad and knocked himself unconscious. He only needed peace and quiet for a day or two. With luck that's all she needs, sir.'

Richard nodded, not quite convinced by the housekeeper's words. He ought to do something, but what? He hated feeling bacon-brained, wanting to impose order but not knowing how. He began to pace up and down.

'Would you be better off retiring to the library, sir? I can look after the young lady.'

The housekeeper's voice roused Richard from his maudlin thoughts.

'Yes, of course, Mrs Wrighton. I'll leave her in your capable hands. When it's convenient, let me have her coat. I'll need to examine the documents the lad said she is carrying.' Before he closed the door behind him, Richard added, 'Let me know if there are any changes to her condition, and notify me when the doctor arrives. If he agrees, I think she should be moved to a bedchamber. Do you think one could be aired and made up for her? She needs to be kept warm. Oh… and one for her brother.'

Mrs Wrighton shooed him away. 'Don't worry, sir. Rooms won't take long to sort. It just needs a light setting to the fires. I always make sure at least four of the bedchambers can be put to use at a moment's notice in case the dowager decides to visit.'

'Do you think you could also engage someone to stay with her? Is there anyone suitable from the village?'

The housekeeper nodded. 'I'll send for Polly. She used to work here as a personal maid to the dowager and still lives hereabouts.'

Richard returned at last to the library and his chair near the fireside. He took a fortifying gulp of the brandy he'd poured for himself before all the uproar occurred. His nerves were stretched, and he needed time to think. On the mantelpiece, two delicate porcelain figures caught his eye, a rather effete shepherd and his dainty shepherdess. To Richard's disapproval, the shepherd's wistful gaze was directed into the distance while his companion's regard was entirely on her mate. The nerve in Richard's eyelid twitched. Setting his glass down, Richard got up and gently turned the shepherd figurine to face his lady-love. His eye no longer twitching, Richard returned to his seat.

It wasn't long before Mrs Wrighton sent her husband in with the young woman's coat. Richard swiftly tore the lining and extracted the bundle of papers secreted there. Examining the water-stained and frayed documents carefully, Richard saw that they indeed supported the boy's claim that he was the missing grandson of the late viscount. Amongst official letters of introduction and formal documents granting safe passage were more personal items. One was a letter dated seven years previously, written by the viscount to his younger son, the Honourable Charles Smythe, at an address in Malta. There was a similar letter from the viscountess to Marie Smythe, her daughter-in-law, eager for news of her grandchildren, Emma and James. The poor lady was missing them desperately. Several more letters in the same vein followed. None of the letters in the bundle had been written within the last five years.

Richard pondered the implications. He was no longer Viscount Easterby, a thought that lifted his spirits. He'd never desired the added responsibilities that the viscountcy would bring. He gazed around at his surroundings – the oak panelling, tired but comfortable armchairs, book presses lining the walls. The furnishings were old and not at all the crack, as Julia, his sister, would have told him, but it was a peaceful space where a man could relax. *Never mind, I've enough comfortable rooms of my own in Cornwall and London, don't need this one as well.* An unwelcome thought intruded. He couldn't leave – not yet. There was the boy and his sister to think about. As their cousin, he had a responsibility to ensure their claims were upheld.

An icy chill ran down Richard's spine. What about those attempts on his life? He'd stopped thinking of them as accidents. They'd only occurred after his new title became public knowledge – were they connected? Richard took another fortifying gulp from his glass. Someone had definitely attempted to kill him, both in town and on the way to Minster Lovell. Something else his solicitor had mentioned nudged at his mind. There'd been rumours about Frederick's fatal accident five years previously, the same year the letters from the old viscount were dated. Odd also that nothing had been heard from Charles or his family from the same year onwards... until now. Didn't Jamie say his parents had drowned? Would the lad be the target for similar attempts once his true identity became known?

Richard leaned back in his chair, pinched the bridge of his nose and closed his eyes, telling himself that his troubles weren't over yet.

Some fifteen minutes later, Wrighton's head bobbed round the library door.

'Excuse me, sir. The doctor will be here shortly. He's been attending the vicar's son, who has suffered a tumble and hurt his leg.'

'Well, let's hope he's not long delayed.' Richard wished no harm to the vicar's son, but as far as he was concerned, the lad had chosen an inopportune moment to have a fall. Richard gestured for the butler to stay. 'I'd prefer it if the young viscount's identity is not made known outside these walls. There've been some, erm, incidents. Too many unfortunate coincidences, shall we say?'

Wrighton's eyes widened.

'Dear me, sir. What do you mean? You think Master Jamie and his sister might be in danger?'

Richard grimaced. It was time to take the bull by the horns.

'Yes. I've strong reason to believe someone may have evil designs on whoever holds the title. There have been several attempts on my life since it became public knowledge that I was the viscount.' The butler gaped at Richard's grim words. 'Until I get to the bottom of the matter, I think it wise not to put James at risk. I shall, of course, contact my solicitor immediately and get some investigations in hand.'

Seeing the strange look Wrighton was giving him, Richard added, 'Don't worry, Wrighton, I'll keep the boy and his sister safe. I don't covet the title. He is welcome to it.'

There was a pregnant pause. Richard could almost hear the cogs of the old man's mind turning.

'I understand, sir. I'll let the other staff know. You can rely on our discretion.'

'I'll do my best to sort this out and reunite the young viscount and his sister with their grandmother. His claim to the title should be straightforward, as the documents and seal seem pretty conclusive, and you and your wife have vouched for their likeness. I have every expectation that their grandmother will do the same.' Richard had an unsettling thought. 'Unless…'

'No worries on that score, sir,' said Wrighton. 'The dowager is not at all dull-witted, though she was blue-devilled for a time after the old viscount died. She'd never be taken in by imposters, but I'd swear on a stack of bibles – begging your pardon, sir – that the lad is who he says he is. She will recognise them for sure.'

'Good. In the meantime, we must keep them safe.'

At that moment, the bell sounded.

'That should be Dr Chesney. Shall I admit him, sir?'

Richard nodded and the butler scurried out.

After the doctor's departure, it was agreed that Emma should be placed in the room already prepared for Richard. After removing his things to his new bedchamber, Richard went to check on the young viscount, who was now ensconced in the chamber across the hallway. Poking his head round the door, he spied the small figure fast asleep in the middle of a large four-poster bed. Satisfied that the boy was safe, Richard returned to the drawing room. It was time to move the young lady, who was still in the deepest of sleeps.

The housekeeper looked up as Richard entered the room. 'I think she's sleeping more natural now, sir, and her colour is returning.'

Richard gazed down at the insensible girl. Her cheeks were indeed a much healthier shade. He bent down and gently scooped her into his arms. To his surprise, she turned her head into his chest and let out a gentle sigh.

At last, with the help of Mrs Wrighton, he placed his slumbering burden on the bed. He stood for a moment watching and then shook his head. How could he have been so stupid to confuse her with a boy, with her jutting cheekbones, dainty chin, and rosebud lips?

'I'll stay here for now, sir, until Polly arrives,' said Mrs Wrighton. 'Poor Miss Emma. She looks all done in. We thought they'd all perished long ago… and now here she is, and dear Master James too.' The old woman dabbed at her red-rimmed eyes with the corner of her apron. 'The dowager will be in alt to know that they're safe. The poor lady clung to the belief that they were still alive long after the rest of us had given up all hope. Inconsolable she was when the courts declared them all dead. She took it far worse than the news of Master Frederick's death.' Mrs Wrighton sent Richard a knowing look. 'If you ask me, sir, begging your pardon, but *his* passing was more like a blessing. Such trouble he caused her.'

Richard quelled his curiosity about the unlamented Frederick and, with a final glance at the sleeping figure in the bed, departed for his own room.

Richard rubbed his eyes. Goodness, he was exhausted. His new bedchamber was chilly, but he was past caring. All he wanted was a good night's sleep. Tugging his boots off, he padded over to the door and placed them neatly side by side. Next came his neckcloth, which was carefully removed and folded, then set on a chair. Just because his valet wasn't around, there was no excuse for disorder, he told himself, stifling a yawn. Next came his shirt and breeches, which he folded and placed with the discarded neckcloth. He smiled as he pulled the nightshirt from his valise. Thank goodness Carter always insisted on packing one. Richard rarely wore a nightshirt, but this night would be an exception. It was damned chilly.

Only regretting that he'd neglected to compose the letters to the dowager and his solicitor – they required a clear head after all – Richard finally crawled under the welcoming covers of the bed. His last waking thoughts were of the young lady's sleeping face.

Chapter 3

THE FOLLOWING MORNING, EMMA was gradually coming to her senses. Thoughts jostled in her head. She'd been walking with Jamie through Minster Lovell. Then there'd been a long, gravel drive. A house… yes, it was Easterby Hall. A front door. Then… nothing. Emma groaned. Her head hurt like the devil, and she couldn't remember anything save reaching Easterby Hall's front door.

'There, there, don't fret now. Everything is well. Would you like a sip of water?'

Emma's eyes shot open at the sound of the woman's voice. She blinked and screwed them shut again. Why wouldn't everything stay still? Was she in a bed or a boat? Someone held a soothing compress to her brow. Taking a deep breath, she slowly re-opened her eyes. Thank goodness the swaying had stopped. Across the room, light peeked through closed shutters, and coals glowed in a large, ornate fireplace, making the room pleasantly warm. She caught the faint smell of lavender.

Emma looked up at the young woman standing at the side of the bed. The woman smiled.

'Here, drink this. Your mouth is dry, I'll be bound.'

Feeling as weak as a kitten, Emma took a sip from the glass that the woman held to her lips. Water had never tasted as good.

'Where am I? Who are you? Where is my brother?'

Holding a finger to her pursed lips, the maid shook her head.

'Speak to me. Tell me what's happened. Where am I?' Emma's voice began to rise as panic gripped her insides.

'Oh, miss, please don't get into a pother, else I'll get into trouble.' The maid's ruddy cheeks reddened even more as her eyes checked the door. 'I've been told not to talk too much because you need to stay quiet.' Smiling shyly, she bent towards Emma and whispered, 'You're quite safe. I was told you stumbled and banged your head, and then you fell into a deep sleep. The doctor saw you last night and he'll be calling again today. He told the master that you will soon be better.'

Only slightly reassured by the maid's words and still feeling sick and slightly dizzy with no memory of what had happened, Emma persisted. 'But where am I, and where is Jamie?'

'Why, miss, you're at Easterby Hall. The new master arrived yesterday. It was he who took you in. If your brother is the young lad who also arrived last night, well, he's in the parlour having breakfast. Shall I go and fetch the housekeeper?'

Emma nodded. The maid cocked her head to one side. 'I'm Polly, by the way, miss. I used to work here, but I had to leave when...' Looking suddenly panic-stricken, she bobbed a swift curtsey and fled the room, leaving Emma on her own.

Emma, frustrated and assailed by stabbing pains in her temples, sank back into her pillows. After a short while, the aching subsided so she risked turning her head in order to inspect her surroundings. Her bed was a large four-poster with soft feather pillows, fine linen sheets, and several blankets. As her gaze trailed round the room a portrait on the wall caught her eye. It seemed familiar. Two golden-haired lads dressed in their best, the older looking sulky, his arm resting on the shoulder of his younger companion who clutched a book. Emma's eyes widened as recognition dawned. It was her papa and his older brother, Frederick. She clutched the bedclothes tighter. Where was her uncle, and why was there no sign of her grandparents?

Chills ran down her spine as fresh fears caught her in their grip. The documents she'd been carrying, where were they? There was no sign of her jacket or her clothes. Emma groaned and slid back against the pillows, dredging her memory for any clues.

Matters had gone awry several years previously when they'd left Patras in haste. Her father had been keen to reach the southern part of the Morea as quickly as possible, knowing that Elgin and his party had already excavated much of the Acropolis and other sites around Athens. He'd been determined to discover something of his own, whatever the cost. On their way to Greece, they'd met Lord Elgin in Rome. Like the Smythes, he was using the peace between Britain and France as an opportunity to travel.

While Emma and her mother had spent Palm Sunday observing the processions around St Peter's Square, her father, Charles, had called on His Lordship. Hearing about his discoveries first-hand fired an unquenchable desire in her father to emulate Elgin's achievements. Emma was certain that her father's determination not to let anything hinder his quest for antiquities – not even the safety of his family – was given added impetus by that unlucky Easter encounter.

They'd taken a ship to Malta and from there travelled to Patras. The British consul had advised against heading deeper into the Morea and certainly not on their own. There were just too many risks – from bandits, uprisings, and even pirates.

But Charles Smythe, like the stubborn man he was, had ignored all wiser counsel, and so the scene had been set for the worst of disasters. Emma swiped away a tear as she recalled her mother's words at their last private conversation. Words that she would never forget.

At the sound of a tap on the door, Emma's eyes flew open. An older woman, attired in a plain, grey wool dress and a pristine white apron, trotted in.

'Well, I'm so glad to see you awake, Miss Emma,' the woman said, her face wrinkling in a smile. 'I'll get Mrs Henning to warm you some milk. But you can't have any food until Dr Chesney says so.' She beamed down at Emma and folded her arms across her middle.

'Thank you so much. Warm milk would be lovely, Mrs…?' Emma gasped. 'Is it really you, Mrs Wrighton?' Emma's mind was so clouded that she couldn't be sure about anything.

Mrs Wrighton chuckled. 'That's right, Miss Emma. I thought you'd remember me. The last time I saw you was just before you set off on your travels.' The housekeeper's smile slipped a little. 'The dowager will be delighted to know that you've both returned safe and well. She was distraught when you left and heartbroken when she was told that you were all lost. I didn't recognise you at first, you were so bedraggled. But now there's no mistaking you – you're the image of your grandmother when she was younger.' She sent Emma a sympathetic look and shook her head. 'You'll look even better when your bruises fade and we feed you up a bit.'

The significance of the housekeeper's words finally registered with Emma.

'People thought we were dead? I don't understand. Father was punctilious in writing to Grandfather, but he never received any replies.' She frowned. 'You called Grandmamma "the dowager". When did Grandfather die?' There were so many unanswered questions.

A knock on the bedroom door saved the housekeeper from replying. The door opened and in stepped a stranger; a rather handsome-looking stranger, despite his saturnine features, dark penetrating eyes, and stern mouth. Emma blinked. Sporting a coat of dark-blue superfine matched with pale buckskin breeches and wearing a snow-white cravat at his neck, he was quite the most distinguished gentleman she had seen in a long time. Dark curls fell across his brow, and a bronzed complexion indicated he spent time outdoors. His strong jaw and aquiline nose betokened a man of character. Emma's heart began to beat faster as he scrutinised her face with intelligent eyes and a curve to his lips.

'I've come to reassure myself that you're recovering. You gave us all quite the fright last evening.'

His disturbingly pleasing voice sent warm shivers down Emma's spine and she almost forgot to breathe. His polished appearance and aura of authority had completely taken her by surprise. If she didn't pull herself together and respond, he'd be sure to think the bump to her head had knocked her silly.

'Yes, I am recovering, sir. Thank you,' Emma said at last. 'Please would you do me the honour of informing me whom I'm addressing?'

The gentleman's smile widened, transforming his appearance from one of cool authority to roguish friendliness. Emma felt the heat rising to her cheeks.

'Of course. How remiss of me. I apologise for my lack of manners.' He bowed. 'I'd quite forgotten that we haven't been properly introduced. I'm Richard Lacey, a distant cousin on my late father's side to Viscount Easterby, who, I understand, was your grandfather.' As the gentleman spoke, he placed a bundle of papers on the writing desk near the bed, which Emma recognised with shock as the letters she'd kept hidden in her jacket. 'May I return these to you? Mrs Wrighton kindly passed them to me last night when you were unconscious.'

Relieved that she had her letters back and about to thank him, she almost missed the significance of his earlier words. Then it struck her. Grandfather was indeed dead. Mr Lacey had confirmed what the housekeeper had unwittingly divulged by referring to Grandmamma as "the dowager". A knot formed in her stomach. She'd never see her beloved grandfather again. Blinking away her tears, she controlled her features, determined not to succumb to emotion before a stranger's gaze, not even a stranger as compelling as Mr Lacey.

Mr Lacey seemed to realise his mistake. He ran a nervous finger round his cravat.

'I'm truly sorry to be the bearer of such sad news, Miss Smythe. I should've recalled that you and your brother were unaware of the viscount's death.' He carried on, as if trying to atone for his faux pas. 'I've written to your grandmother, who I'm sure will be delighted to hear that you and your brother are both alive and well.' There was another smile, this time an apologetic one. 'I'm afraid I'm not informed on the state of her health, so I don't know if she'll travel here or if she'll wish you to join her in London. Of course, I'll be happy to arrange for your conveyance there once you've fully recovered.' Clearing his throat and looking a little sheepish, Mr Lacey added, 'Pending word from your grandmother, I've taken the liberty of sending for my married sister Julia to join us. She's currently in London and should therefore be able to get here without too much delay.'

Emma's head began to spin, and not just because of the attractive gentleman standing in front of her. Something wasn't right. 'But where is Uncle Frederick?' she asked. 'I don't understand how you come to be here, Mr Lacey.' The pounding in her head had suddenly got worse.

A fleeting frown appeared on Mr Lacey's brow, quickly followed by a hesitant smile.

'Please call me Richard, or Cousin Richard, if you will, for we are cousins… though somewhat distant ones.' His eyes flicked to Mrs Wrighton, who shook her head. 'Why don't you wait until the doctor has seen you, and then I'll be happy to explain everything.' He moved rapidly towards the door. 'I'd never forgive myself if I hindered your return to full health.' Before she knew it, he had gone. Mrs Wrighton hurried after him, leaving Emma alone and even more confused. Such shocking news. And who was Mr Lacey? Her cousin? She'd never heard of him. Emma rubbed her aching brow. Matters were becoming more complicated just when she'd hoped they'd become simpler.

Ever cautious when it came to her brother's safety, and mindful of her mother's final warning, Emma couldn't erase her troubling thoughts. Could Richard Lacey be involved in the misfortunes that had overtaken her family? He'd certainly made himself at home here. Indeed, he looked to have gained from their losses. Emma's heart and instincts told her she should trust him, but her head, aching though it was, warned for the need to be on guard until she was sure. Why had she ever believed that getting home would be the end of her problems? The way things were going, these were just the start.

As soon as he reached his bedchamber, Richard took a deep breath. What had come over him? It was surely more than relief at the fact that the young woman was alive. Dolt! He'd been far too familiar. He hadn't intended to unsettle her, but that was plainly what he'd accomplished. He'd shocked her the moment he'd entered the room. Thank goodness some sense of propriety had intervened. Annoyed with himself for blundering in too soon, he questioned why he hadn't waited until the doctor had visited.

Striding to the window, he pushed the sash up, allowing the chilly air to rush in. Perhaps a cold blast would settle his nerves. He couldn't understand it. He was annoyed with himself, and his pulse was racing. What was it about Emma Smythe that made his heart pound and his blood race?

Despite her bruised face, unkempt shorn hair, and boyish figure, she exuded femininity. How could he have mistaken her for a boy? Last night, his first instinct had been to keep her safe. All his protective feelings had been aroused again on seeing her just now. It had taken a supreme effort not to babble that he would take care of everything. She was sure to have thought him completely addle-pated if he'd done so.

As his pulse slowed to a more regular beat, he recalled more of their encounter. Her gaze had remained steady as he'd stupidly broken the dreadful news about her grandfather's demise. What a clodpole! How could he have been so unthinking? The widening of those penetrating grey eyes and the paling of her cheeks were the only indications of the pain he'd inflicted. Most women of his acquaintance would've been calling for the hartshorn and burnt feathers and having the vapours, but Miss Smythe had remained icily calm… at least on the outside. Goodness knows what she'd really been feeling. But then she must be quite exceptional to have survived on her own, to have reached here in one piece and with her brother in tow.

Richard shook his head and took a deep breath of the bracing March air. He was Miss Smythe's cousin and it was his duty to protect her. The fact that she made his pulse race was neither here nor there. He'd made a promise to his father on his deathbed that he would care for his younger siblings.

Richard made another promise, this time to himself. He'd do the same for Miss Smythe and her brother – he'd set all to rights for them, whatever the cost to himself. Because a promise, once made, should never be broken.

Lost in his thoughts and blind to the rolling Cotswold landscape stretching out before him, it was the sudden gust of wind catching the curtains that brought him to his senses. Slamming the sash down, Richard turned and caught sight of his reflection in the cheval mirror. Surprisingly, he didn't look as disordered as he felt. He straightened his cravat and ran swift fingers through his curls. Not as pristine as his valet would wish, but it would do. Satisfied that at least outwardly he looked composed, Richard went to rejoin Miss Smythe's brother in the breakfast parlour. Dealing with another male was much more straightforward.

Chapter 4

LATER THAT MORNING, DR Chesney called on Emma and pronounced her well enough to leave her bed. Fortunately, Mrs Wrighton had discovered a trunk full of Emma's mother's clothes in the attic, left behind when they'd departed on their travels, and Polly had been kept busy adjusting them to fit. Now dressed in a sadly outdated but rather becoming long-sleeved dress of blue jaconet embellished with a wide ruffle collar, Emma sat in a large armchair in what had been her grandmother's favourite drawing room. The cream-and-gold striped curtains had been drawn back from the French windows to give a clear view over the terrace where the green shoots of spring flowers were just beginning to peep over the rims of their tubs. Emma recalled the last time she'd visited. The garden had been in full bloom, and she'd picked a small posy of roses with her mother, which she'd presented to her grandmother in this very same room.

Emma blinked at the sudden appearance of her brother's nose pressed against the window pane. Getting a grip on her still-fragile nerves, she smiled and waved. Jamie's face lit up; he wrenched the window open and hurtled in, almost throwing himself onto his sister's lap.

'Oh, Emm, you're recovered. I'm so glad,' he gasped. 'Cousin Richard told me you were getting better but I... I was afraid.

Wasn't sure whether you'd wake up at all after last night.' He looked up at her through lowered lashes. 'I... I thought I might be left on my own.'

Jamie's words brought home to Emma how frightened he'd been. On their journey, he'd been stoical, summoning goodness-knows-what reserves to appear cheerful and strong. Because he was the taller, he'd posed as the older boy while Emma had played the part of his younger brother. Her lack of curves had helped with the deception, which had worked well, but now she could see the toll the journey had taken on him. The mask he'd donned with seeming ease for all those weeks had slipped... He was a vulnerable boy of thirteen again.

'Jamie, it will take more than a small bump on my head to rid you of me,' she said, injecting her voice with a cheerfulness she didn't feel. Patting his blond locks as he rested his head on her shoulder, she added, 'I just needed time to recover, but I'm well now and I'll soon be walking about once my blisters are healed.'

Taking him by the shoulders, she looked into his eyes. 'Now tell me what you've been doing while I've been lazy and lying abed.'

Jamie's face crumpled.

'Oh, Emm, Cousin Richard told me that both Grandfather and Uncle Frederick are dead. He thinks the war disrupted communications to Patras and that's why we didn't get any news.'

Emma didn't believe that explanation for one minute. Perhaps Richard Lacey had said it to avoid awkward questions from her little brother. She remained silent as Jamie continued, gulping in breaths between each revelation.

'Richard says I shouldn't worry. Grandmamma is still alive. She's in London. We'll see her soon. And Emm...' Jamie's voice quavered, tears coursing down his cheeks. 'This means I'm now viscount, doesn't it? I don't know what to do.'

Emma hugged him.

'Hush, Jamie love. Grandfather was getting on in years, remember. We can't be that surprised that he passed away in our absence, upsetting as it is. But let's not forget Grandmamma, who has had to carry on, thinking we were all lost. She must have been so lonely, wondering what had happened to us.'

'I didn't think. You're right. It must have been awful for her,' came Jamie's muffled reply.

Swiping at his eyes, he straightened up and removed himself from Emma's arms.

'I'm all right now, Emm. I'll look after you and Grandmamma.' Tugging at the cuffs of his jacket, Jamie straightened his spine and puffed his chest out. 'This used to be Papa's when he was my age. Mrs Wrighton found it in the attic. It fits me fine, doesn't it?'

Nearly overset at the sight of her little brother standing proud in their father's jacket, Emma could only force a smile and nod. It took a few deep breaths before she was back in control of her emotions. A cool head was needed now more than ever. It was imperative to discover what had happened at Easterby Hall during her family's absence... and from where the gentleman claiming kinship had suddenly appeared. And despite Jamie's brave assertion that he was now the head of the family, it was her responsibility to see him safely reunited with Grandmamma and acknowledged as the true viscount.

A movement by the open window caught her eye, and she watched as Richard stepped in from the garden. His tall, imposing figure suddenly made the room feel smaller.

'Forgive me, Cousin Emma. Jamie and I were in the garden when he saw you were up. I hope he's not disturbed you. The doctor was insistent that you should rest.'

His smile as he said this set her pulse racing. Emma told herself that she had to stay on her guard; her mother's words of warning were ringing in her ears.

'Not at all, sir. Indeed, I was wondering where Jamie had got to. It was so quiet and peaceful here.' She grinned at Jamie.

Jamie's cheeks flushed. 'I'm not noisy.' He giggled. 'Well, not all the time.'

'Do you object if I join you?' asked Richard, moving towards the fireplace to place a log on the fire. 'I can then relate to you what I've already told your brother.'

Emma bit her lip then nodded. Better to get it all over with. Perhaps he would also explain further his connection to the family.

'Yes, I'd be grateful if you would. I fear I don't know or understand what has occurred in our absence.'

What an understatement that was – they'd heard nothing for years.

Richard watched as the lad, Jamie, settled next to his sister. Richard himself chose to sit on the small sofa opposite the pair. He didn't feel the least bit comfortable, perched as he was on the edge of his seat and attempting a look of unconcern. Thank goodness Jamie had believed him – he was telling the truth, after all. But the lovely Miss Smythe, or Cousin Emma as he should think of her, had been sending him suspicious looks from the minute he'd entered the room. With her hands clenched tightly in her lap, he guessed that she was not as composed as she was pretending to be, but he gave her credit for her easy handling of her brother's terrors at the reality of becoming viscount. Richard's jaw tightened. He'd better get all the bad news out of the way at once. With luck, she'd believe him and let down a few of her defences.

'Well, where do I begin? I should first let you know my place in this, I suppose.' Emma's eyes focussed on his face, making him unaccountably nervous. Would he pass the test?

Richard commenced by explaining his relationship to the Smythe family – how he was a distant cousin on his late father's side. He told them of his immediate family, consisting of his younger brother David, who was just completing his studies at Oxford, and his sister Julia who, at twenty-five, had recently married. How, at the age of twenty-three, nine years previously, he'd become the head of the family, that role being unexpectedly thrust on him by the early demise of his father. Richard finished his account by explaining that he'd only recently been notified of his supposed accession to the title of viscount.

'I don't understand. Your surname is different. How could you have inherited the title?'

He smiled back at the frowning Emma. She was intelligent and sharp.

'Ah, yes, I should explain that anomaly. It was why it took so long for my connection to the Smythe family to be recalled. In fact, I've my solicitor, Blake, to thank for that. He'd been going through some old family papers and spotted the name Smythe, a name he'd also recently seen in the *Gazette* in connection with the court's decision to declare you and your family dead.' Richard settled back into his seat. 'You see, my late father, who was born a Smythe, lost his parents at a very early age. An outbreak of cholera, I understand.'

Emma shook her head in a sympathetic gesture. 'How dreadful for him.'

'Indeed. Anyway, Father and his siblings were taken in by an aunt – his mother's sister – and her husband, Richard Lacey. They were childless, so they raised the children as their own. Father changed his name to Lacey on reaching his majority, in honour of his uncle. He also named his firstborn son after him, which is why I bear his name.'

Emma's face relaxed. 'Aah, now I understand.'

Richard's shoulders felt as if a weight had been removed. He began to hope that she would trust him, after all. He needed her to trust him. Just one more hurdle to go. Richard disclosed the details of their uncle Frederick's fatal accident and the vague but persistent rumours surrounding it, explaining that their grandfather's entirely natural death had come a few months later the same year, no doubt precipitated by his futile attempts to contact his younger son.

'I don't understand. Papa told the consul in Patras – Mr Strane I think his name was – where we were going. And he wrote several times to Grandfather...' Emma paused, looking thoughtful. 'But I admit, Papa soon became so engrossed in his excavations that he stopped writing altogether. Mother and I had concerns that we'd received no replies, but he dismissed us for being foolish.'

Richard inwardly winced. It was Emma's father who had been a complete fool.

'What exactly happened to your parents?' he asked, rubbing his chin nervously. 'Have you been on your own for some time?' He'd refrained from questioning Jamie further – the lad had been upset enough worrying about his sister that he hadn't liked to pry into what were most likely painful matters.

Emma shook her head. 'Goodness me, no. We'd been living in the small village of Gytheion on the southern coast of the Morea. Papa found some exceptional sites there. Six months ago, he decided his work there was complete and we were about to return to Patras.' Emma's voice faltered. 'Th-the afternoon before our planned departure, he and Mama took a caique out for one last sail.' There was another pause as she swiped at her eyes with the back of her hand. 'The weather turned. There was a storm… It was a week before we received news of their deaths.' The colour had drained from her cheeks. She placed her arm round her brother's shoulder.

'I'm sorry. That must have been awful for you both.' Richard's words sounded inadequate even to himself.

'It was. But we coped.'

Momentarily stunned by her disclosures, Richard now started to gather his wits. What she'd told him didn't really tally with what he'd learned. Blake had worked hard to glean every bit of information.

'I understand that your grandfather received a letter from a Mr Bedworth, who worked at the consulate, saying he'd received reports that your family had been attacked and killed by bandits on the way to Sparta. He'd advised that it was too dangerous to send anyone out to ascertain the veracity of the reports and that it would be best to assume it was true.'

'What!' Emma sounded angry. 'That's ridiculous. We weren't attacked.' The colour had now returned to her cheeks. 'Certainly Papa was advised not to travel further south by Mr Strane, the consul. He warned us that it was a risky undertaking, and Mama and I were all for returning home. But then we received a visit from Mr Bedworth. He said he disagreed with the consul's assessment and encouraged Papa to go. Of course, Papa did not need much encouragement, and luckily, we encountered no more than the usual problems – broken axles, lame horses, and suchlike.' Emma frowned. 'This Mr Bedworth... why would he write such things? I don't understand.'

'Didn't you see him when you returned to Patras?' Even Emma's frown was quite attractive, Richard decided.

Emma shot a glance at her brother who shook his head.

'You'd better tell him, Emma. People are bound to find out.'

There was a defiant glint in her eyes, and Richard wondered what she was about to disclose.

'We didn't go back to the consulate. I... I had a bad feeling about Mr Bedworth... about how he'd encouraged Papa to travel south when the consul had urged him not to. And then not receiving any further news from England. It didn't seem right.'

Richard nodded. It all sounded very odd indeed.

'Our housekeeper, Ariadne, had family with trading connections,' Emma continued. 'They took us as far as Gibraltar.

For reasons of safety, as you know, I dressed as a boy. From there, we took the packet back to England, landing at Falmouth. I'd run out of funds by then, so we made our way here on foot. I knew if I could trust anyone, it would be Grandfather.' She sent him another defiant look.

'I see.'

What else could he say? Richard had kept his tone neutral, but inside, his emotions were running riot. Why had she felt the need to disguise herself instead of seeking help from compatriots? A lone, defenceless female with only a boy for company.

'You don't, do you?' She glared at him accusingly. 'I told you that I was uneasy about the lack of communication between Grandfather and Papa. It never seemed right to Mama or me. And Grandfather would never have cut us off. He doted on Jamie.' She squared her shoulders. 'In any case, we are home now.'

Richard's sense of unease was growing, and it wasn't because of his cousin's defiant attitude. Something else wasn't right. Her disclosures had added to his increasing suspicions that somebody held a grudge against the family. Somebody powerful, with far-reaching influence.

As she seemed to be getting her spirit back, he decided to be frank.

'Yes, you're both home, thank goodness. But I'm not sure you're safe.'

Richard watched the shock of his words register in her eyes. Jamie's head, too, shot up.

'What do you mean?' she asked. 'Why would we be in danger now? It doesn't make sense.'

'I don't know the reason, and I agree it doesn't make sense. But I have my suspicions.' Richard took a breath. 'Let me tell you what has happened to me since it was announced that I'd inherited the title.'

After Richard had recounted the details of the attempts on his life to his two increasingly shocked listeners, he stood up and began to pace the floor. 'What also seems odd to me is that the statutory seven years hadn't elapsed before you were all declared dead. It seems that the evidence of Bedworth's statement was taken as sufficient proof.' He halted his pacing and rested his booted foot on the fender, scrutinising his two companions. 'I'm sorry to upset you, but I need to ask... Do you know if your father had any enemies, anyone with a grudge?'

Emma was the first to shake her head.

'No. That's laughable. Who would hold a grudge of that magnitude?' After a moment's pause, she added, 'There was a little rivalry with fellow antiquities enthusiasts. Lord Elgin, as you probably know, had an expedition out there too. We met him in Rome, when he was on his way back to England. Papa and he got on very well, despite the fact that Papa was determined to outdo him. Elgin warned Papa about the inadvisability of venturing south into the Morea, but of course Papa took his warning as proof that there was indeed something there to be found.' She shook her head again. 'No, I can't believe he has anything to do with all this.'

Richard agreed. 'So you haven't heard?' He wondered how much to tell her as he leaned forward to place another log on the fire. 'Elgin was in Paris when the Peace of Amiens broke down, and was held captive like many other Englishmen who had the misfortune to be there at the wrong time. He didn't get home for three years. Then there was his divorce... terrible business.' Richard cleared his throat. 'Forgive me. You don't need to know the details of that. But I agree, I think we can rule him out.'

He turned back from the fire to see Emma's eyes now wide with shock.

'Then who is it?' she whispered.

At last... she believed him. Before he could stop himself, his hand had reached out to hers.

'Forgive my forwardness, Miss Smythe... Cousin Emma. I promise I'll do all in my power to help you and Jamie. I'll protect you both and ensure that Jamie is recognised as the true heir to the title.'

Their eyes locked for a moment until Emma seemed to come to her senses and withdrew her hand from his.

'Thank you... Cousin Richard.' He heard her take a breath. 'Well, what are we going to do about our situation? Jamie and I can't hide away forever.' A glitter of determination appeared in her eyes. 'In fact, I refuse to hide. Jamie and I need to get to London.'

Richard thudded back into his seat on the sofa in disbelief. She believed the threat was real but was talking about taking yet more risks. Would the woman not see sense?

'Look, I know you've done some incredible things, but you're not on your own any more. There's no point in putting yourselves in danger.' He was finding it difficult to disguise his annoyance. 'Leave everything to me. I've written to your grandmother, and my sister will be arriving shortly too, to provide you with some female company.' He forced a smile.

'I've set investigations in motion and I'll soon get to the bottom of things. In the meantime, I don't want you to concern yourself with these problems.'

Even as the words left his lips, Richard knew he'd made a mistake. Emma's grey eyes narrowed and her chin jutted defiantly.

'I really don't think you are in a position to issue orders,' she said through what he was sure were clenched teeth. 'And I hope you don't intend to leave me in the dark with regard to matters pertaining to *my* family.' In glacial tones, she continued, 'I apologise if I sound shrewish, but I'm not going to be ordered about and brushed aside just because I'm a female. I've seen too much of the consequences of that, and I've learned my lesson.'

There was a challenge in her eyes that took him aback. He mentally kicked himself for not handling it better. To achieve what she had showed she was no milk-and-water miss, so why had he foolishly treated her like one?

'I apologise for my peremptory words. But we do belong to the same family, and therefore I should do my part.' Richard spoke softly. 'And I assure you that I wouldn't dream of leaving you in the dark. You have my word that I'll consult you before taking any action.'

Her frosty glare melted, much to his relief, and she nodded her acquiescence. So he'd convinced her of his sincerity, but she'd made it plain that she wasn't going to sit back and let him get on with things alone. As Richard watched her quietly comfort her brother, who'd remained silent throughout the discussion, it dawned on him that he was dealing with a female possessed of a core of steel. Someone a little like his sister, another strong-minded woman. Yet he didn't feel in the least fraternal towards Emma Smythe… no, not at all.

After an excellent dinner, Emma retired to the library with Cousin Richard – much to her own surprise, she was already thinking of him as a cousin. Jamie had already excused himself and had gone to bed some time earlier.

'I'll ask Wrighton to bring some tea, or would you prefer a glass of port?' asked Richard as he led her to a seat near the fire.

'I'd prefer tea, please, but don't forgo your port on my account.' Emma smiled as she gazed round at her surroundings. The book-lined walls, the cosy fire, they'd all seemed only a distant memory just a short time ago. Now she was here at last.

The clock ticking on the mantelpiece and the occasional crackle of wood from the fire were the only sounds as Richard read his book and Emma sipped her tea, revelling in the peace and tranquillity of the moment. She'd persuaded him to read, unsure that she was up to a prolonged conversation. Fortunately, gentleman that he was, he'd understood her need for quiet and had dutifully selected a volume and now appeared to be concentrating on the text. A wave of gratitude swept over her for his forbearance.

Emma told herself that, as cousins, no social codes were being broken by being alone together. She sent him a covert glance. He seemed engrossed in his book, turning the pages and occasionally frowning, which made him appear quite stern. Emma sighed. Despite her cousin's occasionally forbidding mien, this was the first time in an age that she'd felt relaxed and safe.

Richard looked up and caught her gazing at him. The smile he sent her transformed his face.

'Everything all right? Would you like more tea? I can pour if you wish.'

Emma felt the heat rising to her cheeks. 'Oh no, I've had sufficient, thank you.' She'd retained her composure through all sorts of precarious situations on the journey home, but why did her pulse race when he looked at her? She racked her brains to think of something intelligent and original to say.

'What are you reading?' Not her most scintillating conversational gambit, Emma told herself.

Richard held up the volume to show her.

'It's Pope's translation of the *Iliad.* I didn't want to struggle with the original.' He gave a warm chuckle. 'Greek was never my favourite subject at school.' He gestured towards the shelves. 'Your grandfather's library is certainly well stocked. Whoever built up this collection was a connoisseur.'

Emma smiled. Here was someone who appreciated Grandfather's fine taste in books.

'Yes, Grandfather loved his books. Grandmamma reads a lot too, though much to Grandfather's disapproval, she prefers novels.' She tilted her head to better see the book Richard showed her. 'Papa told me that Pope's translation did Homer a disservice, and he forbad me from looking at it. He insisted that I should only read it in the original.' She rolled her eyes and added with a laugh, 'Though, obviously, Grandfather didn't feel that strongly about it if he purchased a copy.'

Richard's eyebrows lifted. 'What, you read Greek?'

'Of course, and Latin too.' Feeling decidedly bold, she resolved to admit all her failings as a female. Better to get his disillusionment over with quickly. 'I was Papa's amanuensis, along with Mama. I had an education normally reserved for sons. There was such a gap between my birth and Jamie's, Papa had given up hope of having an heir.'

She sent him a quizzical look. 'I suppose I've shocked you, and you think I'm a bluestocking? I shouldn't really own up to being educated, should I? Nobody likes a clever female.'

Emma waited for his put-down.

'Not at all! I was surprised, that's all. Pleasantly surprised, if you must know. Young ladies should be encouraged to use their brains and not just lead lives of idleness. My sister Julia has a fine mind, although her talents lie in the sciences and mathematics.' He paused to take a sip from his glass of port while Emma struggled to digest the fact that he didn't disapprove of her. 'She looked after our mining accounts and assisted with some of the estate business before her marriage,' Richard continued. 'I'm happy to say her husband also appreciates her talents.' A wry smile appeared on his lips. 'Indeed, she wouldn't have consented to marry him if he hadn't. And more to the point, I wouldn't have let her.'

Emma's world view shifted on its axis. Here was a gentleman who didn't think she was odd. How unexpected and… how troubling. She gave herself a mental shake and reminded herself of her mother's warning.

'I apologise, Cousin Richard. I didn't mean to be rag-mannered. I mistakenly assumed you were like the other gentlemen of my limited acquaintance who advised Papa that he was making a grave mistake in educating me as if I were a son. They tried to convince him that a spinster's lot was my future.'

Emma didn't go on to voice the dangerous thoughts that the life of a spinster had become her ambition. Better not reveal too much of her mind's workings. With a trembling hand, she set her teacup back on its saucer before risking a glance at Richard's face. Instead of the expected revulsion, she saw only admiration reflected there.

'You're most certainly forgiven for making that assumption. I'm afraid I'm somewhat out of step with a lot of what many of my peers think about females.' Richard settled back in his seat, the book he'd been reading now set to one side. 'I'm happy to say that opinions in society do seem to be changing, albeit slowly. Why, you've only to see the difference in the way views about women's education and an individual's rights to self-determination are being discussed and not immediately dismissed as when they were first put forward.'

Emma blinked. Did he truly believe what he was saying, or was it a ploy to draw her in?

'You've read the Wollstonecraft book?' She tried to keep the astonishment from her voice.

Richard nodded. 'I have indeed. And I think much of what it contains makes a great deal of sense. Others are making the same points, although more obliquely.' His face screwed up in concentration. 'Let me think. What's it called now?' His head tilted towards the ceiling. 'Got it! *Belinda*. Mrs Edgeworth.' He grinned at Emma and then rolled his eyes. 'Julia insisted I read it… all three volumes.' Emma couldn't resist smiling back at him. 'My sister can be quite forceful, you know. Wait until you meet her.' He squinted towards the bookcases. 'There doesn't appear to be a copy here. If you think you might like to read it, let me know and I'll ask my secretary to send one down for you.'

Emma didn't for one moment believe Richard was a man to be bullied by his sister. But he certainly seemed to be a man out of the ordinary, having an infectious sense of humour, for a start, and demonstrating nothing but kindness and concern for her welfare. She was in dangerous territory indeed. Could she manage to maintain her emotional distance from this increasingly attractive man?

Richard drained the last of his glass of port and took a poker to the dying embers of the fire. The clock on the mantelpiece showed it was past eleven. Emma couldn't believe the time had flown so quickly.

'Well, what a lot of interests we share, Cousin Emma,' Richard said, setting the poker back on its stand. 'I don't think I've had a more stimulating evening in ages. Certainly not since Julia left home.' His eyes searched her face. 'You look tired, my dear. Shall I call for Polly to attend you?'

Emma gave her assent, and while she waited for her maid to appear, she examined her own feelings. She, too, had enjoyed the evening and, despite her misgivings, looked forward to spending more time with her new cousin.

When Polly turned up, she and Emma made their way to the stairs.

'Goodnight, Emma. Sleep well. I'll see you in the morning,' said Richard, who'd escorted them into the hallway. Then, much to Emma's astonishment, he suddenly swept her into his arms.

'Noticed you were limping. Easiest if I take you up.' His voice was unusually gruff.

'Oooohhh, really there is no need,' Emma gasped. Though it did feel rather nice, being tucked against his broad chest.

'Nonsense. Save your poor feet. Here we are then,' he answered brusquely, opening the bedroom door and depositing her on the bed. 'Polly, please see to your mistress. Cousin Emma, until the morning.' He bowed and swiftly left the room, leaving Emma staring open-mouthed at the now-closed door.

She became aware of the maid, who was giving her a knowing smile.

'Well…' said Polly with a grin.

Richard strode back to his room, his pulse racing. And not all due to the exertion of carrying Emma up the stairs. What was coming over him? Another second and he would've been kissing her goodnight, despite the maid's presence. He'd definitely told the truth when he'd said he hadn't enjoyed an evening as much as the one spent with her. Their conversation had been stimulating and amusing. And also revealing. He'd guessed she was brave and determined. Now he knew her to be intelligent and educated. What a combination… and in such a beguiling package. He ran his fingers through his hair. Julia couldn't arrive soon enough.

Chapter 5

THE FOLLOWING DAY, EMMA was woken by loud noises coming from downstairs. It had taken her an age to fall asleep the night before, with her mind tossing and turning all the events of the previous day. Her overriding anxiety was caused by the inevitable conclusion that someone was intent on destroying her family. Who and why? She'd racked her brains but could come up with no explanation. Perhaps Grandmamma would be able to shed some light.

The unsettling thoughts of Richard Lacey were another reason for her sleeplessness. The impulsive way in which he'd swept her upstairs had left her quite confused. To say her emotions were a little heightened that morning would've been a gross understatement. The experience had been quite overwhelming. But, she told herself, it probably meant nothing to him. He was just a man demonstrating that he could physically control a female.

She bristled as she lay in bed, recalling how he'd attempted to impose his will earlier in the day. True, he'd apologised, but wouldn't he think it natural to exert control and have authority over the females in his life? Wasn't that what all men expected? She'd seen with her own eyes what had happened to her mother, heard her mother's words. Would never forget them.

Emma's mind drifted back to her journey with her brother. While at times it'd been terrifying, it had also been liberating. She'd been in control, and she'd achieved something that a few months earlier she wouldn't have dreamed herself capable of. She'd planned and made decisions – decisions that their lives had depended on – and they'd got through it. After years of being a biddable daughter whose opinions were either ignored or disdained by her father, it was exhilarating to know that she didn't need a man's guidance at all times. She had no desire to relinquish this heady feeling of controlling her own destiny at last. Emma smiled to herself. Yes, her new-found cousin was attractive – dangerously so – and on the surface, at least, totally unlike her father in his attitudes. She would have to be careful.

Emma swung her legs out of bed and peered at the clock on the mantelpiece. Its fingers pointed to half past ten. A light tap sounded on her door and Emma guiltily bade whoever it was to enter.

'I thought you might be awake now, so I brought your hot water,' said Polly, tripping into the room bearing a steaming pitcher. 'You were fast asleep earlier, dead to the world, you were, miss. Didn't stir at all, even when I dropped the poker.' The maid grinned conspiratorially. 'The dowager would've had my hide for that. Now, would you like me to bring you a bite to eat and drink, miss?'

'No. I'll wash and dress, then breakfast in the parlour. What is all the disturbance downstairs, by the way?'

Polly bobbed her head, full of excitement. 'The master's sister has arrived. Such a lovely-looking lady. She's waiting in the drawing room for the master to return from his ride.

The master's valet and his man of business have also arrived, so we're getting quite a houseful.'

Nervous at the prospect of meeting Cousin Richard's sister, and wondering how much she should tell her, Emma made her way behind the screen to wash and brush her teeth. She put on another of the dresses that they'd discovered in the attics. This one was a high-waisted white cambric underdress with a matching long-sleeved overdress edged with blue and yellow ribbons. Polly had made good progress in shortening them all. Emma grimaced at her reflection in the mirror. Why hadn't she thought to ask Cousin Richard for his sister's married name last night? She'd been distracted, that's why, and totally absorbed in talking with him and hearing about his life, quite forgetting that Julia might be arriving today. Quelling her nerves, Emma took a final look in the mirror to ensure she was presentable... or as presentable as was possible for someone sporting an impressive purple bruise and a dress meant for somebody blessed with a more Junoesque figure.

An elegantly dressed brunette was gazing pensively out of the French windows when Emma entered the drawing room. Emma, acutely aware of her own outdated and somewhat shabby appearance, resisted shrinking when the young woman turned to face her.

The young woman's face, framed by chestnut curls, broke into a friendly smile, her brown eyes sparkling with the same good humour as her brother's.

'You must be the mysterious lady Richard wrote to me about.' Her smiling expression turned to one of concern. 'Oh dear, your poor face. How did you come by that bruise?' Without waiting for an answer, the young lady pointed to the sofa. 'Come and sit down next to me. I'm simply dying to hear all about you.' Emma, overwhelmed by her new companion's exuberance, meekly did as she was told. It was evident by Julia's forthright manner that she was a lady accustomed to taking charge.

'What, Julia, taking over already?' came a familiar voice from the open doorway.

'Richard!' Julia rushed towards him, her arms outstretched. 'You wretch, I'd only just arrived in London to join George when I got your missive. I abandoned my unpacking and set off immediately, leaving George on his own to take charge of David.' Laughing up at her brother, she shook her head. 'Goodness knows what they'll get up to without my restraining influence. Now, what's this all about? And do introduce us, my love.'

Richard, who was undoubtedly accustomed to his sister's gushing manner, obliged.

'Cousin Emma, may I present to you my sister, Mrs Julia Morton. Julia, this is Emma Smythe, sister to the current Viscount Easterby.'

Julia made a curtsey and turned and frowned at her brother. 'But I thought... You wrote...'

Richard made a dismissive gesture.

'Yes, I know, but it seems things are not as they first appeared. Come, join us for breakfast.' He crooked his elbow for Emma to take and, with the other hand, tugged his sister towards the door. 'I would hazard Mrs Henning has provided us with a wonderful repast judging by the marvellous smells wafting past my nose. I'm quite ravenous. Cousin Emma, I'm sure you haven't eaten yet, have you?'

Once both ladies were seated at the table, Richard dismissed Wrighton and went over to the laden sideboard. 'We can speak more freely on our own,' he told them. 'Well, Emma, what can I tempt you with – beefsteak, collops of bacon, sausages, kidneys, eggs? Or would you prefer some cold meats? Mrs Henning has really done us proud.'

Emma's mouth was watering at the seductive smell of the bacon. She didn't care how unladylike it was to eat more than birdlike portions in company; she was going to enjoy her first English breakfast in ages.

'Oh, just some bacon, a sausage, and an egg, if you please. It's been so long since I tasted an English breakfast. In Greece, we had yoghurt and honey. Nothing like this. I did miss it.'

Julia smiled, then her brow creased in a frown.

'You've been living abroad in these troubled times?'

Emma nodded as she took the laden plate from Richard's hands.

'Yes, for almost eight years. We left here when I was seventeen, during the short-lived peace. Everybody was travelling then, so Papa deemed it was safe. We went briefly to Paris and then continued travelling south to the Italian states, then the Kingdom of Sicily. From there, we crossed to Patras and then southwards again into the Morea.'

Julia's eyes sparked with interest.

'Goodness me. Did you visit Athens? I've heard that it's very beautiful.'

'No. I've never been there.' Emma's voice was tinged with regret as she answered – she'd always harboured a desire to see Athens. 'We lived in a small village on the southern coast. Father's passion was archaeology but, according to him, Athens was far too crowded with other enthusiasts. He wanted to make his own discoveries. He'd heard rumours of a promising site in the Morea and decided that he would locate and document it.' She sighed. 'That is what kept us there for so long.' She didn't mention that he'd led them to several other prospective sites before he'd made his big discovery, ignoring all her mother's entreaties for them to return home. Or their impoverished existence there.

Julia's cup of coffee halted on its way to her mouth.

'Surely that was quite dangerous, was it not? I've heard that the land there is somewhat lawless. The Greeks resent being subject to Ottoman rule, and there are frequent insurrections. Were you not afraid?'

Emma swallowed. How could she frame an answer that didn't make Father sound like he'd been obstinate and single-minded in the extreme? Even though it was the truth.

'I… I don't think Father ever thought about the danger, not really…' Seeing the look of shock on Julia's face, she quickly added, 'Oh, he always looked after us as best he could, and fortunately we did not encounter any troubles. I had some misgivings, of course, but the village where we stayed was friendly. My real fears were for Jamie when we were left on our own. I knew it was my responsibility to get him home safely.'

Emma's eyes flicked to Richard who'd stopped what he was doing at the sideboard and was giving her a curious look.

'We found people ready to help us. Our housekeeper Ariadne had family who saw us safely to Gibraltar where we then took a ship back to England.' She forced a bright smile. 'And now here we are.'

A grim-faced Richard turned back to filling plates. He found himself cursing the late Charles Smythe for being so outstandingly selfish. Honestly, the man must've had windmills in his head. If it wasn't for the fact that he was already dead, Richard would quite happily have throttled him. A shudder went through him as he considered how Emma and Jamie had come so close to disaster, and it took an effort of will to compose himself before he returned to the table. He placed a plate in front of his sister.

'Now, Julia. That's enough questions. Let's eat something first. We can return to the subject later over coffee.' Richard's tone was pleasant but firm. To his relief, Julia didn't object, and the grateful smile Emma sent him confirmed that he'd said the right thing.

Emma sipped at her coffee, only vaguely aware of the continuing chatter between Richard and his sister. They were doing their best to make her feel at ease, and it was lovely to feel part of a family again. She'd recounted most of the details of her journey back to England, and Richard had told his shocked sister of the suspicions of wrongdoing and possible murder. Emma could hear Julia's voice as she gazed around the familiar room, a comforting buzz in the background. It reminded her of previous family meals taken at that very same table. A lump formed in her throat as a thought struck her. She would never be part of a true family again… now there was just Jamie and Grandmamma. Her cheeks felt wet and she realised she was crying.

'Oh, you poor dear girl.'

The next thing Emma knew, she was being held in a fierce hug as she sobbed into Julia's shoulder.

'Have a good cry. Don't mind us, my dear,' Julia's voice soothed. 'You need to grieve, and that will take time. Let me be a friend to you. I'm sure my brother has said the same.'

Emma, getting her emotions under control at last, drew away and swiped at her eyes with the dainty lace handkerchief that Julia handed to her.

'Yes, I've assured Cousin Emma that I'm at her disposal,' responded Richard. 'I'll do my utmost to discover who or what is behind this dreadful turn of events. That's why I sent for you, Julia. Would you be so kind as to keep Emma and Jamie company for a while? It's an imposition, I know, but I might need to get to London as quickly as possible, and I don't wish Emma and Jamie to make the journey until arrangements have been made for their safety.'

Julia didn't hesitate.

'It's no imposition. Of course I'll stay.' She paused and sent Emma a questioning look. 'If that's all right with you, Cousin Emma? You can't stay here on your own. It sounds as if it might not be safe.'

'It's very kind of you, Cousin Julia, considering we've only just met. I'm very grateful. Though, please call me Emma. "Cousin" sounds so formal.'

At that moment, a flushed and clearly excited figure bounded into the room, catching everyone's attention. Disregarding the two ladies, the boy Jamie, for that was who it was, fixed his eyes on Richard.

'I say, Cousin Richard, those horses of yours are magnificent.' Momentarily taking a much-needed breath, the lad belatedly took in Richard's grim expression. He cast a quick glance at the figures at the table and, to his credit, noted the presence of a stranger. 'Sorry, I didn't know we had a visitor.'

He squirmed under Emma's reproving look as she made the introductions.

'Jamie, allow me to present to you our cousin Mrs Julia Morton, Richard's sister. Julia, this is my brother, James. Viscount Easterby.'

Remembering his manners at last, Jamie made a creditable bow.

'I'm honoured to make your acquaintance, Cousin Julia.'

Her lips twitching, Julia returned the gesture with a graceful incline of her head.

Formalities over and with barely a pause for breath, Jamie renewed his address to Richard.

'I've been helping Joe groom them,' the lad gushed. 'He says they're prime goers.' He sent Richard a pleading look.

'Do you think I might ride one... please?' At last, the boy's roving glance took in the laden dishes of food on the sideboard, and he eyed them with relish. 'I say, I'm starving. Have you started without me?'

Emma was about to reprimand him, but Richard spoke first.

'Young man, please mind your manners. You are a viscount now. You must behave like one.' He softened his reprimand with a smile. 'First, you should apologise to your sister for being late for breakfast, then you must change if you've just come from the stables.'

A chastened Jamie replied, 'Yes, of course. Sorry, Emma. Sorry, Cousin Julia. I meant no disrespect.' He walked dejectedly to the door, then turned with pleading eyes to Richard. 'Will you let me ride, Cousin Richard?'

'Yes, of course. But not those two in the stables. They're far too lively. Now be off with you and get cleaned up, sir!'

Jamie grinned. 'Thank you. You're the best, Cousin Richard.' The door slammed behind him.

Julia squeezed Emma's arm and rolled her eyes.

'Boys!'

Richard grunted and said, 'By the way, Emma, I thought it best if it wasn't spread abroad that you've arrived here, or certainly not your true identities. I don't want you or Jamie at risk. I've asked Wrighton to speak to the staff, and they will put it about that you are distant relatives. Hopefully, I will continue to be the sole target for any mischief.'

Julia's face clouded.

'Oh Lord!' she gasped. 'Now I remember. George said something about footpads. I thought it likely you were both probably foxed and you'd been careless.' She fixed gimlet eyes on her brother. 'But this is what you mean, isn't it? From the moment your connection to the Smythe family was announced, you've been targeted too.'

Richard grimaced. The cat was amongst the pigeons now. Emma confirmed Julia's suspicions.

'Richard told me someone tried to run him into a ditch on the way here. And the girth on his saddle was cut in London.' Emma turned imploring eyes to Richard. 'I can't let you take all the risk for us. It wouldn't be fair. You've only just discovered your connection to the family. I can't ask you to put yourself in harm's way.'

'And what sort of fellow would I be if I left a young boy to deal with this nonsense?' he answered sternly. 'The fact that I didn't know of your side of the family before now means nothing.' His jaw set in a determined attitude. 'I know now, and I intend to help.'

Emma opened her mouth to protest, a martial look in her eyes, so Richard adopted a more placatory tone.

'It may be that it's all just a set of dreadful coincidences, but if not, I'm determined that the scoundrel responsible will be discovered and made to pay.' Richard didn't believe it was coincidence for one minute, but nor did he wish to have two females arguing with him. One was bad enough. 'Permit me to judge the risk. I'll take every precaution, I assure you.' He smiled to soften his next words. 'But I ask that all three of you take care. I request that you remain within the confines of the house and gardens.'

Julia looked shocked but remained silent. He guessed she was planning to ring a peal over his head when they were alone. He hoped that Emma, at least, would see the sense of his words.

'You're very kind, Richard, and I appreciate your help,' said Emma in clipped tones.

He sensed there was a "but" coming.

'But may I remind you that it is more my responsibility than yours to discover what has been going on.' A tight smile appeared on her lips. 'I don't wish to sound ungrateful, but I cannot allow you to take the whole burden on yourself. I've managed to get Jamie back safely, and I therefore must insist that I play my part in any further investigations.' Her chin jutted out. 'I will, however, do as you request… for now.' The challenge in her eyes was unmistakeable.

Clenching his fists at his side, Richard managed not to snap out a terse retort. A quick glance at his sister told him that she was clearly enjoying this battle of wills. What could he say? Just like his sister, Emma was opinionated and forthright and – much as he loathed to admit it – she had a point. Damn! He couldn't just wrest control from her, not after what she'd disclosed of her life with her father. The formidable chit had more than proved herself by getting her brother back home. Besides, he understood more than most her wish to retain some control.

He sucked in his cheeks.

'Very well, Emma. Of course I understand that you wish to play a part in discovering what's been going on.' He kept his tone even. 'However, you must also see that, with my contacts in London, I am better placed than you to initiate any investigations.' Before she could object, he rushed on, making a commitment that he hoped he'd not come to regret.

'I promise, furthermore, that I'll keep you informed of all developments, and I'll not take any steps before consulting you. Is that acceptable?'

To his satisfaction, not to say relief, Emma answered, a gleam of triumph in her eye.

'Yes, that is acceptable. Thank you, Richard.'

Julia gave him a knowing smile. 'Nicely done, Richard. You're learning.'

He snorted.

'I've only agreed because Emma possesses a rare intelligence and incredible determination.' He wasn't saying it to flatter. He meant every word.

'Just like me, you mean?' inquired Julia, her face all innocence.

Chapter 6

THE NEXT FEW DAYS passed quickly. Emma's face lost its pinched look, her bruise was fading, and she was pleased to be feeling a little stronger. Her feet, too, had recovered, and it no longer pained her to walk. A welcome letter from her grandmother had explained why that lady was unable to travel to Oxfordshire, desperate though she was to be reunited with her grandchildren. Confined to her bed with an ague, she hoped to be recovered sufficiently to journey to Easterby Hall by the week's end. The dowager begged them to wait for her arrival, seeming concerned that a further journey on her grandchildren's part might cause them to disappear again.

In the meantime, Emma enjoyed spending time with Julia, a friendly and intelligent companion who entertained her with lively accounts of her life in London. Emma's respect for her grew when Julia confessed to attending not only Royal Academy exhibitions but also numerous public lectures on mathematics, astronomy, and philosophy. How Emma yearned to do the same. With Julia as a friend, this perhaps would be a possibility. Emma, for the most part, had been content with her life of classic scholarly pursuits. Now with Julia's vibrant company and her talk of theatre trips, lectures, and entertainments both serious and frivolous, it was becoming more obvious how narrow her own life had been.

They were seated in the library, Julia flicking through a copy of the *Lady's Magazine* and Emma ostensibly checking an inventory of the linen cupboard. Mrs Henning had been insistent that now there was a mistress in residence, her household accounts should be presented on a regular basis. The lines on the carefully written pages were beginning to blur, and Emma's mind was filling with dismal thoughts of the years and opportunities she'd missed, when she was roused from this introspection by Julia's casual mention of a trip she intended to make.

'Sorry, what did you say, Julia? I'm afraid I was wool-gathering.'

'Just that I'm hoping to visit Scotland later this year. I'm part of a committee pressing for better conditions for workers, you see.' Julia's mouth turned down. 'Honestly, you wouldn't believe the conditions in some factories, Emma. Absolutely terrible.' She shook her head. 'I believed the chimney boys' situation was quite bad enough, but it seems that for those of the lower orders, life is very harsh indeed.'

Emma agreed. It had come as something of a shock when she'd read in the newspapers that the England she'd so looked forward to returning to had a dark side that she'd never been aware of before.

Julia was chattering on, her face now glowing with enthusiasm.

'Richard has been very progressive with our mines and manufactories. He says there's no reason children or anybody else should suffer when trying to earn their crust. To that end, I'm set on visiting a model factory at New Lanark to discover if there are improvements we haven't thought of.' She gave a rueful smile. 'That is, when I can persuade George to travel all the way up to Glasgow.' Her expression turned dreamy. 'He does admit that I can be very persuasive when I want to be.'

Emma, while admiring Julia's altruism, couldn't help feeling a tad jealous. How nice it would be to have a relationship of the sort that Julia had with George. Richard's face came to mind. Over the last few days, he'd impressed her with his punctiliousness, keeping her informed of all the reports he received from his solicitor's investigators. He hadn't patronised her or tried to shield her from any unpleasantness, admitting frankly that he'd strong reason to suspect her uncle's death had not been accidental. In all respects, Richard treated her as an equal, a new experience for her. Her father had never asked for advice or listened to her opinions, something Richard did as a matter of course.

He was also kind to Jamie, teaching him to ride and taking him around the estate to familiarise him with the land that came with the viscountcy. With Joe Henning's help, the boy was being taught to care for horses. He'd never had a horse of his own, as their father, unlike Uncle Frederick, hadn't been a keen rider. Admiration now shone out of Jamie's eyes whenever he spoke to or about Richard. Emma chuckled inwardly. If she wasn't prepared to lay her heart and independence at Richard's feet, her brother certainly was.

Now her initial distrust had been dismissed, she found herself drawn more and more to him. But only as a friend, not as a husband, she told herself.

Emma was certain that beneath Richard's mostly serious exterior lurked an engaging personality. Why else would his lively sister think so highly of him? Kind and considerate, his occasional flashes of wit indicated he possessed a sharp sense of humour that matched Julia's. Julia had indicated as much when she confided in Emma one day as they were strolling round the garden.

'It was very difficult for Richard when Father died. He had so many calls on his time, what with the estate and the mining business. But David and I never felt neglected. Richard was always there for us. Now I worry that he's missed out on things.' She pulled her shawl closer round her shoulders and patted Emma's hand. 'Richard can be very serious, but…' She paused, a blush stealing up her cheeks. 'Well, these last few days, I can see some of his light-hearted humour has returned, despite the current problems we are facing. You seem to have had a good effect on him, Emma, and for that I'm very grateful.'

Emma, rather taken aback, gave a hesitant smile but remained silent.

Richard lingered in the study for a few moments after reading the latest report from Blake. Dressed for riding, he was shortly intending to journey to Oxford. He glanced critically down at his new boots – hessians, ordered against his valet's advice from a new bootmaker in St James's. In fact, Carter had barely hidden his contempt when he unpacked and presented the boots to Richard that morning, having brought them up from London.

Richard paced up and down the Turkey-carpeted floor trying not to grimace. The boots pinched, but he was not going to mention it to Carter. The man would most probably gloat because his advice had been ignored. With luck, they would stretch.

Squinting down at his feet, he admired the glossy leather. Despite their tightness, the boots looked as good as any others he'd seen. Besides, he'd made up his mind not to patronise Hoby again. In his opinion, the man had become a pompous fool since Prinny had become one of his customers. Wincing slightly, Richard stepped gingerly over to the window and spied Emma and Julia strolling round the bare rose beds. It was time to tell the ladies of his plans.

He hailed them as he strode across the terrace. 'There you are. I didn't expect to find you outside. It's not very warm.'

Julia dismissed his comment with an airy wave of her hand.

'Oh, pooh, we're not so fragile that we can't enjoy a brisk walk on a chilly day, and we're both wrapped up well, as you can no doubt see. Besides, sitting in the library was becoming tiresome, wasn't it, Emma? We decided that we were both in need of some fresh air after being cooped up.'

Richard's dark eyes twinkled. 'I'm not questioning the robustness of your constitutions, Julia. I was merely wondering why, unlike me, you were not hugging the fireplace. I must be getting weak in my old age.' He made a parody of rubbing his arms.

Julia rolled her eyes and groaned. 'Yes, you're such a weakling.'

He winked at Emma and was pleased to note the blush that rose to her cheeks.

'Well, I'm glad I've found you together,' he continued. 'Emma, I've just received Blake's latest report. He's arranged for me to meet someone who might have further information about both your uncle's death and the chap Bedworth.' At Julia's questioning look, he added, 'Bedworth's suspected of intercepting letters.'

Emma started heading towards the house. 'Where are you meeting? I'll come with you,' she said over her shoulder.

Richard grasped her arm as she moved past him.

'I don't think that would be wise.' He tried not to sound too domineering. Emma stopped in her tracks and spun round to face him, her eyes blazing.

'What?'

'I'm meeting the chap in a tavern in Oxford. So it's not very suitable for you to be seen there.' Her mouth began to open, so he rushed on. 'He's terrified of being discovered, and your presence in such a place would occasion some gossip. You do understand, don't you?' He sent her an apologetic smile. 'This meeting would be difficult to rearrange. He might even change his mind about speaking altogether. It took a great deal of persuasion on Blake's part to get him to agree at all.' A nerve twitched in his cheek. He played his final card. 'This might be the only chance we get.'

'Very well,' she answered at last. It was plain that she was unhappy.

Glad not to have to argue, he nevertheless recognised the effort she'd made to concede to his wishes. 'Thank you.'

'You will take care, won't you… and give me a full report on your return?'

'I will indeed take care. What's more, I'll return as soon as my meeting is concluded.' His eyes held hers, trying to decipher the emotion behind her steady gaze. The silence was broken by Julia.

'When are you going?'

Richard tore his gaze from Emma's face and turned to his sister.

'I'm planning to set off straightaway. I shouldn't be gone more than a day or two. Blake has arranged everything. The informant should be arriving there tonight, so I expect to meet with him first thing in the morning. If matters go well, I'll be back tomorrow night, or at the latest Wednesday. I'll stay at the Mitre.'

He moved between the two ladies, tucking Emma's arm round his and doing the same with Julia on the other side. He was acutely aware of Emma's body, her hand clutching his sleeve. Injecting a lighter tone into his voice, he added, 'I'll be back before you know it. Just make sure you stay within the confines of the estate, and if you do venture out of the gardens, ensure one of the manservants accompanies you. I've ordered them to be on the alert.'

He didn't want to leave them on their own, but this meeting was the only way to find out more. And he wouldn't let her down.

Emma watched from the front drawing-room window as Richard prepared to set off. His mount, a spirited chestnut stallion, snorted and pranced as it was led to the front steps. She watched as Richard checked the girth before swinging up into the saddle and immediately bringing the horse under control. He sent a jaunty wave to Julia, who'd insisted on seeing him off, then his eyes raked the windows until he caught sight of Emma. A jolt of fear went through her, but she forced a smile and returned his wave, inwardly praying that he would come to no harm.

She'd wanted to go with him, but Julia's presence had made it difficult to argue her case. With any luck, this meeting would reveal the identity of the malefactor and she'd be able to take her own steps to deal with him, allowing Richard to return to his steady, controlled life.

She heaved a sigh. Richard was not meant to go gallivanting about the country. Everything she'd learned about him told her he was not made for intrigue and adventure. A steadier man she couldn't imagine. Emma recalled Julia's words about how Richard took care with everything, down to the slightest detail. She herself had wryly noted how the ornaments in the drawing room were all perfectly aligned along the mantelpiece whenever Richard had graced it with his presence.

Now Richard had the use of it, her grandfather's desk, which had always been covered with a welcoming jumble of account books and papers, held neatly stacked documents sorted alphabetically. She would swear Richard should've been an archivist rather than an engineer.

Emma's heart gave a lurch. This was the man who even now might be riding into danger, meeting a dangerous informer and putting himself at risk for her sake.

Emma slumped down on the sofa, her mind in turmoil. She needed to stay detached, but her thoughts kept returning to the man she'd just waved off. She'd found him to be intelligent and perceptive, not to mention kind and patient with Jamie. He didn't think he was right all the time either, unlike her father.

Emma frowned and twisted the fringe of her shawl, telling herself that she couldn't afford to be too drawn to Richard. Her mother had warned her that all men made themselves agreeable until they had their ring on a woman's finger. But Julia speaks so highly of him, she reminded herself. Julia wouldn't do that if her brother ignored her opinions or treated her like most men treated women – like children who needed to be constantly told what to do.

Emma looked down to see that several strands of the fringe of her shawl had become knotted together. How had that happened? Smoothing them out, she continued her musing, recalling Richard's warm, dark eyes and the unexpectedly attractive smile that lit up his face. His hair curled in such a way that there'd been times when she'd wanted to run her fingers through it and her keen eyes couldn't help but notice his manly physique and how well the muscles in his arms and legs displayed in his tailored clothes. Emma's eyes took on a dreamy expression.

'What's brought that smile to your face?' Julia grinned at her from the open doorway. 'You look as if you're miles away.'

Emma, mortally embarrassed, turned pink and mumbled something about recalling her childhood before standing up and taking Julia's arm in her own.

'Shall we return to the garden and make the most of this mild spell before the day departs?'

'Why not? Perhaps we can find Jamie if we walk round to the stables,' agreed Julia. 'Your little brother is certainly horse-mad, isn't he?'

Emma, pleased that she'd so easily deflected Julia's attention, agreed that her little brother was indeed horse-mad. She didn't notice Julia's knowing smile.

Richard had enjoyed his ride to Oxford. The weather, though bracing, was fine, and the surrounding countryside consisted of well-tended fields and pleasant, open vistas. He had made good time travelling on the turnpike road from Witney and then on to Eynsham, where the toll bridge took him over the Thames and on towards Botley. He had arrived in Oxford by mid-afternoon. Turning on to the High Street and heading towards the Mitre inn, his progress was slowed by the volume of carts and carriages crowding the road. The noise of the drovers contrasted sharply with the peace and tranquillity he'd recently enjoyed at Easterby Hall.

'Hey, Lacey! Is that you? Lacey, Halloo!'

The booming voice made him turn. A tall, distinguished man of around his own age, dressed in regimentals, hailed him from the pavement. Richard edged his horse closer, no easy feat in the crush.

The gentleman grinned up at him, his green eyes twinkling in his weather-bronzed face.

'It is you, Lacey, as I live and breathe. Didn't expect to see you here. It's been a long time.'

Richard grinned back. Indeed it had been a long time. Nigh on nine years since he'd last seen Nathaniel Crawford, his friend from university days. They'd continued to correspond intermittently, but Richard's responsibilities on the death of his father and Crawford's decision to purchase a commission had precluded them from meeting in person. Richard drew his horse to a halt and surveyed his friend who was still grinning up at him. There was a cane in Crawford's hand and Richard briefly wondered why his friend had taken up that affectation.

'Hello, Crawford. Yes, what a turn-up. It certainly has been a long time.' He pointed up the street. 'I'm just off to take a room at the Mitre. I'll be staying the night. Do you fancy joining me there for some refreshment?'

It'd be good to spend a couple of hours catching up, and he'd missed the camaraderie of his university days.

Crawford didn't hesitate.

'Great idea. I'm just off on a small commission. I'll see you… what… in about half an hour?'

'Look forward to it. It'll be good to exchange our news. Thought you were still out in Spain, so I'm pleased to find you safely back home.'

His friend's expression took on a closed, more sombre mien.

'I'll tell you about it when I see you, Lacey.'

Crawford turned back into the crowd. The reason for the cane became apparent as he lurched in an ungainly manner along the footpath.

Richard's smile froze as he watched his once nimble and athletic friend disappear into the crowd. Feeling chastened, he gathered his thoughts to the task in hand and urged his horse on to the Mitre's stable yard where there was much jostling and noise, as a coach had just arrived. Tired, confused, and short-tempered passengers mingled with drivers and guards, all trying to avail themselves of the facilities in the short time they had before travelling on. Richard easily attracted the attention of one of the ostlers who, spotting this well-dressed and hopefully generous patron, quickly relieved him of the reins and assured him his mount would be well cared for. Richard made his way into the taproom and managed to procure a decent room.

'The last one available, sir. We're very busy today,' the landlord, a man named Grover, assured him. Richard then bespoke himself a private parlour and ordered food.

'You're lucky, sir. The rush is just subsiding. Once the coach pulls out, it'll quieten down, so you won't have to wait long for your meal. I'll bring it in myself.' He cocked a speculative look at Richard. 'Would you care for a tankard of ale while you wait?'

It seemed the landlord had decided that Richard, although not showily dressed, was a gentleman of quality. His prime horseflesh had declared him unlikely to be light in the pocket. Richard thanked him and, after being shown his bedroom and approving it, allowed himself to be ushered into "one of our better parlours, sir". This was a small, panelled room with an open fire at one end, a couple of comfortable chairs either side of the fireplace, a long oak table, and a settle. The windows faced on to the busy High Street.

Richard settled himself in one of the chairs near the fire and held out his hands towards the flickering flames. Before long, a young waiting woman brought him his ale. Through the open doorway, Richard heard a commanding female voice issuing instructions. It seemed the landlady of the Mitre was not as happy as she could be with her husband's efforts.

The maid bobbed a curtsey. 'Mrs Grover says your dinner will be ready shortly, sir. She don't like to keep customers waiting.'

Richard nodded and flipped her a coin, which the maid received with a grateful smile. He settled down to enjoy his drink. Riding was thirsty work, he decided.

It wasn't long before Crawford joined him, a brimming tankard of ale already in his hand. Richard looked up and waved his friend in.

'You look very smart in your regimentals, Crawford. I wager all the ladies are impressed. But what are you doing here? Thought you were out in the Peninsula with Wellesley – or, I should say, Viscount Wellington.'

He gestured to the chair opposite, and Crawford, his cane tucked under his arm, levered himself down carefully after setting his tankard on the side table.

'No, I've decided to sell out.'

'Any particular reason?' Richard had guessed, but he thought he'd better ask in any case.

Crawford pulled a face and pointed to his leg.

'Mainly this. Got a ball to the leg at Talavera. Bit of a close call, that was. We lost a quarter of our men.' He shrugged. 'Then we had to withdraw to Portugal, even though we'd won. Backwards and forwards.'

Crawford shook his head and paused for a moment, lost in his thoughts. Richard studied his friend. The sun-bronzed face was more lined and drawn than he remembered it. Streaks of grey now threaded his dark hair. No wonder, if all the reports of the horrors of that battle were accurate.

As if recalling where he was, Crawford looked up and grinned – a rather forced grin, in Richard's opinion.

'Well, anyway, I came back. Many of my companions weren't so lucky. Got a bit of a limp, but I'm fine now, so Father requested I come home. Said he needed my help.' Crawford chuckled and shook his head.

'Is he ailing?' asked Richard.

'Not a bit of it. Fit as a flea. I think he just considers I'll do better at home.' Crawford's eyes slithered away, and he continued in a more matter-of-fact tone. 'I've been working on the staff at Horse Guards for a few months, but I've agreed to give that up and help him more with the estate. I came over to Oxford to see an old friend for a couple of days.' He grimaced. 'He lost his arm, poor wretch. Anyway, I'm back to London shortly to tidy up my affairs at the War Office before I head off for Warwickshire.'

Crawford gazed pensively into the fire for a moment, and Richard tried hard to think of something inconsequential to converse about to change the mood. Fortunately, Crawford roused himself and began speaking in a more jovial tone.

'I have to say, being on the Beau's staff at headquarters was a bit too much like being with you here at Oxford.'

Richard sent his friend a quizzical look. Crawford grinned, his white teeth contrasting against his bronzed complexion.

'That's what we call Wellington – behind his back, of course.' Crawford gave a throaty chuckle. 'He's just like you. A complete perfectionist, always wants to know every last little detail. Doesn't like not being in total control.'

Richard inwardly squirmed. Was he really that bad? He'd made great efforts to control his obsession. Was it so obvious to others? Before he could respond, his friend added, 'Mind you, he gets results. Not surprised he was made viscount.'

Crawford laughed and then ducked as Richard threw a cushion at his head.

'Just because I like to understand matters thoroughly doesn't make it a bad thing, you know. I helped you through a few scrapes, didn't I, when we were at Balliol?'

Richard, too, was now beginning to see the funny side. They were like two schoolboys again.

'Which reminds me. Heard you've now got a title, right?' Crawford managed to get the words out between gasps of more laughter.

'Correct. Wasn't expecting it. Don't really know much of that side of the family.' Richard inclined his head in a gesture of condescension and pulled a haughty face. 'You may address me as Easterby, by the way.'

Crawford grinned and tugged his forelock in a mocking acknowledgement. Richard decided it was best for the present to keep up the fiction that he was the viscount, even though Crawford was one of his oldest and most reliable friends. He felt a little guilty at the deception.

'The estate is just west of here, Easterby Hall by Minster Lovell, if you know it? It's a bit run-down. No-one's been there since the last viscount died, and then there was some legal business over his missing heir.' Richard puffed up his chest. 'Well, I've now been declared the legal heir, so here I am.'

'Thought I recognised the name when I read it in *The Times*.' Crawford leaned forward in his seat. His voice went down a notch. 'Father was here with Frederick, the oldest son, years back, y'know? When he read the notice of his death, well... I'd better not say. Know you're related and all.' Crawford's mouth clammed shut, an uncomfortable expression on his face.

Richard spoke. 'Spit it out, man!'

His friend shifted in his seat. 'Well, Father said that Frederick's death was for the best. Turns out he couldn't stand the chap. He told me that there was some suspicion he cheated at cards. And there was a scandal, just after he finished here, but it was all hushed up.' Crawford took a swig from his tankard. 'Sorry. Speaking out of turn. Forget I said anything.'

At that moment, the landlord, looking harassed and accompanied by a young waiting woman, entered the parlour. They were both carrying trays laden with steaming dishes, which they proceeded to place on the table. Delicious aromas filled the room, reminding Richard that it had been several hours since he'd eaten.

'Here you are, gentlemen. Shall I carry your drinks over to the table? Just give me a shout when you've finished and I'll bring the puddings and cheeses,' Mr Grover advised in a breathless voice. Out of the corner of his mouth he hissed to his assistant, 'Come along, Molly. Help me clear the table in the other parlour before Mrs Grover finds something else to complain about.'

Richard had been about to question his friend further about Frederick Smythe, but the landlord's untimely interruption had made it impossible to talk. His nerves tingled at the thought Crawford might know something useful for his investigation. Masking his interest, he smiled in a nonchalant fashion as he took his seat at the table where Crawford was already making himself comfortable.

'Don't worry about recounting scandal, Crawford. As I said, I hardly knew that side of the family. It sounds quite diverting. I'd no idea.'

Crawford took another pull at his drink.

'If you're sure. I wouldn't call it amusing exactly. It's certainly sad, if it's true, and I'm only repeating what Father told me.' He rubbed his chin thoughtfully. 'I wouldn't speak of it to anyone else... not a gossipmonger, you know?'

Richard nodded in agreement as he helped himself to a hefty slice of game pie. Inwardly, he urged his friend to get on with his tale.

Crawford folded his arms across his chest and began.

'The story is that Frederick Smythe got a respectable young lady into trouble, if you know what I mean. When confronted by the lady's father – and I understand she was a lady – the cur denied everything. The shock of it all caused her father's early death, and the young woman herself was sent to live in seclusion somewhere in the country. I'm afraid that's all I know.'

Richard took a helping of broccoli, then pushed the dish towards his friend. His mind was whirring. A tale like this could very well lead to the source of the grudge.

'Did your father know the identity of the young woman?' he asked tentatively.

'Oh yes, but he never disclosed it to me,' replied Crawford. 'She was a friend of my father's sister. They went to school together. Aunt Dorothy said she'd never known a more genteel and shy young woman. The young woman had been swept off her feet when Frederick showed an interest in her.' Crawford snorted. 'What sort of chap ruins a girl from a respectable family and then refuses to do the proper thing?'

Richard shook his head, agreeing with the sentiment. Who indeed? A gentleman should face up to his responsibilities.

Crawford was still speaking. 'When he spoke to me, Father was adamant that the lady was totally above reproach until Frederick started to court her. When accused, he claimed she'd welcomed his advances. Even said he suspected someone else had caused her fall from grace, and he wasn't going to be made the scapegoat. Poor girl didn't have any brothers to defend her honour, and when her father died, she'd no option but to disappear from society.'

The food Richard had been looking forward to all afternoon was now sticking in his throat. Was he really related to such a worm?

Crawford quirked an eyebrow. 'Anyway, according to my father, those who really knew Frederick and his ways guessed the truth of it and cut him from their lives.' He picked up his fork and stabbed a piece of chicken. 'Father never told me any of this until he saw the obituary in the papers. I've never seen him so vehement in his hatred of someone.' His eyes flickered across to Richard and he smiled apologetically. 'Sorry, old chap. But you did ask.'

Richard grasped his friend's hand. 'Thanks for telling me. It's best that I know.' He gestured to the food. 'Let's forget about him for now. How about making a start on some of this before it gets cold?'

The remainder of the afternoon passed most enjoyably, the two friends exchanging reminiscences.

A sly grin appeared on Crawford's face as he set his tankard down on the table. 'Do you still see anything of that Scottish chap? He was trying to build a self-propelled steam engine, wasn't he? Or was that just another of your tall tales? You used to tell such bouncers!'

Richard made a face of mock outrage. 'Never! But you must mean William Murdock? That story is true. Father took me to the King's Head hotel in Truro when I was about seven years old, and I swear we saw it working.'

Richard had a vivid memory of a large, noisy machine. He'd hidden behind his father's legs as the crowd of gentlemen he was with tried to make themselves heard above the thudding of the engine and the hissing of the steam. He grinned at Crawford across the table. 'Of course, now the talk is all about engines running on rails, not roads. Sounds a bit safer that way, if you ask me. Engines on roads would surely scare the horses.'

They both roared with laughter.

After sharing a bottle of the inn's finest claret, the pair at last decided to call it a day. It was gone eleven o'clock. Before they took their leave of each other, they agreed to meet up again in London.

Feeling more than a little foxed, Richard retired to his room to compose instructions for his solicitor. He was sure the clue they needed lay in Frederick's past. He wondered about the child his friend had spoken of and whether it had survived. Blast! He'd forgotten to ask Crawford when it had all happened. He made a mental note to get Blake to look into it.

Richard found himself picturing Emma's face and smiled; for some reason, she was never far from his thoughts. His smile rapidly faded when he wondered how on earth he could tactfully reveal the unsavoury details of her uncle's life.

Shrugging that unpleasant notion aside – there was time enough to work that problem out – he blessed the day that he'd met her. It'd been pure chance that they'd both arrived at Easterby Hall at the same time. Were all life's connections built on such tenuous links? he wondered. Whatever happened, he was going to stay with her until all was sorted. He'd given his word.

Letters written, Richard readied himself for bed. Untying his neckcloth, he folded it and carefully placed it on the chest of drawers together with his jacket and kerseymere waistcoat. It was a struggle getting his boots off – *damn, they were tight* – but he managed it at last, picturing Emma's face to dull the pain of his aching feet.

He smiled lazily as he stripped off his shirt, smoothing out the creases before it, too, joined the tidy pile. The smile turned to a scowl as he recalled Emma's wretched state on that first dreadful night. Pent-up anger against the unknown blackguard responsible for her misfortune welled up inside him; his breeches, wrenched off in one violent movement, were slung across the room. He vowed that if it were up to him, she'd never suffer the like again.

Chest still heaving, he regained control of his emotions and padded over to retrieve his breeches from where they'd fallen, placing them with his other discarded clothes.

At last, ablutions completed, he clambered unsteadily into bed. He doused the candle and hoped his dreams would be of the young woman he'd departed from that morning. A smile formed on his lips as he drifted off, thinking how close he'd been to kissing her that night he'd carried her up the stairs and wishing that he had.

Chapter 7

The next morning – washed, shaved, and impeccably dressed, even down to his tight-fitting boots – a slightly bleary-eyed Richard strode purposefully to the parlour and ordered breakfast. There was time to kill before his meeting with…? The alcohol from the previous day still befuddling his brain, Richard screwed up his eyes in concentration, trying to recall the informant's name through the thudding of his head. It'd been a while since he'd overindulged, but the fortuitous renewal of his friendship with Crawford and the discoveries about Frederick's past had made it all worthwhile. Richard had never had the habit of drinking to excess and no intention of forming one. The sensation of not being in control, especially of himself, was something he didn't enjoy.

At last it came to him. *Bill Rogers, that's right.*

Unlike his head, Richard's stomach did not suffer from the effects of the previous night's indulgence. After eating his fill of eggs and thick slices of ham and finishing a second cup of coffee, a stroll into the hazy early daylight of the High Street seemed in order. His feet took him towards the Physic Garden, then a turn along the footpath beside the river beckoned, where the early-morning mist hovered over the grey, flowing water. The gravel footpath crunched beneath his boots as he made his way back towards the High Street, taking in lungfuls of crisp, cold air as he went. He'd always considered Oxford to be at its best in the early morning, before the workers started their day and the commoners reluctantly roused themselves to attend their lectures.

Richard strolled along the footpath up the side of St Mary's church towards the Radcliffe Library, halting briefly to admire that building's monumental circular dome. He turned onto Catte Street, which finally brought him in sight of his destination. The White Horse inn had been one of his haunts when he'd studied in Oxford, which seemed a lifetime ago. He paused for a moment, letting his gaze drift over the familiar view of the Sheldonian, the Printing House, and the empty expanse of Broad Street, before turning his steps towards the inn's open door. Ducking his head, he entered the smoky taproom and peered about. A fug of smoke hung in the air. At a table in the far corner, a shifty, weasel-featured individual looked up from the tankard of ale he'd been contemplating and scrutinised Richard through narrowed eyes. He gestured to Richard with his pipe.

'You be Mr Lacey, sir?'

Richard nodded and, after catching the tapster's attention for two tankards of ale, made his way over to join the fellow who'd beckoned him.

'Yes, I'm Lacey,' Richard confirmed. 'And you must be...?'

The man's eyes darted round before he answered in a whispered rasp, 'Rogers, Bill Rogers.' Scratching his head – the sparse grey hair adorning it looked none too clean – he added, 'Your man Blake told me you'd make it worth my while to talk to you. He'd better be right.' Rogers' eyes took on a furtive glint. 'I'm risking my life coming here. If *he* finds out I've told what I know…' Rogers pulled a finger across his throat. 'Well, I know how ruthless his nibs can be.' Rogers' pipe trembled as he raised it to his mouth to take a long pull.

The cynical side of Richard questioned whether this was just an act to get him to part with his money, or was Rogers truly in fear of his life? Neither prospect was pleasant. He decided to give him the benefit of the doubt.

'If you've got anything useful to tell me, I'll be generous,' he said, jingling the purse of coins in his greatcoat pocket.

Rogers shot him a suspicious look.

'Show me. I'm not saying more till I've seen your blunt.'

Disliking the chap's manner, Richard nevertheless placed two guineas on the table. Rogers' hand shot out and the coins disappeared.

The man's lips parted in a sly smile, revealing crooked teeth. 'That'll do for starters.'

'There'll be no more until you tell me something.' The menace Richard injected into his next words was unmistakeable. 'Now… talk, or else.' It wasn't often he got angry.

Rogers blinked, then began to speak in a wheezy, panicked whisper.

'Well, I've worked for his nibs ten years now, and I've done some things for him, I can tell you.' He mopped his brow. 'But that's it, no more.' Rogers' eyes darted across to the tapster, who was lounging near the door. Assured that he couldn't be heard from that distance, he continued, 'Thought he'd changed at last. There'd been no nasty business for a fair while. Not since… never mind. But this was the limit for me.'

An icy shiver crawled up Richard's spine.

'Who are you speaking of, man? Tell me.'

There was a pause as Rogers' throat bobbed up and down convulsively, then his eyes lifted and met Richard's.

'The Duke of Wheatley, that's who.' Rogers seemed not to hear Richard's sharp intake of breath as he continued. 'I've worked for him for years… or rather, for his man of business. I saw his correspondence.' Rogers shrugged. 'Well, most of it. He's always been very good at getting what he wants.' He sent Richard a knowing look. 'All rich, powerful men pull strings, don't they?'

Richard squirmed inwardly. Wasn't he also such a one, pulling strings? Banishing the uncomfortable thought from his mind, he rapidly tried to recall everything he knew about Wheatley. It wasn't much.

The aristocrat was a shadowy figure, rarely seen in society, but the rumours that had reached even Richard's ears were that the man was ruthless. It was also said that he had a penchant for haunting the more unsavoury gaming hells and brothels when he did visit town. It wasn't sounding good.

Resting his chin on his hands and trying to project an air of insouciance, Richard prompted Rogers for more.

Leaning forward across the table, Rogers continued in an undertone. 'A few years ago, things began to change. Wheatley ordered investigations to be made about the Smythe family. In p'ticular, Frederick, the oldest son.' Rogers winked. 'Bit of a wild one, by all accounts, though I couldn't see what Wheatley had against him. Not his usual sort.' There was a pause as he sucked on his pipe, blowing out a cloud of smoke from the side of his mouth. 'Anyways,

I was told to take a message to someone from Seven Dials to do away with this 'ere Frederick and to say that his death should be made to look like an accident.'

Richard raised a quizzical eyebrow.

Rogers blinked rapidly. 'So I 'appened to read it. I can read, you know.' He sent Richard a sly look. 'Besides, you never know when things will become useful, do you?'

Richard's eyes narrowed. The man was shameless… a good thing really, considering. He focussed back on what Rogers was now telling him.

'Next thing I hears, Frederick had a fall from his horse and broke his neck.' Rogers leaned back into his seat. 'Told you I'd make it worth your while. But I'm not saying more until…' Rogers' gimlet eyes lingered on the pocket where Richard had his purse.

Richard was thunderstruck. *Good God, there was more?* He slid another two guineas across the table, and they disappeared just as quickly as before.

Satisfied with his remuneration, Rogers began again.

'Just after the celebrations for Trafalgar, when all sorts was going on, Wheatley was in London.' There was a snigger and another pull on the evil-smelling pipe. 'Letters were sent to the consulates in Athens and Patras. Seemed the duke was looking for the younger Smythe brother too.' Rogers' eyes flickered as he met Richard's steely gaze. He held up his hands. 'I know, I know. I read 'em before they were sealed.' In a more belligerent tone, he added, 'It's lucky for you I did, so don't come the 'igh and mighty with me.'

The nerve in Richard's cheek twitched. 'Just tell me what you know. I don't care how you came by the information.'

'Well, Wheatley paid someone at the consulate in Patras to intercept all mail between the Smythe family members and to re-direct it to himself instead. I reckon he expected that the family would get caught up in the local troubles there and people would forget about them. Probably assume they were dead.' A smirk appeared on Rogers' face. 'They did die, didn't they?' Rogers drained his tankard and wiped his mouth with his sleeve. His lips pursed and his eyes locked knowingly with Richard's. 'You're the viscount now, ain't I right?'

'Yes, I'm the viscount now.' Richard's lie came easily.

'Then I'd be careful if I were you, my lord. As for me… I'm going to disappear.'

Despite his dislike of the man, Richard was curious.

'Why did you decide to talk?'

Rogers shrugged. 'Murder ain't right. Why should a duke get away with it when us common folks would hang? Anyway, I need the money.' He sent Richard a meaningful look.

Richard shook his head. 'In good time. I've a few more questions. Did anything happen in the duke's household before he started on this quest with the Smythe family? Think. Anything at all?'

Rogers pulled a face.

'Can't really think of anything.'

Richard's fingers twitched. He'd a strong desire to get them round the man's throat and choke the truth out of him.

Sublimely unaware of the anger he'd provoked, Rogers took another puff of his pipe and gazed into the distance. Then he cleared his throat. 'There was the new chap,' he muttered, scratching his head, then examining his fingernails. 'That's right,' he added in a more animated tone. 'He was taken on a year or two before the business with the Smythe family started. Started helping His Grace at the War Office.' At Richard's questioning look, he added, 'Forgot to mention, Wheatley has an office there. He works with Lord Liverpool. Something to do with what's going on abroad. Never managed to discover much about that.'

Richard was privately grateful that the inner workings of the government's War Office were immune to the pryings of men such as Rogers. Otherwise goodness knows what secrets would be revealed to His Majesty's enemies.

'Anyways,' said Rogers. 'This chap I was telling you about is Wheatley's private secretary now. Good-looking young cove.' He sniggered again.

A shiver of excitement swept through Richard. He was getting close, he knew it.

'What's this young man's name, this secretary?'

Before answering, Rogers blew out several more smoke rings that curled gently upwards to the tobacco-stained ceiling.

Richard's fists clenched under the table.

'Hesketh... Holiday... no, that's not right,' teased Rogers, before noting the dangerous gleam in Richard's eye. 'Heslop, Francis Heslop. That's right. He's still there, as far as I know. Wheatley takes him everywhere. But he's a right nice cove. Not high in the instep. Always civil to those beneath him... not like some.'

Richard kept his face emotionless, hiding his elation at having a name and far more information than he'd ever expected. He decided it was worth another push.

'Anything else you can tell me about Wheatley, anything at all?'

Rogers snorted. 'Nah. He's a man of routine. Doesn't have many visitors. Spends most of his time at his Warwickshire estate. When he's in London, he often visits Horse Guards. Probably to see Lord Liverpool.' Rogers wagged his finger. 'I don't know everything, you know. I only dealt with some of the paperwork, after all.' He cupped his chin. 'There's a young sister, or 'alf-sister, I should say. Looked after her since their father died, he has. Saw to her education with governesses and such, then sent her to a school in Bath. Visited her regular. Not many single men would bother themselves about their sisters if they could pay someone to do it for them. But he always has time for her.' His eyes, now holding an avaricious gleam, fixed on Richard's.

'Now, about the blunt. I've told you all I know.'

As he stood up to leave, Richard dropped a handful of coins on the table, where they landed with a noisy clatter. 'There's ten guineas. If you remember anything else, contact Blake.'

As Richard reached the door, he heard Rogers' voice.

'Remember what I said, won't you?'

He turned back to see the smirk on Rogers' face. 'What's that?'

'Better be careful, my lord.'

Richard paid his shot at the Mitre, collected his things, and set off, expecting to reach Minster Lovell well before nightfall. By mid-afternoon, the Eynsham toll bridge was in sight.

From his vantage point atop his horse, Richard gazed over the bridge's parapet. The Thames beneath sparkled in the crisp afternoon air, dazzling his eyes, and for some reason he was reminded of Emma. He wondered what her reaction would be to the news he brought. Would she have any idea as to why a duke or his secretary might be involved in her uncle's death and the recent attacks on himself?

Drawing level with the toll booth, Richard fumbled in his pocket for coins. Impatient to be on the move, his mount snorted and pawed the ground.

'Steady, Caesar.'

The toll keeper, who'd stepped out of the booth, took a hasty step back. He'd obviously been in the job a while and knew all about horses and their tricks. The sound of hooves clattering over the bridge behind him caused Richard's mount to prance about. Whoever it was, they were not slackening their pace. Richard caught only a glimpse of a muffled figure as a bay horse skirted past him and charged onwards through the open toll gate.

Richard stared in disbelief at the rapidly disappearing rider.

'Well I never! Of all the cheek.' The old toll keeper shook his fist in the rider's direction, then hawked and spat on the ground.

'Does that happen often?' asked Richard, shaking his head.

The old man squinted up at him.

'Nay, most folks are honest, though there's always a few bad apples.' He thumped his chest and gave a raspy cough. 'Always one or two young bucks think it fun to distract me while their cronies race through.' The look in his eyes turned suspicious. 'Friend of yours, is he?'

'Certainly not,' answered Richard in haughty tones. 'But have this in any case.' He tossed down sufficient coins to pay for two riders. The toll keeper's expression transformed from suspicion to bonhomie. With a toothless grin, he touched his forelock.

'You're a true gent, sir. Have a safe journey.'

'Thank you. Good day to you.'

Richard dug his heels in and spurred his horse into a gallop. But there was no sign of the impatient rider on the road into Eynsham. Quelling his anger – he'd been ready to give the chap a piece of his mind – he told himself that there was no point in getting involved in further trouble. He'd enough to deal with as it was. Slowing to a gentle trot, he followed the signpost for Witney, where the empty road stretched into the distance and there was nothing to see but bare fields and the occasional clump of woodland.

Richard decided instead to concentrate his thoughts on Emma, a more pleasant subject than reckless riders. He'd much to share with her, and questions too. Did she know if Wheatley had any possible connection to the Smythe family? Perhaps her father had said something?

Lord, he was eager to see her again and not just to question her about Wheatley. She was so different from most other young ladies of his acquaintance. There was a reserve about her coupled with sensitivity. Yet he'd also seen steely determination in her eyes. He pictured her enigmatic smile and sparkling, intelligent grey eyes. Her dark-brown hair had felt gloriously soft and silky against his cheek when he'd carried her – to think she'd blithely hacked most of it off in order to pass as a boy! Something about her drew him like a moth to a flame. Something more than duty, more than the attractions of her body... more even than the promise he'd made.

Richard sighed and frowned, glancing at the sky ahead. Grey clouds were gathering in the west. The church spire in the distance told him it wasn't much further to Witney. With luck, he'd be back at Easterby Hall before the storm broke. And what a blessing it would be to remove his boots, he acknowledged to himself wryly, even though he'd be obliged to put up with Carter's smirks for some time to come.

Richard bent his head to scrutinise the offending articles. As he did so, something whistled past his ear and embedded itself with a loud thud into the trunk of the tree on the far side of the road. A curse left his lips as Caesar reared up, nearly unseating him. Regaining his balance, Richard got control of the panicking horse and turned his head in the direction of the shot... for that was what it was, he was certain. Someone had fired at him.

Through the growing gloom, he spotted a figure on horseback lurking in the copse at the side of the road. Richard guessed that, whoever it was, they were reloading their pistol. He didn't hesitate. Spurring his mount into a gallop, he headed straight for his attacker. The rider looked up, wheeled his horse around, and set off across the fields. His temper riled, Richard's first thought was to pursue, but common sense told him it would not be a wise course of action. Better to return in one piece to Easterby Hall and make sure Emma, Julia, and Jamie were safe.

His face set in grim determination, Richard returned to the road.

Night was drawing in by the time Richard reached Easterby Hall. Thankfully, the remainder of the journey had been uneventful. Apart from a carrier, his wagon laden with Witney blankets bound for Burford, Richard had encountered no-one. Leaving his horse with a groom, he entered the house by one of the side doors, pausing only to check with one of the manservants whether all had been well in his absence. Reassured that everything was as it should be, he continued up to his room to change before seeking out Emma and Julia. It wasn't long before Carter arrived bearing a welcome pitcher of hot water.

'Welcome home, sir. Thought you might like to tidy up with a wash and a shave.'

'You do anticipate my needs, Carter. It's most unsettling that you seem to read my mind.'

'Just doing my job, sir. How are the boots, by the way?'

Was that a smirk on the man's face?

'Funny you should ask, Carter. I think they may have saved my life.'

Chapter 8

HAVING CHANGED INTO MORE suitable clothes for dining at home, Richard headed for the library, drawn by the sound of voices and laughter. There, he found Jamie on the rug in front of the fire playing spillikins, while Julia and Emma were together on the sofa, huddled over a copy of *La Belle Assemblée* and laughing at the illustrations of the latest styles.

'I couldn't possibly wear that. Why, it's positively indecent. Are the fashions truly now so extreme?' Emma's words of mock horror reminded him how long she'd been away from England.

'Oh, some are much worse,' said Julia with a chuckle. She caught sight of her brother and leapt up to greet him. 'Richard! You're back!'

Enveloped in his sister's hug, he saw a blush appear on Emma's cheeks as she too rose from her seat and smiled her welcome. Jamie's spillikins were abandoned as he rushed to greet Richard, nearly overbalancing him with his exuberance.

'Oh marvellous, you're back. I can go out riding again.' Jamie's tone became indignant. 'You wouldn't believe it, Cousin Richard. They wouldn't let me go further than the paddock, and even then I had to have a groom with me. I'm not a child, you know.'

One of the drawbacks of family life, mused Richard, was having to act the authority figure from time to time. He'd gone through much the same thing with David.

'Steady on, old chap. How are you? Still in one piece, I see. I'm glad to hear the ladies have been taking my instructions seriously.'

Jamie's look became incredulous. 'Your instructions? You mean you told them to keep me by the house? Why?'

Before Richard could reply, Emma briskly cut in. 'Jamie, I told you. Someone seems to be causing trouble for our family, and we need to find out who it is before any more accidents occur.'

Richard was pleased that Emma didn't dissemble. She'd also used the words "our family". Did that mean she fully accepted him?

Jamie's mouth opened to object, but Richard got in first. 'Your sister is correct, Jamie.'

The lad looked at him in surprise and shut his mouth again, so Richard decided to continue. Might as well get it over with while they were all together, he told himself. 'Talking about accidents... something happened on my way back from Oxford.'

Emma blanched. 'My goodness, are you all right, Richard? I'd never forgive myself if you suffered because of our family connection.'

He sent her a reassuring smile. 'Yes, I'm all in one piece and fine. Well, apart from my feet and possibly my pride.'

Julia, in her decisive way, demanded, 'Tell us what happened, Richard, for goodness' sake. Can't you see Emma and I are worried?'

'Someone took a shot at me as I was coming back. Fortunately, they missed.' There was a collective gasp, but Richard ignored it and carried on. He'd far more important news to disclose. 'I only caught a glimpse of the fellow before he raced off. As it was getting late, I thought it best to come straight here to make sure you were all safe rather than risk chasing after him.' His eyes focussed on Emma. 'Besides, I think I may have discovered who is behind it all.'

Emma's heart had leapt when Richard appeared in the doorway of the drawing room, looking very handsome. She'd missed his company the previous evening, despite her efforts to keep herself occupied. Now she felt positively ill. He'd been put in danger because of her. And here he was, saying he knew the identity of the culprit.

'Wh-who do you think it might be?' she asked, trying unsuccessfully not to betray her nerves.

He guided her by the elbow back to the sofa. The moment his hand touched her arm, a feeling of calm settled over her. Somehow, his presence made her feel safe.

'Did you ever hear your father speak of the Duke of Wheatley?'

She racked her brains but came up with nothing.

'Not that I can recall. Father moved in academic circles. He and Mama rarely attended social events, and I don't remember the duke's name in connection with any of his scholarly pursuits.' Emma sucked her cheeks in and frowned. 'Is he an antiquarian too?'

Richard's face was grim. 'I'm fairly certain he has no interest in antiquarian matters.'

'Why do you think Wheatley is responsible then? Surely there's no other reason for anyone to hold a grudge against my father. It might just all be some terrible misunderstanding.' To her surprise, two spots of colour appeared on Richard's cheeks, and he tugged at the edges of his neckcloth as if it were suddenly too tight. She made her mind up. 'I'll speak to His Grace and clear the matter up.'

'Good grief, no!' was Richard's abrupt and loud response.

'How dare you!' The words were out of Emma's mouth before she could stop them. She wasn't going to be ordered about. Glancing at Julia's white face, she could see she was shocked too, but whether at her brother's words or her own, Emma couldn't tell.

Richard bit his lip.

'I'm sorry. I didn't mean to raise my voice.' His tone was conciliatory. 'It's just that… well, I want to be absolutely certain before we make accusations. If he is innocent, that could cause us more trouble – something we don't need at the moment. But if he is the culprit, there's no telling what he might do.' Richard's eyes narrowed in a warning. 'He's a very powerful and influential man, after all.'

Emma was gratified by his apology, but she wasn't going to be fobbed off. It was her brother who was in danger, and so it was her responsibility to solve the problem. She'd proved that she could achieve things that women were not supposed to be able to do. It would take more than an oblique warning from Richard to divert her from her purpose.

'Yes, I understand what you're saying. But what *shall* I do?'

Richard's jaw tightened and she could tell he was going to scold, but before he could say anything, Julia stepped in.

'Perhaps we should discuss that after dinner. Here's Wrighton now.'

Emma, not wishing to cause a scene, nodded her agreement and allowed herself to be led into the dining room by a now rather grim-faced Richard.

Richard leaned against the mantelpiece and took a sip from the glass of port in his hand. The lines of his face had relaxed somewhat.

'That's settled then. Tomorrow we'll head off to London.' He looked at his sister. 'Julia, if you'd be good enough to reside in my townhouse, then Emma and Jamie will be suitably chaperoned. I'm sure George will be happy to join you there.'

'But I still don't see why I cannot stay with my grandmother,' remonstrated Emma. She'd been engrossed in pouring the tea when his words caught her attention. How would she be able to make her own investigations under Richard's constant scrutiny? He meant well, and she was grateful for his help, but she felt compelled to play an active part and not just be a passive bystander. She was not a helpless female waiting for a man to come and rescue her, even though it would be so easy to let him take control. Memories of her mother stiffened her resolve.

Julia answered Emma's question.

'But you don't know how her health is yet or whether she has recovered from her ague. Think of the shock if any more attempts are made.'

Emma flushed. Julia was right.

'Oh, I didn't think. You're correct, of course.'

No, Emma didn't know at all what state her grandmother was in. It seemed that she'd no option but to agree to Richard's plans… for now.

She glanced at Richard, still lounging by the fireplace. If she wasn't mistaken, he was looking somewhat smug.

He addressed her directly. 'No-one knows that you and Jamie have returned safely to England. If you stay with your grandmother, word is bound to get back to the duke… or whoever it is who's responsible for our current problems.' He set his glass down and began to pace back and forth in front of the fire. 'Her servants may talk. Whereas my staff are paid well and know where their loyalties lie.' He paused his pacing to twitch the ormolu clock on the mantelpiece into a better alignment. 'I've been thinking that we could pass you off as distant cousins, come to spend time in London, which is true enough. By keeping as near to the truth as possible, we shall get by.' Richard turned to face her, a look of pleading in his dark eyes. 'You'd be able to visit your grandmother quite openly that way, as I'm sure no-one will recognise you after all this time. Come on, what do you say to that?'

Emma took a breath and considered the smooth words delivered with a most engaging smile. Richard's tone had been coaxing, persuasive. A dangerous man. She'd have to maintain her guard. There was no telling what else he could persuade her to. It was also infuriating how he'd anticipated all her objections.

Feeling thoroughly outmanoeuvred, she answered, 'You seem to have thought of everything. But do you agree, Julia? I feel bad at disrupting your life too.'

'Nonsense, my dear,' said Julia, putting her arm round Emma's shoulder. 'We're friends, are we not, and cousins, in truth? I'm perfectly happy to stay in the family townhouse with you. It's much more modern than the Morton townhouse, with every convenience.' Her eyes crinkled as she giggled. 'Besides, I'm sure George won't have any objections. In fact, he'll be in heaven. He's been trying to tempt Richard's cook away for ages, so to dine there every day… well!'

Richard arched his eyebrow at Emma. 'That's settled, then? No more objections to my plan?'

Emma, knowing she was beaten, nodded.

Later, alone in her room, Emma pondered what she was going to do. Happy that she would see her grandmother at last, she was more than a little anxious about Richard's plans to involve himself in what she considered to be her problems. He was a distant cousin, after all, and it was her responsibility to protect her brother. But the infuriating man was set on risking his own life by continuing the fiction that the title was his. Should she really have agreed to let him do so? Her brow wrinkled in a frown. On the other hand, it might keep Jamie from danger. Lord, what a conundrum. She didn't want anyone to get hurt. She'd been shocked beyond measure at Richard's account of the attempt on his life on his way back from Oxford and sick at the thought of him being killed.

Her mouth set in a firm line. Somehow, with or without Richard's blessing, she'd sort matters for her family.

Left on his own, Richard took his time finishing his port, musing on the best way for them to travel on the morrow. He decided Emma and Jamie should go with his sister in her carriage, while he rode alongside on Caesar. Philip Cullen, his man of business would follow in the curricle.

Richard smiled to himself. Phil was rather more than a man of business, though what he was Richard couldn't entirely be sure, but he had his suspicions. Phil's life outside of his work for Richard was shrouded in secrecy. Contacted by Lord Liverpool to take Phil on, Richard had readily agreed when it was made known that Phil was working for the government. Important work in the war against Napoleon.

All Richard had known about the personable chap was that he was a younger son, from Cornwall like himself, and with no estate to inherit. Free of ties, he was the perfect government agent. At least, that had been the case until a short time ago when Phil's older brother had unexpectedly died, leaving Phil with an estate and responsibilities, a situation which would have to be resolved.

Since being taken on, Phil had impressed Richard with his intelligence and application. In return, Richard was happy to turn a blind eye to Phil's irregular hours, as long as the job Richard paid him for was completed. So far, all had worked well. Phil also happened to be a regular at Gentleman Jackson's and was a pretty good shot – handy if they were waylaid on the journey. Richard fervently hoped Phil's martial skills wouldn't be required.

Phil's connection to the War Office had been another reason for Richard's surprise on learning of Wheatley's involvement with the same department. He'd spoken to Phil about Rogers' claims about the duke, but Phil had been sceptical and urged him to be cautious.

'I'm only small fry there,' Phil had told him, 'but I can tell you that Wheatley is very well thought of. I'm not quite sure what he is responsible for – as you know, we're only told what we need to know and no more – but you can be certain he is more concerned with pursuing French informants than personal vendettas.'

Richard had been inclined to agree.

Richard returned to working out his plans for the following day. He'd decided that Carter and the two maids should travel in the large carriage with the luggage. They were unlikely to be targets. He calculated that they would require one overnight stop before reaching his house in Bedford Square.

Richard set his glass down with a satisfied smile. Now he'd convinced Emma to agree to his plans, it wouldn't take long for him to get to the bottom of things. She'd be unable to get up to any dangerous nonsense while under his roof. He'd promised to keep her safe, and he was a man of his word. He yawned as he made his way upstairs. Yes, soon all would be well.

Chapter 9

A LATE, HARD FROST greeted them the next morning. The carriage horses, eager to be off, stomped on the iron ground and tossed their manes. Joe Henning was having a time of it keeping them under control.

'Easy, boys, easy.'

'Everything all right there, Mr Henning?' asked Richard. Dressed against the cold in his travelling greatcoat and a curly beaver hat, he'd come out to oversee the final preparations and to escort Emma and Julia into their carriage.

Joe grinned and raised his hand to his forehead. 'Yes, sir. They're raring to go. Should be able to keep up a brisk pace if it stays dry and clear. We should make Maidenhead easily by nightfall.'

'Good man. That's what I thought.'

At the sound of voices, Richard turned to see Emma arm in arm with Julia coming down the steps. They, too, were warmly attired, and both sported jaunty hats. He blinked in appreciation, for Emma was looking particularly fetching in a dark-red velvet turban and matching pelisse, which he recognised as belonging to his sister. The turban gave a glow to Emma's pale complexion and framed her elfin face. Richard's smile disappeared as he caught their conversation.

'Are you sure you're fine, Julia? You're looking a bit peaked.' Emma's voice sounded anxious. 'I'm sure we can hold off travelling if you're not well. Richard surely won't mind.'

Julia, with an airy wave, dismissed Emma's suggestion. 'No, no. It's just a little tummy upset, I'm sure. I probably indulged in too much dessert last night.' She gave what sounded to her brother like a very forced laugh. 'George always says I eat more than I should when it comes to pudding.' Julia held a defiant look in her eyes as Richard stalked towards her, forcing him to question why all the females in his life could be so troublesome.

'Now, don't you start fussing too, Richard,' she said rather acidly. 'I'm perfectly fine to travel. Susan shouldn't have mentioned it.'

'Oh, please don't blame Susan,' said Emma, looking worried. 'Polly just happened to notice that your breakfast was untouched and told me that you might not be feeling quite the thing. I'm sorry, I didn't mean to upset you.'

Richard was curious. Emma looked awkward and embarrassed. His sister was unusually pale. Richard pulled off his riding gauntlets, ready to postpone their journey if Julia was ill. What he couldn't understand was why Julia was being so defensive. Before he could say anything, his sister spoke.

'I'm sorry for snapping, Emma.' Julia's eyes were now apologetic. She turned to him. 'Richard, I have a slight headache, that's all. I shall be as right as anything once we're on our way. I don't mean to be a sourpuss.'

Emma, still looking concerned, said, 'Don't worry, there's nothing to forgive. But do let me know if you begin to feel unwell again. Mama often suffered with headaches, so I know a few remedies, and I'd be perfectly happy to travel with the curtains drawn if it helps.'

Julia's mouth twitched. 'I'm not as bad as that, I assure you. Come on. Give me your hand, Richard.'

Richard frowned, perplexed as to why his sister, who'd first claimed it was a stomach upset that was causing her to look unwell, was now saying that it was a headache. He suspected something else was going on.

Richard gave her a long, penetrating look. 'If you're quite sure, Julia?'

Her eyes flickered away from his as she answered briskly, 'Of course I am. Now give me your hand, Richard, if you please.'

Thoroughly nonplussed, he took her proffered hand and helped her into the coach. Julia hardly ever suffered from headaches. Out of the three siblings, he considered her to have the strongest constitution. He hoped this wasn't something else he was going to have to worry about. They needed to reach London as quickly as possible.

'Don't worry. I'll look out for her.' Emma's words, spoken in warm, hushed tones brought him back to the present. He acknowledged them by giving her hand a quick squeeze as he handed her up into the carriage. The smile Emma sent him told him that his sister was in safe hands. Such a capable young woman and an attractive one too, despite her propensity for alarming him with her dangerous notions.

The sight of Jamie's slight figure, shoulders hunched and hands jammed in pockets, spoke eloquently of the lad's thoughts on travelling with the ladies and gave Richard an idea.

'Jamie, how would you like to ride in the curricle with me?'

The boy's face lit up.

'Really? I say! Thanks, Richard. You're a good sport.'

Richard grinned at Jamie's beaming face. At least one of the party was happy.

Richard walked up to Phil, who'd just brought the curricle round from the stables.

'Phil, would you mind riding Caesar while I take Jamie up with me?'

Phil's face showed surprise. 'Certainly, though I'm honoured that you entrust him to me.' Phil jumped down and headed towards the frisky chestnut stallion who was dragging behind him a panting and red-faced stableboy.

Richard laughed. 'I've seen you ride, remember. And if you can control that beast you keep back in Falmouth, I'm sure you can manage Caesar.'

Soon, the cavalcade set off.

It was getting on for evening when the carriages at last drew into the yard of the King's Arms. The day had gone without incident, much to Richard's relief, and he was pleased to note, as she alighted, that the colour had returned to Julia's cheeks.

Emma saw him watching his sister and whispered as she passed him, 'Don't worry, she seems fine now. And I'll look after her if she becomes unwell again.'

'Thank you. It's good to know I can rely on you.'

He continued to watch as Emma's slight figure disappeared into the inn, unable to drag his eyes away. There was definitely much more to her than met the eye.

After a welcome night's rest, Emma woke up to the sound of a cockerel crowing and wheels turning on the cobbles in the yard below. She lay still for a moment, enjoying the sensation of not being constantly jolted around. As well sprung as Richard's travelling carriage was, she would be glad to reach their destination, for there'd been several times during the previous day's journey when she'd been convinced that Julia would faint. Despite her denials to the contrary, Emma was certain that her friend was ailing.

Rubbing the sleep from her eyes, Emma sat up to see the huddled shape that was Polly curled up on the truckle bed nearby. Emma smiled at the sound of the maid's gentle snoring and decided to let her sleep a while longer.

Then another sound caught her ears, which seemed to be coming from Julia's room next door. It sounded very like someone retching. Panic-stricken, Emma flung off the blankets, threw a shawl over her shoulders, and set off to discover what was going on. She tapped lightly on Julia's door.

'It's only me, Julia. May I enter?'

There were sounds of muffled voices, then Susan opened the door, in her hands a covered bowl. She bobbed a quick curtsey and slipped past a startled Emma, heading for the stairs. Stepping inside the dimly lit room, Emma saw that

Julia was upright in the bed, her head bent over another receptacle.

Julia groaned and waved her in, without looking up. 'I see you've found me out.'

Emma moved nearer, a concerned expression on her face. 'What do you mean? I heard you being ill.' She moved to the window and pulled at the shutters to let in some light. Her eyes widened at Julia's ashen face. 'Goodness me, you look pale. Is it something you've eaten?' A puzzled frown creased her brow. 'Though we both ate the same things last night and I seem to be fine.'

Despite her obvious distress, Julia managed a smile as she wiped her mouth.

'You really haven't guessed? I'm increasing, of course. But don't tell Richard. He'll only insist on taking it even slower. Besides, I want to tell George first.'

Emma stared and her mouth dropped open. She knew nothing about pregnancy. It was not a subject that her mother had ever discussed with her. There'd been no need, after all. She'd never had a suitor, and there'd been no plans for her to wed. And now she never would, she told herself. She knew babies came after marriage but wasn't sure exactly how it all came about. As for the signs of pregnancy, well, she hadn't a clue. Her mouth twisted. No marriage meant no babies. Emma forced that thought away.

Climbing onto the bed, she gave Julia a hug and they both giggled with pleasure, delighted with their shared secret.

Emma decided that she might as well learn more.

'Do you mean to tell me that one is sick when one is expecting? Is it like that all the way through?'

Julia gave a wan smile.

'Only at the beginning, or so I've been told. I'd a suspicion I might be increasing when Richard's letter arrived. My courses hadn't come and I'm never late.' Her eyes twinkled with mischief. 'I didn't say anything because I knew George wouldn't be happy for me to travel. But honestly, apart from this beastly morning sickness – which Susan assures me is perfectly normal – and being a little tired, I feel really well.' She grasped Emma's hand. 'So, please, you won't say anything, will you?'

Quelling her misgivings, Emma promised. 'Not if you don't wish me to, of course I won't.'

Julia beamed at her. 'Thank you. I knew I could rely on you.'

Emma winced inwardly at this echo of Richard's words. Would he still trust her once he discovered that she'd kept quiet about his sister's condition? Well, it was Julia's secret to keep, and she wasn't going to break a confidence.

Julia continued, her face radiating excitement. 'I've been dying to share my good news with another female. I'm so glad we're friends. I always wanted a sister, and now I feel I've got one.'

'As do I,' replied Emma, smiling. 'Travelling abroad meant there weren't young ladies of my age that I could mix with. In any case, Papa preferred to avoid society. For the last few years, there were no English people at all living near us.'

As she returned to her room, Emma pondered on whether, once life got back to normal, she could remain good friends with Julia, for it would also inevitably mean continuing to see Richard, a man who had a disturbing effect on her emotions. Dare she take the risk? But, she told herself, he might not want an unmarried, independent-minded female keeping company with his sister. Come to that, neither might the saintly George. She rolled her eyes. It was beginning to dawn on her that heeding her mother's words would have repercussions on all aspects of her life, not just her friendships. There was no acceptable role for an unmarried lady of her class other than as a maiden aunt or a lady's companion. It was almost unheard of for a female to make her own way in the world independent of male guidance and control. She frowned to herself. And what would Grandmamma say?

Yes, it was all getting very complicated.

Down in the parlour, the party enjoyed a hurried breakfast. Julia wasn't the only one feeling not quite the thing. Richard was suffering the effects of a disturbed night. Who would've guessed that Jamie, with whom he'd shared a room, was subject to thrashing about and talking in his sleep? From the boy's disjointed ramblings, Richard deduced that the lad was having nightmares about his journey back from Greece – nightmares so vivid in their terrors that Richard had been forced to tuck the lad back into his truckle bed several times during the night.

Richard gazed round the table with bleary eyes, noting happily that at least his sister's face showed no sign of illness. She was smiling brightly, even eating a little toast and drinking a dish of tea.

One less thing to worry about at least, he told himself, blissfully unaware that his sister's glowing cheeks were the result of a judicious application of rouge. Finding nothing else to concern him in his companions, apart from Emma's beguilingly disturbing smile, he decided that they should continue their journey.

Soon they were on their way again and making good time, thanks to the fine weather and dry roads. But as the day wore on, clouds gathered and a storm threatened. The first heavy spots of rain were felt just as they were nearing Hounslow, and it wasn't long before the heavens opened. Richard, who was driving the curricle with Jamie beside him, had given the lad his own heavy waterproof to wear while he made do with a spare cloak and a hat pulled down over his brow.

'Not far to go now, Jamie,' said Richard in a bolstering tone. 'We'll stop shortly to dry off and get some food, and with luck the rain will blow over.'

The forlorn, bedraggled figure at his side nodded in agreement. Richard smiled despite his own discomfort. Jamie was getting over his excitement at riding outside. Richard fervently hoped that the weather would clear, as he was wet, tired, and hungry too.

To add to Richard's troubles, rainwater had collected in the brim of his hat and streamed down his face with every jolt of the wheels. Gritting his teeth, he tried to ignore it, but soon even his calm temperament was sorely tried. With a grimace, Richard fumbled for his handkerchief, and as he did so something whizzed past his head.

There was a scream from Jamie.

Richard's eyes shot to the boy who was now slumped down clutching his arm. Blood seeped through the sleeve of the lad's coat, and his face was deathly pale. Richard felt an icy shaft of fear.

Not the boy. Not the boy.

Richard strived to keep his voice calm. 'Steady, Jamie, hold on. Let's stop and see what's happened.'

Phil cantered up to Richard's side, his pistol drawn.

'I heard a shot. Are you all right?' Phil's eyes widened at the sight of Jamie's bloodied arm, and he pointed to a copse at the side of the road. 'I think it came from there.' Without waiting for an answer, he wheeled his horse round and added, 'I'm going over,' before galloping off in a hail of mud and dirt.

All Richard could think was that it should be him dealing with the problem, but his first concern had to be for Jamie, who was now whimpering.

'Can you remain still for a moment until I can come round and lift you down?' asked Richard gently. He didn't want to panic the lad.

Jamie gave a slight nod, his face creased in pain. Satisfied that Jamie wouldn't tumble, Richard tied the reins off and climbed down. By this time, Henning had brought the travelling carriage to a halt, leaving it in charge of the under groom, and was making his way towards Richard.

'What's the problem, sir?' Henning's mouth dropped open as he caught sight of Jamie. 'Good grief! What happened? Where's Mr Cullen?'

Richard was brusque. 'Never mind that for now. Can you help me get the lad down? We need to take care with his arm. He's been shot.'

Henning sprang into action, much to Richard's approval, and deftly manoeuvred Jamie into Richard's waiting arms.

The rain was still coming down, but thankfully not as heavily as before.

A female voice called, 'What's happening? Is everything all right? Why have we stopped?'

Emma had stepped down from the coach and was starting to pick her way through the puddles when her eyes alighted on her brother. Before Richard could call out a warning, she was running towards him. Richard braced himself. He wasn't in the mood for female hysterics.

To his surprise, she didn't faint or scream, but seeming to grasp the situation at once, she started to issue orders.

'Get him into the coach where he can lie down, please,' she said briskly. 'I'll tell Julia to clear the seat.' Spinning on her heels, she trotted back towards the coach. Her instructions to Julia were calm and concise. 'Julia, would you mind terribly making room for Jamie to lie down? I think there's been an accident, and we need to get him warm and dry.'

Stunned and not a little awestruck at her composure, Richard swiftly followed and placed Jamie in the carriage in the space Julia had quickly vacated. The lad was being very brave, biting his lower lip in what looked like an effort to restrain himself from crying out. Richard was beginning to understand how the pair had overcome the perils of their journey back to England.

Emma tugged on Richard's sleeve. 'What happened?' Her voice was commendably steady.

Richard grimaced. 'He's been shot. But no doubt it was meant for me.' He sent worried eyes towards the lad, who was pale and staring anxiously at his sister. 'Would that the ball had found its true mark rather than him.'

Julia gasped and Emma's eyes flickered. 'Nonsense,' she said. 'He's been wounded in the arm. All is not lost. We must get his coat off to see what damage has been done. Would you do it, Richard?'

Richard nodded. It wasn't often that he took orders from a female.

'Of course. Come, gently does it, Jamie. I'll try not to hurt you, old man,' he murmured to the lad, who now appeared to be rallying.

There were more gasps from Julia as Jamie's blood-soaked shirtsleeve was revealed.

'Let me have your cravat, Richard,' Emma instructed.

Richard wordlessly complied as Emma carefully pulled up the blood-soaked shirtsleeve to examine the wound.

She let out a breath. 'It's only a flesh wound, thank goodness. Look, it seems to have skimmed the top part of his arm. I think the ball must have missed embedding itself. Have you got any alcohol? It will help until he sees a doctor.'

Richard hurried back to the curricle to retrieve his flask. Filled with guilt, he was blaming himself for not taking better care of Jamie. Emma's composure had also shaken him. Who would guess from her fragile appearance that here was such a determined and purposeful woman? She'd behaved as if a shooting were an everyday occurrence, taking charge in an unobtrusive way, issuing instructions, and all the while reassuring her brother. He'd never met anyone like her. Even Julia had wilted, and up to now she'd been the strongest female he'd known.

He sprinted back with the flask as Emma was cutting the last of the sleeve from Jamie's arm with a pair of needlework scissors. She took it from him and proceeded to pour a liberal amount over the wound.

Jamie yelped. 'Devil take it, Emma! What are you doing?'

'Hush, mind your language, Jamie,' scolded Emma. 'I remembered seeing one of the village women treating a boy who'd been shot. She told me it helped the healing process. Of course, it wasn't brandy; I think it was ouzo. But this might help until we get you to a doctor.'

The sound of horses' hooves approaching signalled Phil's return. There was a grimace on Phil's face as he reined in his panting horse.

'Sorry, Richard. I couldn't catch him. The devil of it is that I nearly had him at one point. But with his head start and the light fading…' Phil's shoulders slumped.

Although he was disappointed that the would-be assassin had escaped, Richard was glad that Phil had returned in one piece. One victim was quite enough for one day.

'Never mind that now.' He grasped Phil's hand. 'Thanks for trying.' Richard returned to the coach and spoke to Emma and Julia. 'We'll head off now before it gets too dark. It shouldn't take long to reach London.' He cocked his head to one side and looked inquiringly at Emma. 'Or do you think we should try to find a doctor in Brentford?'

She answered without hesitation.

'The bleeding has stopped and the wound doesn't look too deep. So I think it better that we continue to London and get a doctor there to look at his arm. He should be fine once we get him settled in a proper bed.'

Richard nodded, impressed again by Emma's calm and decisive manner.

'It shall be as you wish. Would you prefer me to travel in the carriage with you?'

Emma looked at Julia. Julia shook her head.

'No, we'll be fine. Emma is proving to be a very efficient nurse.' Julia smiled at her blushing friend, then wagged her finger at her brother. 'Just make sure nothing happens to you.'

'No fear. Be sure to let Henning know if you require anything or if Jamie's condition deteriorates.' Richard headed back to join Phil.

Back in the coach, Jamie had drifted off to sleep. Emma, who excelled at showing a calm face to the world regardless of the turmoil she was feeling, was currently a seething mass of nerves. What if the ball had hit him in a more critical spot? What if the assassin had hit Richard, his intended target? She couldn't bear to contemplate it. It could so easily have been fatal for either of them. She had to get to the bottom of this as soon as possible before someone was seriously hurt. Lost in her thoughts, she was startled when Julia grasped her hand.

'You're very quiet, Emma. Don't worry. Richard will see us safely home.'

Julia's utter confidence in her brother's abilities made Emma feel wistful. If only she had someone she could rely on completely. But experience had taught her that she couldn't rely on anyone, not even her father.

'I'm sorry. Don't worry about me,' Emma whispered in reply, trying not to disturb her sleeping brother. 'I should be taking care of you, especially in your condition.'

'Nonsense. I'm fine,' replied Julia. 'Now, try and get some sleep. It shouldn't be too long.'

Meanwhile, in the curricle, Richard was mentally berating himself. He couldn't forgive himself for not spotting the culprit who'd obviously been lurking at the side of the road. It was his fault that the boy had been injured; if only he hadn't leaned back when he did. Would Emma ever forgive him?

His mind continued in circles. Could it have been down to Wheatley? Why? What motive did the man have? And why had no other suspects presented themselves? Richard knew that he had to sort this mess out as soon as possible, for Emma's sake.

The curricle gave a sudden lurch as its wheels went over a hidden pothole and Richard was almost thrown out of his seat.

Phil, who was riding alongside, grinned.

'Steady there. You'll never make the Four Horse Club at that rate.'

'Don't think they'd have me in any case. It's a good thing that we're nearly there. I've had enough shocks for one day.'

Chapter 10

THE HORSES HAD BARELY halted in front of the Bedford Square townhouse before Richard leapt down and was hammering on the door. A footman stood to attention as Grimes, Richard's ever-efficient butler, greeted him with a bow.

'Good evening, sir. Welcome back. We received your message, and the guest rooms have been prepared for Mrs Morton and the young lady and her brother. Mr Morton is already here, by the way.' The butler took Richard's greatcoat and handed it to the footman as he continued speaking. 'I took the liberty of settling him in the library to await your arrival. Your brother is also here.'

Richard nodded. Well, it seemed everyone was present and correct, even David.

'Thank you, Grimes. Would you arrange for hot baths to be prepared for the two ladies? I'll have one later. I have some things to do first. Most importantly, send one of the footmen to fetch Dr Donaldson immediately.'

The butler's face turned solicitous.

'I hope nothing is amiss, sir. Is one of the ladies unwell?'

'No. We suffered an accident on the way. My young cousin hurt his arm. I'm sure it's nothing serious, but I want to set his sister's mind at rest.'

'Of course, sir. I'll see to it right away.' Grimes gestured to another of the footmen, gave him whispered instructions, and the man sped off into the dark. The rumble of wheels on the cobbles heralded the arrival of Julia's coach, which had been following close behind. Julia beckoned from the coach window and Richard's stomach lurched, wondering what other disaster had occurred. Vaulting back down to the street, he flung open the carriage door, astounding the footman who'd been poised to let down the steps.

'What is it, Julia? Is Emma unwell? How is Jamie?' Had the lad taken a turn for the worse or Emma succumbed to shock? His heart raced as these fears crowded his thoughts. When had he become such a nerve-racked fellow?

Julia held a finger to her lips. 'Shh. Nothing is amiss,' she whispered.

He peered past her into the gloom of the coach. Both Jamie and Emma were slumbering.

'Oh. They're both asleep.'

'Very observant of you, Richard,' was his sister's tart reply. 'No wonder you manage to do so well.' She held out her hand. 'Here, help me down.'

Richard's racing heart returned to its normal pace.

As he escorted Julia into the vestibule, he smiled and said, 'I believe George is in the library.'

Julia gave a little gasp and sped off up the stairs, lifting her skirts as she ran. Richard shook his head and chuckled. She'd definitely recovered from her indisposition of the morning. Richard turned briskly to the footman, who was now shuffling his feet and gazing up at the star-filled sky.

'Take the young gentleman up to the room Mrs Wilson has prepared for him. Mind his arm as you go. He's suffered an injury.'

Jamie barely stirred as the burly chap hefted him in his arms and took him inside. Emma was still fast asleep. She didn't stir at all when Richard picked her up. Cradling her against his chest, he manoeuvred her out of the coach and up the steps. As he climbed the stairs with his burden, he caught her subtle scent. It reminded him of summer roses.

Disturbed by the movement, Emma opened her eyes, blinking in the light of the resplendently lit stairwell.

'Where am I?' she asked, alarm in her eyes. 'Goodness, what are you doing? I can walk perfectly well. Please put me down.'

He hissed into her ear. 'Keep still, for pity's sake, or I'll drop you. I'm taking you to your room.' She gave a frustrated groan but stopped struggling. 'You were fast asleep and Julia didn't want me to disturb you. Jamie is being settled, and the doctor is on his way to see him.'

At last, to his relief, he reached his destination. Emma wasn't heavy, but for some reason, his pulse was racing and he was finding it difficult to breathe. He pushed open the bedchamber door with his knee and caught his breath. It still gave him a jolt seeing the familiar furnishings with their colours of springtime.

'Oh, what a beautiful room.'

Emma's whispered exclamation brought him to his senses. He set her on her feet, but somehow his arm remained around her waist as she joined him in admiring the bedchamber.

'This used to be my mother's room,' he murmured wistfully. 'It's on the quiet side of the house, so you shouldn't be disturbed by the noise of tradesmen in the morning. She loved it because it catches the morning sun… said it was like waking up in a garden. I'd quite forgotten how lovely it is. It's an age since I've been in here, not since Mama…' His gaze met Emma's upturned eyes, and he became suddenly aware that he still had his arm about her. He released her and she moved swiftly away. It had felt good, her being so close to him. Her body fitted neatly against his. He could get used to that. Richard gave himself a mental shake. Emma was far too independent-minded for him. He was just being ridiculously fanciful. Wasn't he?

It was Emma who broke the silence between them.

'I'm sorry. I'll move to another room if you prefer. You'll want to keep her room as it is.'

'No. You misunderstand me,' he said. 'I miss her, but I can't help but think she would approve of you having her room.'

He stepped nearer, taking in every detail of her face.

'She would have liked you, I'm sure,' he rushed on, the words tumbling out of his mouth. 'And I'm certain she would expect me to take care of you. What I mean to say is, I want to…'

The unexpected intrusion of two footmen bearing a heavy trunk cut his words short.

'Shall we put it here, my lord?' one of them asked, mopping his gleaming brow.

Richard gathered his disordered wits and nodded to the man. Deciding that he'd already said too much, he bowed to Emma and departed.

Emma gaped as Richard left the room. They'd been having a conversation, and she was beginning to feel as if she was getting to know him better, when he'd suddenly clammed up. His moving words about his mother had almost managed to dispel the crushing embarrassment of waking up and finding herself in his arms. Emma flushed at the memory, recalling dark, intense eyes and a mouth with the hint of a smile – the closest she'd ever been to a man's lips. The stubble on his chin made him appear darker and very masculine. The wonder of it was that she hadn't felt frightened. Rather, like the evening she'd spent with him at Easterby Hall, she'd felt safe.

Wrapping her arms around herself, Emma gave a deep sigh. She'd have to be careful. Richard was a compelling and attractive man, and if she didn't heed her mother's warning, she would be in great danger of falling under his spell.

Once clear of Emma's room, Richard mentally berated himself. It was becoming a bit of a habit. What had he been thinking, telling Emma about his mother? Those were the sort of confidences one only disclosed to a female one had feelings for, not a headstrong miss like Emma. For a cautious man like himself, his high-spirited sister had been enough of a strain on his nerves. He wasn't going to choose the same qualities in a wife.

Richard entered his bedchamber and started to remove his travel-stained clothes. Untying his neckcloth, he folded it neatly for Carson to take to be laundered and placed his jacket on the back of his chair before sitting down, one booted foot resting on his knee.

Try as he might, he couldn't help thinking about Emma, picturing her delicate features. What was it about her that kept drawing him in? Every time he looked into her eyes, it was as if he was drowning, and it put to flight all his rational thoughts. What should he do? This mental confusion was beyond his experience. His only passions up to now had been engines and science, not females. He'd intended that his search for a wife would be undertaken rationally and not involve a maelstrom of emotion. He cupped his chin in his hands and frowned. He was thoroughly confused.

A short time later, with a change of clothes and a clearer head, Richard bowled into the library, only to find Julia and George there entangled in an embrace. Reversing sharply, he made a great play of rattling the door handle and coughing. By the time he entered again, they were seated decorously on the sofa, holding hands. Only George's tousled hair and rumpled neckcloth stood evidence of his previous activity, while Julia's flushed face beamed. Richard wondered why his brother-in-law had the appearance of a man who'd just been granted a knighthood.

'Good to see you, George,' he said. 'You look… well. I see Julia found you.'

George grinned back at him. 'Yes, and she's brought wonderful news.'

Richard sent him a puzzled look. Surely the fact that they'd been attacked wasn't that wonderful, or was he missing something?

'What do you mean? Don't quite understand, old man.'

'What he means, my dear Richard,' cut in Julia smoothly, 'is that you may soon be an uncle. I'm expecting a happy event. Before autumn's end, I think.' She turned with a smile to her husband, who gazed at her with besotted eyes.

Richard's mouth dropped open. He was delighted at the prospect of being an uncle, but the thought of what could have gone wrong on their journey back to London made his blood run cold.

'So that's why you were feeling unwell?' he managed to get out at last. 'It's wonderful news, of course. But you should have told me,' he said sternly. 'What if something else had gone wrong? Believe me, George, if I'd known, I'd not have permitted her to travel.'

'Precisely why I didn't want you to know,' his sister flashed back at him. 'I thought George should be the first to learn of it, in any case. I wasn't entirely sure myself until a couple of days ago.'

Richard pursed his lips, struggling with his contrary thoughts. How could he keep his family safe if they didn't tell him things? The headstrong minx. She'd always gone her own way. Richard saw that George was still grinning inanely at his wife. At least he didn't seem angry that his spouse's life had been placed in danger.

'Well, congratulations to the two of you,' Richard said gruffly.

George patted his wife's hand. 'To tell the truth, I'm glad I didn't know. I wouldn't have let her travel up to visit you. You're going to have to be more careful now, Julia, my love.'

'Fiddle!' answered Julia. 'I hope you're not going to be boring and insist I rest all the time.' She smiled mischievously at her spouse. 'I'm not planning on doing anything dangerous, you know.'

'No, I know you won't. It's just that… well, you're even more precious now.' George sent her an adoring look.

Richard, certain he was *de trop* at this point, decided to leave them to it.

They didn't notice him depart.

Meanwhile, in her room, Emma was still a little dazed from the agitations of the journey. She'd hoped that a short trip to London would be uneventful. There'd been sufficient excitement on the journey from the continent, enough to last her a lifetime. Well, perhaps a little excitement in the future would not be too bad, she thought, provided it did not involve loved ones getting shot.

A knock sounded on the bedroom door. Thinking it might be news about Jamie, Emma called for whoever it was to enter. She found herself confronted by the sharp, penetrating blue eyes of a slightly built gentleman sporting sparse grey hair and an air of self-importance.

He pushed at the spectacles perched on the end of his nose and inquired, 'Miss Smith?' His voice had a Scottish burr.

'No… I mean yes, that's me.'

She'd almost forgotten Richard's advice about assuming a different surname.

The gentleman frowned. 'I'm Dr Donaldson. I was instructed that you should be told of your brother's condition as soon as I'd assessed him. I'm happy to say that he's doing well. The wound he sustained is only slight, and providing infection doesn't set in, he'll not have much scarring.' Donaldson gave his spectacles another shove. 'Apart from that, he seems to be a fit young man, so I'm hopeful he'll make a complete recovery. I've left the wound open to the air, which should aid healing.'

The doctor cocked his head to one side and sent her an appraising look. 'I understand you had the presence of mind to wash the wound with alcohol. Where did you learn to do that?'

'That's correct. I've seen that sort of thing done to good effect on my travels in Europe.'

Donaldson scratched his chin, a thoughtful expression on his face. 'Yes, in the circumstances you wouldn't have been able to cauterise the wound, so you did reasonably well, I suppose, for a female.' He wagged his finger at her. 'But I'd have preferred it if you'd used cider vinegar instead.'

Emma bit her tongue. Why did men always feel that anything a woman did well was despite their sex? She pasted a smile on her face.

'May I see him now?'

'Certainly. But as I have given him a draught of laudanum, he is likely sleeping.' The doctor pulled himself up to his full height and gave her a condescending smile. 'If that is all, I'll say good evening. Send for me if any swelling or feverishness develops, as it may be necessary to bleed him.'

Dr Donaldson gave a bow and made his stately way towards the stairs.

Emma hurried to Jamie's room, which she'd been told was next to hers. The maid seated at her brother's bedside looked up as Emma entered and whispered, 'He's gone to sleep just this minute, miss. I'm to stay with him for now, and one of the other maids will be with him through the night.'

'That won't be necessary. I'll stay with him,' replied Emma. She wasn't going to neglect her duties.

'But, begging your pardon, miss. His Lordship insisted you were not to be troubled. I'm sorry, miss. I have to stay here. I promise I'll call you if the young gentleman's condition changes.'

Seeing the anxiety on the maid's face, Emma reluctantly capitulated. Inside, she was angry. Why did Richard feel it necessary to order things without consulting her? She'd cared for Jamie successfully up to now, but it seemed as if Richard wanted to take control. Her mother was right, she told herself. If she didn't want to live a life of total subjugation, she should avoid marriage at all costs.

Some time later, Emma joined the others in the drawing room, where she was at last introduced to George. Emma couldn't see why Julia had said he resembled Richard. Physically, he was quite different, being stockier and blond, whereas Richard was tall and dark. She didn't fail to notice the glances he kept giving his wife and the careful way he tended her. A pang of jealousy shot through Emma. How nice it would be if someone cared for her like that. What was she thinking? she reprimanded herself. She wanted to be independent, didn't she?

The clock struck nine, Grimes announced that dinner was ready, and they all trooped into the adjacent dining room. Emma was placed next to Richard, who was at the head of the table. A further place had been laid next to hers. George and Julia were already seated on the opposite side of the table, so she wondered whom the vacant place was for. The minutes ticked by. Grimes hovered near the door, awaiting his instruction to serve the meal. Emma could see Richard's frown as he made distracted small talk with George. Julia was contemplating the ceiling and tapping her fingers on the knife beside her side plate. When Emma at last caught her gaze, Julia rolled her eyes.

Then the dining-room door swung open, nearly oversetting the footman stationed beside it, and a tall, young gentleman entered, clutching a book that he appeared to be reading. His dark, curly hair identified him as a member of the Lacey family, but unlike the carefully groomed and precisely attired Richard, this young man's creased jacket, dishevelled hair, and carelessly tied neckcloth declared that they were totally dissimilar in character.

'David, so glad you could join us at last.'

Richard's ironic welcome roused the young man from his intense contemplation of his book. Emma smiled at his look of surprise. It was as if he hadn't expected to find himself in a dining room with four pairs of eyes staring at him.

'Oh hello, Richard. You're back. Good evening, Julia. You're back too. Evening, George.'

The young man caught sight of Emma and squinted, as if trying to recall her name. Emma smiled at him and he coloured up.

'Yes, I'm back,' said Richard. 'And not a moment too soon. What have they been teaching you in Oxford? Not manners, I see. You're late, David, and we've been waiting for you.'

David dragged his gaze away from Emma and looked awkwardly at his brother, who added, 'Anyway, you're here now, and we must be grateful, I suppose, that you've managed to tear yourself away from your books.' Richard chuckled. 'Well, apart from the one in your hand. Emma, may I present to you my brother David who, as you can see, takes his studies very seriously. David, this is Miss Emma Smith, our distant cousin. She and her young brother will be staying with us for the time being.'

Richard didn't elaborate further, and David didn't question anything he'd been told. His book was shoved into a frayed pocket – a pocket which, by its condition, had been similarly ill-used on a regular basis. Now unencumbered, David made her a courteous bow.

'Pleased to make your acquaintance, Miss Smith,' he said as he took her hand. 'I apologise for keeping you waiting. I'm afraid I was rather engrossed.'

Her eyes twinkled in amusement. 'I think you must be studying something very important if it keeps you from your food.'

David's eyes lit up as if he'd discovered a kindred spirit. 'Yes, very important indeed. Some colleagues and I have just discovered a text in the Bodleian that sheds important light on our understanding of some of Galen's theories.' He sat down beside her and added confidentially, 'We're all very excited, and I was just checking a more recent interpretation to refresh my memory. I intend to submit a paper on it—'

'David, I'm sure Cousin Emma will be interested to hear more about your discovery later, but please may we start?' Richard cut in. His mild reprimand came with a smile. 'My brother is a scholar like yourself, Emma, though he favours the scientific classical texts.'

A gleam of something like respect appeared in David's eyes. 'You're a scholar too, Cousin Emma? What is it you study?'

Gratified that he didn't express astonishment at her learning, Emma relaxed and enjoyed chatting with him throughout the meal.

Once dinner was over, David announced that he was meeting with some friends and made his apologies before departing.

'David is a bit of a law unto himself, I'm afraid,' Richard explained. 'Lives in a world of his own most of the time. Still, at least he's not part of the dandy set. Doesn't really cause me an ounce of worry.'

He and George decided to take their port with the ladies in the drawing room. Richard took up a stance by the fire, with one foot resting on the fender and his elbow on the mantelpiece. Emma, who was seated nearby, tried not to let her eyes wander towards his muscled thighs encased in form-fitting kerseymere breeches, instead forcing her gaze up to his face.

Richard took a sip from his glass and smiled down at her. 'I've sent word to the dowager, and she expects your call tomorrow. In fact, she'd been planning to set off for Minster Lovell herself at first light, in contradiction of her physician's advice.' He chuckled. 'She sounds quite the intrepid lady. Just let Grimes know when you're ready to leave and he'll have the coach brought round.' He looked over at his sister, who was engrossed in something else entirely, namely her husband, who was whispering into her ear. 'Will you be able to accompany Emma, Julia?'

Julia, all flushed cheeks and sparkling eyes, started at the sound of her name.

'What's that? Accompany Emma? Of course. I'd be delighted.' She sent Emma a searching glance. 'Unless you have any objection, Emma dear?'

Emma, stifling her indignation at Richard's taking charge yet again, answered sweetly.

'Thank you for arranging that, Richard. Yes, Julia, I'd very much like you to accompany me.' She shrugged. 'I don't know why, but I'm anxious about meeting Grandmamma after all this time.'

Richard, a troubled look on his face, interjected.

'There's no need, I assure you. I've arranged for two armed grooms to attend you at all times when you're out.' He gave her an earnest smile. 'I'll come with you if you wish, though I had other plans to take matters further with regard to the investigation.'

Emma was exasperated at the high-handed manner in which he'd arranged things without consulting her again. How on earth was she going to make her own investigations if she was to be watched at all times? She had to think of some way to speak to Wheatley without Richard finding out.

Her reply came out through clenched teeth.

'You misunderstand, Richard. I merely meant I'm a little apprehensive about meeting Grandmamma. I don't know what her true state of health is, and I don't want her to be shocked at my appearance. I'm certainly not anxious about going out and about.'

Richard looked deflated. She almost felt sorry for him.

'Of course. I understand,' he said, blinking. 'I'm sorry. It's my fault entirely.' He cleared his throat and tugged at his neckcloth. 'I should have consulted you, I know. I've become unaccustomed to consulting others, I'm afraid. Especially since Julia left to get married.' He shot Julia a rueful look. 'Tell me I used to take account of your feelings.'

'Yes, indeed you did, silly man. As if you could've ignored me!'

George guffawed and rolled his eyes, whereupon his loving wife gave him a sharp dig in the ribs. Emma, taken aback by Richard's very handsome apology – had she misjudged him? – decided it was time for her to return to her room. She needed to think.

'I'll retire for the night, if you don't mind, everyone. I'm feeling a little wrung out.'

Richard held out his arm. 'Come, I'll accompany you upstairs. In fact, why don't we check on Jamie, make sure he's fast asleep?'

Emma, relieved that she hadn't completely alienated him and not wanting to lose his friendship, felt an apology of her own was in order as they climbed the stairs.

'How thoughtful of you. This house is so large. I confess I would find it difficult to find my own way back to my room.' She tipped her head up to him, but he resolutely continued to look straight ahead. 'By the way, I'm sorry for being a little sharp. I know you only mean well.'

His fingers rested briefly on her arm, sending quivers of excitement through her.

'I beg you, don't think any more about it. I know I can be a bit overbearing at times,' he said gruffly. 'I don't mean to rule you. I just want to sort this mess out, for all of us. You must know that I have the highest regard for you.' There was a moment's pause. 'I hope you've not lost your good opinion of me?'

'Of course not,' she answered. 'I… I just find it difficult being told what to do. There is no need.' There. She'd told him, made it absolutely clear she was not a docile female, not suitable wife material for any man.

By now they'd reached the landing and Richard, without speaking, took both her hands in his and looked down into her eyes. Emma frowned. Had her words not repelled him? His thumbs caressed the backs of her hands. The intense look in his eyes made her skin tingle and her pulse race. She swept her tongue over her lips, which had suddenly become very dry. She shouldn't be doing this, Emma told herself. She pulled her hands away and the spell was broken. As if coming to his senses, Richard took a step back. He coughed. Emma wondered if his throat was as dry as her lips.

He gestured to the door, not meeting her eyes. 'This is Jamie's room. Go and check on him, and I'll see you tomorrow. Sleep well, my dear.' He planted a chaste kiss on her forehead, resting his hands on her shoulders. For one deliciously agonising moment, Emma thought he was going to continue. She wasn't at all sure she'd resist if he did. Instead, she heard his deep intake of breath before he released her and strode away.

Chapter 11

AFTER A RESTLESS NIGHT, Emma rose and took breakfast alone in the smaller of the parlours. Richard had left a note to say he was pursuing inquiries with his solicitor. She pondered what had happened the night before. Had she upset him with her declaration of independence? He'd given no clue but had then surprised her with a kiss. Not a lover's kiss, she knew – though her experience of those was non-existent – but it hadn't been entirely brotherly. Emma trembled, recalling how gentle he'd been and the troubled look in his eyes. What had he meant by it?

But she needed to focus and keep her mama's words in mind. She couldn't afford to succumb to a gentleman's charms unless she was prepared to live her life as little more than a chattel.

Emma was still lost in her thoughts when Julia bounced in, full of smiles.

'What a lovely morning. How are you? Did you sleep well?' her friend asked as she helped herself to a bread roll.

'Yes, it is. And I did, thank you.' Emma sent Julia a quizzical look. 'You're looking a lot better than I expected for this time of day.'

Julia blushed. 'Yes, well, I have been up some hours. I thought if I got the sick part over with early, the rest of the day should be fine.'

'Is George joining us?'

Julia blushed even more.

'Er, no. I think he's decided to lie abed a little longer.' Julia walked over to the window and looked out. 'Why don't we go out for a stroll before calling on your grandmother? It's such a fine day. I'll ask for the carriage to meet us at the park gate, if that suits you?'

Emma thought a walk to settle her nerves was just what was required, so an hour before she was due to make her call, both ladies left the townhouse for the nearby park. Daffodils were on the point of coming into bloom and fading snowdrops were being replaced by colourful crocuses scattered amongst the flower beds. Emma tilted her head up to gaze at the clear blue sky as her breath condensed in the air.

'I forgot how beautiful England can be in the springtime. I did miss it.'

'Yes, I can see you would miss all this.' Julia gestured to the still-bare trees and the puddles on the pathway.

'You know what I mean,' said Emma, laughing.

The two friends continued their stroll, ignoring as best they could the two burly footmen who followed a few steps behind. After completing their leisurely circuit of the flowerbeds, the ladies headed for the park gates and the awaiting coach.

The elderly butler who greeted them at the front door of the Easterby townhouse ushered them into a drawing room on the first floor.

'I'll just inform the dowager of your arrival, Mrs Morton, Miss Smith.'

He bowed and backed out of the room. They had deemed it wise to keep Emma's true identity a secret from the staff, not knowing how loyal they were. Emma hoped none of them would recognise her. Surely she'd changed beyond all recognition from the gauche girl she'd been when she left? But what if Grandmamma didn't recognise her? What then? The thought set her pacing the floor.

At that moment, the door opened and a petite, stately lady of advanced years sailed in. Her sharp eyes swept over Julia before alighting on Emma, who'd now ceased her pacing and was staring back. The dowager's eyes widened and she gasped.

'Is it really you, Emma dear?' she asked, her voice husky with emotion. The old lady moved nearer, her arms reaching out. 'Let me look at you… Yes, yes, it is. To think that I'd given up all hope. Come closer, Emma dear. Let me see your face.' The dowager gently cupped Emma's face, scrutinising her with intelligent blue eyes – eyes brimming with unshed tears.

'Oh, my dear, dear Emma. You're home at last.'

'Yes, Grandmamma, it's me. I'm home now. Oh, how I've missed you.'

The pair of them dissolved into tears as they hugged each other.

Emma pulled herself together first, acutely aware that Julia, still awaiting an introduction, was no doubt feeling awkward at witnessing such an outpouring of emotion.

'I beg your pardon. I didn't mean to upset you, Grandmamma. I know you've suffered too.'

'Nonsense, my child. I'm older and more resilient,' the dowager replied briskly, though it was noticeable that her grip on Emma's arm remained. It was as if she were concerned that her granddaughter would disappear if released. 'I've had the support of friends. By all accounts, you've coped on your own and with the added responsibility of keeping young James safe all these months.' She beamed at Emma and stroked her hair.

'What a brave, capable young lady you've become. I'm so proud of you.' The dowager's face suddenly clouded. 'But where is James? Is he not with you?'

'He's well, Grandmamma,' Emma reassured her. 'He is just er… slightly indisposed this morning, so we thought it best that he stay away.'

Her grandmother gave her a sharp look.

'Please don't offer me Spanish coin, my dear. Tell me the truth.'

Julia stepped in, breaking all the rules of polite society by addressing a lady of higher rank without an introduction. She gave a deep curtsey.

'My lady, please forgive me. I'm Mrs Julia Morton, sister to Richard Lacey. Our families are distantly related. I'm afraid Jamie… er… sustained a slight injury on the journey from Easterby Hall to London.' The dowager's eyes widened as Julia continued to explain. 'A shot intended for my brother unfortunately struck Jamie instead. The doctor who saw him has assured us that it is but a flesh wound. Thanks to Emma's quick actions, he will be up in no time.'

The dowager's face had paled, but her response was robust.

'Thank you for explaining, Mrs Morton. I'm pleased someone is being honest with me.' She rolled her eyes at her granddaughter. 'I'm not made of porcelain, you know, my darling.' Taking Emma's hand, she squeezed it, then smiled at Julia.

'Now, do let us all sit down and take some tea.'

Some time later, when emotions had settled, the dowager leaned in and confided to Emma, 'Don't be shocked at my present lack of tears for your parents, my darling. I can assure you I've shed them many times, especially when we lost touch and, of course, when they were finally declared dead by the courts.' She gave a deep sigh. 'It's something of a relief to me to discover exactly what happened. I've suffered many a sleepless night wondering, you know.' The dowager pursed her lips and shook her head. 'It pains me to say it, but Charles was a fool to travel abroad. And why he insisted on taking you all with him, I'll never understand. But he would not be dissuaded. Stubborn like his brother.' She gave another deep sigh and set her teacup down before addressing Julia. 'And now your brother has written to me that Frederick's death may not have been an accident.' She gestured for Emma and Julia to help themselves to more of the dainty pastries that had been served with the tea. 'I had my suspicions at the time. Such a troublesome boy. I guessed that he was bound to have enemies. He kept some very queer company. But your grandfather, bless him, insisted on shielding me from any unpleasantness.' She gave a harsh laugh. 'As if I wouldn't hear the whispers and gossip. I knew Frederick had a poor reputation.' Almost to herself, she added, 'What a trial sons can be.'

Suddenly perking up, the dowager turned to Julia. 'Now, Julia. I believe I owe your brother an immense debt of gratitude for taking care of my grandchildren. Furthermore, it appears to me that my grandson's arrival has denied him an inheritance, making your brother's kind behaviour even more generous. When may I meet with him?'

'My lady, my brother did what any decent gentleman would have done,' replied Julia. 'He didn't have expectations of an inheritance, so he's not at all disappointed. He's asked me to convey his deepest regards to you. He's rather occupied at the moment with the investigations into who is behind these attacks and begs your understanding for the delay in coming to see you.' Julia's expression became more serious. 'Furthermore, Richard is strongly in favour of Emma and her brother remaining in his household for now… for their safety, you understand?'

'Oh dear.' The dowager's mouth turned down. 'I was so hoping you'd both come to live with me as soon as you arrived here, Emma.'

'We will soon, Grandmamma, but I agree with Cousin Richard. I think it better that this matter is settled first.' Emma took hold of her grandmother's hand. 'We don't want to put Jamie at risk. You see, no-one else is aware that we survived.'

The dowager appeared to consider, then, smiling grimly, she at last spoke. 'Yes, you're right to be cautious. I do understand. And, of course, we must continue the fiction that Richard is the viscount.'

Emma, who'd expected more opposition from her grandmother, was relieved, not relishing another battle of wills. However, the dowager hadn't finished.

'In that case, Julia,' she said sweetly, 'I'll call on your brother the day after tomorrow, and at the same time, I'll expect to see my grandson. After all' – she shrugged – 'who would deny a frail elderly lady inquiring after the health of a very distant young relative?'

Emma nearly choked on her tea.

As this happy reunion was occurring, Richard was occupied with his solicitor. The man had offices off St James's, and Richard had enjoyed the early-morning walk through Green Park. This was despite the presence of Phil Cullen who'd insisted on accompanying him, even though Richard thought it unlikely an assassin would attack in broad daylight in the middle of London.

Richard settled into the leather chair facing Blake's desk and crossed his legs. Blake covered his surprise at the presence of Richard's well-built companion who positioned himself like a human barrier near the door.

Richard steepled his fingers. 'Well, Mr Blake, do you have any news?'

'Not much, I'm afraid, my lord.' Blake blinked, his eyes darting between the two large gentlemen crowding his office. He started to shuffle papers about on his desk. 'There have been rumours and talk, of course.'

Richard tensed.

'Oh yes? What rumours?'

'Well, I've heard that Frederick Smythe kept rather unsavoury company, and there have been hints that he visited places kept under observation by the War Office.'

Richard's ears pricked up. This was getting interesting.

Blake continued. 'I've also discovered that the Duke of Wheatley some time ago approached the Dowager Viscountess Easterby to see if she was interested in selling Easterby Hall. He apparently thought it was not in the entail, but it turned out he was mistaken.' Blake picked up a pen from his desk and rolled it in his fingers. 'One of my informants works as a footman in White's and overheard some talk. Seems the duke was quite put out about it, though I can't understand why he'd want the estate. It's been somewhat neglected, as you've no doubt discovered.' Blake set his pen back down.

Richard frowned. These were yet more pieces in the puzzle linking the duke to the Smythe family. What in the blazes did the duke have against them? And what of Frederick? What was he doing visiting places under suspicion by the War Office? Was he somehow involved in spying?

'Do you happen to know if Wheatley is in town at the moment, Blake?' asked Richard.

Blake's head bobbed. 'I believe he is, my lord. He was seen in White's only the other day. A rare occurrence, I understand... caused a bit of a stir.'

'Indeed,' said Richard, sucking in his cheeks. 'I think I'll call in at my club. Phil, what do you say?'

Phil chuckled. 'That sounds like a good idea.'

Richard stood up. 'Good man. Let's go and reacquaint ourselves with the cream of London society and maybe have a drink or three.'

The two distinguished-looking gentlemen sauntered up St James's towards White's. On the way, Richard made a detour into Hoby's where he ordered a new pair of boots, gritting his teeth as the great man himself condescended to attend to him. Now Hoby had his measurements, he wouldn't be required to visit the shop in person for future pairs. He'd send Carter to collect them and serve him right.

At White's, they were greeted by a footman in the foyer.

'Are many in today?' Richard affected a bored demeanour.

'A tolerable few, my lord,' the man replied in lowered tones. 'Most of the gentlemen are in one of the card rooms. I understand there is some high-stakes play going on.'

'Sounds interesting.' Richard quirked an eyebrow at Phil. 'Shall we?'

Richard led the way to the rear card room. He needed to see if Wheatley was present and remind himself of whom he was up against. Peering through the fug of cigar smoke and suppressing his urge to cough, Richard headed for the main table, around which hovered a small group of onlookers. Drawn by the palpable air of tension, he moved closer to see who was playing. A young man – eyes bright with excitement, or was it perhaps fear? – was perched on the edge of his seat and eying the languid gentleman across the table.

Richard recognised Wheatley at once. A handsome man with strong but cadaverous features and no colour to his complexion, he lounged in his chair, every inch the aristocrat. A smile played at the corner of his mouth. His icy blue eyes flicked over his opponent before lowering them to the cards in his hand.

'I fear you may have won, my dear Gibson,' Wheatley drawled.

The young chap exhaled. Too soon.

'Ah, no, let me see.' Wheatley made a play of looking at his cards again. 'No. My mistake. I think you owe me…' His lips curled in a smile. 'What was it again? A thousand guineas?'

The young man gasped.

'But I was sure… You can't have.' His mouth snapped shut as his opponent's blue eyes narrowed.

'Are you suggesting that something underhand is going on?' The hint of menace in Wheatley's softly uttered words sent a chill through the crowd. Had the temperature dropped several degrees, or was it just Richard's imagination?

A hush descended as the young chap at last opened his mouth to speak.

'Not at all, Your Grace. M-m-must have lost my concentration. T-t-too much t-t-to drink, don't you know?' The young man's forehead beaded with sweat. 'Will you take my vowels for now, Your Grace? I'll settle with you b-b-by week's end.'

Wheatley nodded, his face impassive. The tension in the room dissolved, and even Richard started to breathe normally again.

The young chap rose from his seat, pushing his chair back awkwardly, and staggered across the room towards the door. The buzz of conversation recommenced.

Wheatley's cold gaze roamed around the room, registering the newcomers. His eyes caught Richard's and his expression faltered for a moment, or so it seemed. Then Wheatley turned to the younger gentleman standing beside his chair, who Richard guessed was his secretary by his expensive but sober dress, and Wheatley's austere features broke into a smile.

'Got to teach these young pups not to gamble all their inheritance away. Perhaps he'll be more careful next time.' The younger man nodded and laughed, very much at ease with his companion.

Wheatley leaned back and yawned, splaying his legs out beneath the table and stretching his arms above his head.

'Egad, I've had enough for one day.' He quirked his eyebrow at his companion. 'Why don't you stay awhile, and I'll see you later?'

'Are you sure, Your Grace? I should really return too.' There was a hint of anxiety in the younger man's voice.

Wheatley rolled his shoulders before answering. He'd the look of a man who'd sat too long at the gaming table.

'No, I insist. You do far too much. Take advantage of my good mood and enjoy yourself.' Wheatley's tone softened as he patted his companion's arm. 'I'll see you this evening.'

About to drain the last of his glass, Wheatley's hand started to shake uncontrollably as it neared his mouth. The glass slipped from his fingers, sending rivulets of red across the baize table and crimson splashes on his waistcoat.

'Damn. Not now.'

Wheatley's words were hissed but audible. His face tightened as he stared at his hand, almost as if it didn't belong to him. The onlookers had dispersed; the excitement for them had been over when the novice had left the room. Only Richard, Phil, and Wheatley's companion had observed the incident.

The younger man grabbed a footman and ordered him to get some water and a cloth, then he leaned in to Wheatley and said, 'Henry – I mean, Your Grace – are you well?'

'Don't make a fuss,' Wheatley growled as he flexed his hand and looked at it accusingly. Seemingly satisfied that it was now obeying his will, he used it to smooth down the front of his magnificently embroidered waistcoat. Wheatley's eyes lifted and he again caught Richard's gaze. Richard schooled his face to look impassive. After the slightest pause, Wheatley's gaze moved on. For a man who'd looked shocked to the core a moment ago, he now appeared totally composed.

Richard and Phil made their way over to a free table, all the while keeping a surreptitious eye on the duke, who was calling for his jacket. His companion was hovering nearby, shifting his weight from foot to foot.

Wheatley's face relaxed back into a smile.

'For goodness' sake, Francis, I'm quite well.' He clapped the young man on the back. 'Take that expression off your face. I'm not about to expire just yet.'

Giving Richard the briefest of glances as he strode past their table, Wheatley waved his hand in dismissal.

'I'll see you later, Francis. Now do as I suggest. Enjoy yourself.'

The young man gazed forlornly after his departing friend, then he headed off into the dining room, his shoulders hunched.

'Well, Richard, now you've seen him, what do you think?' whispered Phil.

Richard frowned. 'I don't know. He's obviously unwell but doesn't want anyone to know. Why would he bother trying to buy the Easterby estate when he must have enough responsibilities and some sort of affliction? Anyway, let's go and get something to eat.'

The pair sauntered into the dining room, where they found themselves a table and sent for cutlets, potatoes, and a bottle of claret. Out of the corner of his eye, Richard studied Wheatley's erstwhile companion, who was seated alone. Looking rather disconsolate, he glanced up nervously when anyone wandered too near his table. His features had the stamp of an aristocrat, with a pale complexion and prominent cheekbones. Straight blond hair swept across his forehead, and his pale blue eyes roamed the room as if searching. He was slimly built, and Richard put his age at about the same as his own. He reminded Richard of someone, but he couldn't recall who.

Richard was just musing on whether he should take the bull by the horns and go over and introduce himself when he was hailed by a familiar voice.

'Lacey, I mean Easterby, thought it was you. How are you? See you made it back to London pretty quick. Was the countryside too quiet for you?'

Richard looked up to see a grinning Crawford, leaning heavily on his cane and hobbling towards him. He leapt up to pull out a chair for his friend and started to make the introductions.

'Phil, let me introduce Major Nathaniel Crawford. We were at Balliol together. Crawford, this is my good friend and man of business, Philip Cullen. He's a Cornishman like me.' Richard pulled a face at the major. 'I'd better warn you, Crawford, we're both mad about engineering. And Phil's a Cambridge man, by the way, but don't hold that against him.'

He waved for a waiter to bring another glass, but Crawford held his hand up in a staying gesture.

'Be with you in a minute. I've seen someone else I know.'

To Richard's surprise, Crawford limped over to speak to the young man he'd been covertly observing. Richard watched as the chap's eyes widened, then crinkled into a broad smile at his military friend.

'Nate, fancy seeing you here. I heard you were out in Portugal,' said the young man, getting to his feet.

'How are you, Francis? It's been a long time, though you've not changed a bit,' answered Crawford, slapping him on the back. 'I've just sold out...' Crawford gave a rueful smile. 'Long story. Are you living in London?'

His friend nodded.

'Yes, but only for a few weeks. I'm secretary to the Duke of Wheatley... been with him several years. I'm, er... mainly to be found at his estate in Warwickshire.'

Crawford's eyes sharpened. 'Then you must have seen my father. Strange that he's never mentioned you.'

The man's eyes flickered away, and he shifted on his feet.

'I didn't like to presume, you know? Once I'd finished at university, well, I didn't wish to...' Francis reddened. 'You do understand, don't you? Your father was always kind to me when I was a boy. But I wasn't sure he'd want to continue the connection once I'd left home and Mama died.'

Crawford clapped his friend on the back again. 'Nonsense, you oaf! Of course he'd want to see you.' Tapping the handle of his cane on the table as if to reinforce his words, he added, 'Now promise me you'll call when you're in Warwickshire. I'm returning there shortly and I'll take great offence if you neglect to visit.'

Francis looked up at his friend and gave a shy grin.

'Well, if you're sure.'

They pumped hands and Crawford turned back towards Richard's table. 'That's settled then,' he said. 'Would you believe that I've just met another old friend, Francis? The chap he's with was at Cambridge too; you might know him. Now, why don't you join us?' Without giving his friend a chance to refuse, Crawford sat down at Richard's table, a broad smile on his face. 'Well, this is grand, meeting two old friends on my first day back in London.'

The young man hesitated, then, much to Richard's relief, for this would be a heaven-sent opportunity to discover more about Wheatley, he came over and joined their table. Crawford introduced the diffident young man as Francis Heslop, secretary to the Duke of Wheatley. Richard caught the flicker of shock on Heslop's face when he was presented as Viscount Easterby.

'How do you and Crawford know each other?' Richard asked, after taking a sip of his wine.

Heslop sent Crawford a shy smile. 'Well, we were boys together. Our families lived near each other and we both attended the same school. Sort of lost touch when Nate went to Oxford and I went to Cambridge.' Looking serious, he turned to Phil. 'I believe you were at Cambridge, Mr Cullen, is that right? Don't recall seeing you there. Perhaps you were ahead of me?'

Richard guessed there was more behind Heslop's seemingly innocent question and wondered what it was.

'Probably.' Phil grinned. 'I'm pretty ancient. Thirty-four years old, so quite decrepit. My Cambridge days are but a distant memory.'

'That'll be it then.' The tension left Heslop's face. 'I must have started when you were in your final year.' Heslop nudged Crawford. 'When I heard you'd bought a commission, I made sure to check the *Gazette* for news of your regiment. I knew you'd been wounded at Talavera but understood you'd made a full recovery. I assumed you'd gone back.'

Crawford's fingers tightened round his glass. 'That was the plan, but... well, never mind. Father insisted I return to the fold. Says he's getting too old to manage on his own, so that's why I'm heading home.' He heaved a sigh. 'Suppose I'm lucky really. Too much blood, too many good men lost.'

Crawford's eyes misted over, as if remembering. Richard knew his friend had probably seen sights that were better not spoken of – war was an ugly business, after all. They sat for a moment in uncomfortable silence until Crawford seemed to become aware again of his companions.

'How did you become acquainted with Wheatley, Francis?' Crawford asked. 'Heard he didn't mix much outside his own circle.'

Richard silently blessed his friend. Crawford had asked the very thing he needed to know.

Heslop seemed to consider for a moment before answering. 'Met him by chance a few years ago. Something I'd been working on brought me into contact with him.' Francis toyed with his glass and smiled as if remembering the occasion. 'Anyway, my work pleased him, so he offered me the post of secretary and, well' – he shrugged – 'here I am.'

'Heard Wheatley is a difficult man to deal with.' Richard kept his tone bland.

'I've never found him difficult.'

Richard held up his hand. 'Sorry, old man, no offence intended. Only repeating what I've heard. Haven't a notion what the man's really like.'

Crawford cut in, trying to smooth things over.

'Wheatley's patronage is no less than you deserve, Francis. I congratulate him for recognising your worth.'

Francis sucked in his cheeks and sent Richard and Phil a keen look.

'I shall tell you something about myself, gentlemen. Nate already knows and he doesn't hold it against me.'

Richard wondered what Heslop was about to disclose – he'd lay a monkey that it would be nothing so useful as admitting that he knew about the murder attempts.

Francis spoke in an undertone.

'I'm telling you in case you want to cut the connection with me. I'm illegitimate. Indeed, it's only because of Wheatley's patronage that I'm welcomed here.'

'Nonsense, Francis. Of course you'd be welcome in any case,' Crawford interjected. 'It's only because of your overdeveloped sense of pride that you hold yourself apart from society.'

'I'm not so mean-spirited as to hold a man accountable for his father's sins. Any friend of Crawford's is a friend of mine.' Regardless of Crawford's assurances to the contrary, Richard guessed that the poor devil probably received the cut direct from many when Wheatley wasn't with him.

'Same goes for me too,' added Phil, raising his glass.

Crawford refilled his own glass and, smiling at them all, said, 'We all need friends. Let's drink to friendship.' The four men raised their glasses and made their toast. It wasn't long before general conversation resumed.

Another bottle of claret later and Heslop checked his pocket watch, a very expensive-looking timepiece, to Richard's discerning eye. How did a man in his situation afford such luxuries? he asked himself.

'Is that the time? I'd better get back,' said Heslop, getting up from his seat. 'Wheatley expects me to attend him in the evenings.' He laid a hand on Crawford's shoulder. 'It's been good to see you, Nate.' With a smile and a gracious inclination of his head, he acknowledged Richard and Phil. 'I'm glad to have made your acquaintances, gentlemen. I've enjoyed our conversation.'

'I hope we meet again, Heslop,' replied Richard, racking his brains for a way to engineer another meeting. 'Do make yourself known to me when you're in here next. I come over most afternoons.' He quirked his eyebrow hopefully. 'Might I see you in Jackson's or Angelo's?'

Heslop smiled. 'His Grace enjoys a bout with the foils, but I'm not up to his standard, so I intend to have some lessons at Angelo's. I plan to visit Manton's too, but you won't find me at Jackson's.' He gave an awkward grin. 'I'm afraid I don't enjoy getting beaten to a pulp.' With a final wave, he headed for the door.

'He seems like a good sort, Crawford,' ventured Richard.

Crawford nodded. 'Yes, he is, you can depend upon it. His mother was a lady of good family sent to live in the country. Not sure who his father is; Francis never spoke of him. We spent much of our youth together. I'm glad he's doing well.'

Richard became thoughtful as Crawford continued reminiscing.

'We did everything together... you know, the sorts of things all boys get up to. But he was never in the petticoat line.'

Crawford grinned. 'Unlike myself. I always enjoyed flirting with the barmaid. But Francis never joined in… said he wasn't interested. He has very high principles.' Crawford sighed. 'Each to his own. Can't claim my principles are that high.'

'Why don't you join me for dinner at home this evening, Crawford?' offered Richard. 'You, too, of course, Phil.'

'Not me, thanks all the same,' answered Phil. 'I've lots of paperwork to catch up on.'

'You make me feel guilty, Phil, making you work so hard.'

'Not at all.' Phil winked. 'It's just that I like to keep on top of things. Also, I've a few matters of my own that need sorting.'

'Very well, but if you change your mind, you'd be very welcome. How about you, Crawford?'

'Yes, I'd be happy to,' replied Crawford, an amused twinkle in his eye. 'I was wondering how I'd fill the hours this evening, not many people in town yet.'

'So I'm the last refuge of the lonely, am I?' Richard slapped Crawford on the back. 'I'll expect you at about eight.'

The three men made their exit, Crawford heading off to his lodgings at the Albany, while Richard and Phil retraced their steps through Green Park.

Chapter 12

After the visit with her grandmother, Emma and Julia went shopping. The dowager had decided that nothing would do but for Emma to be fitted out with the latest styles, entrusting the supervision of this task to Julia and insisting that all bills be directed to her.

'Though you will have a significant inheritance, Emma, once all the paperwork is sorted,' the dowager disclosed. 'I insisted that your grandfather oversee the details of Charles' will before you all left for France, and he assured me that you were to be well provided for.'

Emma was secretly elated. She could avoid marriage and would not have to become someone's companion after all. She'd have funds to live an independent life.

Julia escorted Emma to her own modiste, who, despite looking with misgivings at Emma's slight figure, assured both ladies that she would be transformed once in the right attire. Emma was not quite convinced.

'Grandmamma said I was to spend what I needed, but I do feel guilty,' she confided to Julia later in the carriage. 'Do I really require all those dresses? I swear, I've never had so many in my life.' Julia laughed at her friend's qualms.

After the modiste, they visited other shops, selecting hats, shawls, gloves, shoes, undergarments, and nightwear. Hearing Emma voice her reservations yet one more time, Julia became impatient.

'Nonsense. I've only helped you select the bare minimum for the moment. You can't attend some of the social events I plan on taking you to without the right clothes.'

Emma's heart skipped a beat. 'Oh, but I thought I was not to go out and about too much until the matter with… well, you know, is sorted?' She couldn't bring herself to say "murder attempts". Besides, she wanted time to herself to develop her own plans, still adamant that Richard should not shoulder the entire burden of sorting out her mess. She'd even thought out how she might confront the duke.

Julia, who was now preoccupied trying on a rather attractive hat, said abstractedly, 'Richard has agreed for you to attend a few select social gatherings, under your assumed guise, of course. He and George will also be there, so I really can't see that there'll be much risk. There will be too many people about.' She gave Emma's arm a reassuring pat.

Emma smiled, but inside her stomach churned. She'd put all thoughts of her predicament out of her head for a few hours, enjoying the novel sensation of trying on different gowns and deciding which of the fine fabrics and beautiful colours would suit her best. Now reality was intruding again.

Several hours later, Polly had put the finishing touches to her hair. Emma was wearing a dress that she'd been persuaded to purchase immediately – an Albanian robe in Sicilian blue crêpe, which Julia had insisted brought out the colour of her eyes. Silver buttons adorned the front from bodice to hem, and the sleeves and bosom were embellished with a Vandyke border. Drawing a matching silk scarf in the same hue around her shoulders, Emma surveyed herself in the mirror.

Her eyes widened. Goodness, she looked almost elegant. No, dash it. She was elegant. Putting her shoulders back and lifting her chin, she no longer saw herself as the frightened young woman she'd been just a few weeks before. Would Richard like what he saw? she wondered. Why did his opinion matter? She'd every intention of remaining an independent woman… didn't she? She bit her lip. Good grief, it seemed she didn't know her own mind. Oh, it was all his fault. Why was he so attractive? Merely seeing him turned her thoughts awry. Telling herself not to be such a goose, Emma took a deep breath and went to join the others in the drawing room.

George rose to greet her.

'Julia was about to come and fetch you, Emma. I must say, you look particularly lovely. Is that one of your purchases from your shopping expedition? Julia told me you'd bought all manner of things.'

The heat crept into Emma's face, blushing at the thought of Julia sharing all the details of the shopping expedition… the underwear, the stockings.

'Don't mind George,' said Julia. 'He's always teasing. But you do look lovely, Emma. That colour really suits you, as I told you it would. It was so lucky Madame Gilbert had a cancelled order.' She turned towards the door. 'Now, I wonder where Richard has got to. Dinner will be served shortly.'

No sooner had the words left her mouth than the door opened and Richard entered, accompanied by another gentleman using a cane. Despite his pronounced limp, he held himself erect as he came forward to be introduced. By his bearing and commanding presence, Emma guessed he was a military man.

'We've not delayed you too long, have we?' said Richard, laughing apologetically. 'I'm afraid Crawford and I were caught up in conversation and I quite forgot the time. Please forgive me.' He gestured to his sister and her spouse. 'Julia, George, you remember Crawford, don't you? No need for introductions.'

Crawford bowed.

'Emma, may I present my good friend Major Nathaniel Crawford? Crawford, this is my cousin, Miss Emma Smith.'

Major Crawford smiled and took her hand. His arresting green eyes held an interested and appreciative gleam.

'Very pleased to make your acquaintance, Miss Smith. Richard has not mentioned you before now. Has he been hiding you away?'

Emma suppressed a feeling of panic, feeling the blood rushing to her cheeks. She'd no experience of flirting, yet this gentleman wanted to flirt. She braced herself. She could deal with this.

Richard, who up to now had been looking forward to a convivial evening, was suddenly assailed with doubts. He hadn't invited Crawford in order for him to flirt with Emma. As much as he liked him, a military man like Crawford was not the man for her. She needed someone more… like himself.

Richard sucked in his breath. He shouldn't feel so possessive, he told himself. She was far too independent-minded and impetuous for him. They would never suit.

He eyed her wistfully. She did look stunning in that blue dress. It had taken an effort of will for his jaw not to drop open when he'd first seen her on entering the room. No wonder Crawford was turning on the charm. Who wouldn't when faced with such a vision of loveliness? In the past, he'd enviously watched Crawford charm the most reluctant of females. Some had been so smitten with him that they'd been practically begging for a kiss. Surely Crawford wouldn't try for the same with Emma? Richard scowled. Of course Crawford would. He cursed himself for inviting his friend. Emma had no experience. Her life had been sheltered from predatory males like Crawford. Richard made his mind up. There was nothing for it… it was up to him to protect her and pray that Crawford had lost his touch. His ears tuned to their conversation as he hovered nearby.

'I'm happy to make your acquaintance too, Major Crawford,' said Emma. 'So, you were at university with Richard. What did you study?'

Crawford sent her one of his easy smiles. Damn the man, thought Richard, glowering in the background. Unclenching his fists, he forced himself to act nonchalantly and swept an imaginary thread from his sleeve. Listening to their conversation was torture.

'Oh, the usual. Classics, mainly.' Crawford gave a throaty chuckle. 'That's where Lacey and I tended to part ways. He was always more interested in engineering and mechanicals.' To Richard's smothered outrage, Crawford smoothly took

Emma's arm. 'Mind you, the classics never really held much for me either, apart from helping to occupy me when I was bored.'

Richard gaped as Crawford guided Emma to the sofa and sat beside her. He frowned. Was it his imagination, or was Crawford sitting just a little too close?

Emma gave a light laugh. 'Yes, it's nice to escape from everyday cares, isn't it? What authors do you read?'

Richard cursed inwardly, thinking that the pair had far too much in common. Emma could read Latin and Greek, and he'd forgotten that Crawford had come top of his year in classics.

Crawford's face glowed with admiration. He was clearly impressed with both Emma's looks and her learning. Emma's eyes sparkled as she steered the conversation. In short, they were getting on famously. Richard moved glumly towards the fireplace. He'd lost all appetite for dinner.

A few minutes later, Grimes announced that the meal was ready to be served. Richard's head whipped round at this heaven-sent opportunity, and he crooked his elbow towards Emma, at the same time shooting a menacing look at his friend.

'Let me escort you in, Emma. Crawford, you don't mind, do you?'

Crawford, with a knowing smile, waved at his friend to proceed.

Dinner was taken at the smaller of the dining tables. Richard was at the head, with Emma seated to his right. Next to her was George, while across the table sat Julia and Crawford. Richard felt pleased with himself for arranging matters thus.

His cook had excelled herself. There was white soup, followed by poached salmon and turbot, roast fowl, and a couple of prime rabbits, together with side dishes of potatoes, spinach, and broccoli. To finish, there were jellies, sweet pastries, and a rather fine Stilton cheese. The conversation had been lively, with Crawford recounting some of his escapades – those that were suitable for mixed company – and George had brought Richard up to date with news of their mutual neighbours in Cornwall. By the meal's completion, Richard was once more feeling benevolent towards his friend and readily agreed that the gentlemen should take their port and brandy in the library with the ladies.

Taking her arm, Richard deftly manoeuvred Emma into a chair near the fire, where he intended to linger.

Crawford took the seating arrangement in with a glance and smirked at Richard, saying sotto voce, 'Why didn't you tell me about this lovely cousin? Marking your territory, you sly dog? Oh well, perhaps she has a sister?' Without waiting for a reply, Crawford sat on one of the remaining sofas, a look of amusement on his face. Shooting a quick glance at Richard, he leaned forward and asked, 'Do you have any other family, Miss Smith? Apart from Richard and Julia, of course?'

Emma blinked. 'Erm, yes, I have a brother. He's much younger than I, so he did not join us this evening.'

'And your parents – where do they reside?'

Richard made a swift decision. He'd known Crawford for years. There was no-one more upright and reliable. He was a war hero and could be trusted with the truth. Richard leaned down and, in an undertone, spoke to the now worried-looking Emma.

'Let me tell him, Emma. I know Crawford well enough to say that what we disclose to him will go no further than these four walls.'

She regarded him from under her lashes for a moment.

'Very well,' she replied. 'I trust your judgement.'

Crawford's face clouded. 'Is something amiss?'

It didn't take Richard long to reveal to his astonished and horrified friend all the details.

'You should've told me sooner about these attempts on your life, Lacey.' Crawford was now very much a commanding officer concerned about one of his men. 'I insist you let me know if there's any way I can be of assistance. I'll certainly put off returning to Warwickshire until the culprit has been run to ground.' His head swivelled to Emma, a new look of respect in his eye. 'And you, Miss Smythe... I just wish we'd had more officers with your pluck back in Portugal.'

Julia, who'd been listening with an attentive ear, piped up. 'Major, I agree. Emma certainly has pluck. I don't think I could have managed to pull it off, despite my tendency for adventure.'

George patted her hand. 'There'll be no more adventures for you, my love.' In response to the outraged look she sent him, he quickly added, 'At least not for a while.'

Richard grinned and took his friend's hand.

'Thanks, old man. Knew I could rely on you.'

Crawford dug Richard in the ribs.

'So, you're not a viscount after all? Never mind, I'll still treat you the same.'

The evening, after a precarious start, was going well as far as Emma was concerned. She'd found Richard's friend, Major Crawford, a little intimidating at first. But then they'd discovered mutual interests and were getting on famously. It was only when the major started asking more personal questions about her background that she'd started to panic again. But Richard had come to her rescue, and it seemed as if the major, now he knew the truth, also wanted to help. How was she going to sort this out? Things were getting trickier by the minute.

Her ears pricked up at Major Crawford's words. Richard had shared their suspicions about Wheatley.

'Are you absolutely sure?' Crawford's tone was incredulous. 'He's a very powerful man – but to do such a thing, why would he? And if he is the culprit, well… you'd best be careful.'

A chill shot through her. Wheatley must indeed be dangerous for the major to issue such a warning. She'd intended somehow to engineer a meeting with the duke, but this was sounding riskier by the minute.

Crawford flashed Richard a knowing look. 'I see now. That explains your surprise at my greeting Heslop this afternoon. And why you tried to question him about Wheatley.'

Richard nodded. 'Was it that obvious?'

'It seemed to me that Francis thinks very highly of his employer, but I can't believe him guilty of having a part in anything so nefarious.' Crawford shook his head. 'No, not Francis. He's not like that at all.'

Richard shrugged.

'People change.' He slapped his forehead, as if remembering something. 'Wait a minute, Crawford. Think about what you told me recently. When we met in Oxford.'

Crawford frowned and scratched his head. 'Sorry, old man. We spoke about so much.'

Richard set his glass down on the mantelpiece, his eyes glowing with excitement.

'Think, man. You said your father disliked Frederick Smythe intensely because of what he'd done to that young woman.'

Emma's eyes swivelled to Crawford.

'What young woman? What did Uncle Frederick do?' she demanded. She'd guessed her uncle had been a bit of a loose screw from some of the comments her mother had let slip, but she was clueless as to what he could've done to attract the enmity of a duke.

Understanding dawned on Crawford's face. He swallowed hard and ran a finger around his neckcloth.

'Well, I blush to tell you, Miss Smythe, and you too, Julia.'

Emma's eyes hardened. Whatever it was, and it seemed it was bad enough to unsettle a seasoned military man, she needed to know.

'I think we may dispense with the formalities, Major,' she said cordially, 'especially now that you know all our family secrets. You may call me Emma. And please don't worry about shocking me with your tale. I'm no wilting violet.'

Crawford's eyes sped to Richard before he answered. 'I'd be honoured, Emma. Please call me Nate.' The major took a breath. 'My father told me that Frederick Smythe had a particularly poor reputation. The strong rumour was that he' – here Crawford cleared his throat – 'well… he got a very respectable young lady into trouble, if you understand my meaning.'

'You mean he got her with child?' interrupted Julia, not mincing her words.

'That's it exactly.' Crawford mopped his brow. 'I do apologise for distressing you with this sordid tale.'

'I'm not distressed,' Emma reassured him. 'Well, only for the young lady involved. What happened? Uncle Frederick didn't marry.'

'That's correct.' Crawford's voice held a tone of disapproval. 'He denied any involvement. Even accused her of lying. Nobody believed him, though. According to Father, the young lady was beyond reproach.'

Emma nodded. 'Now I understand why my father had little time for his brother.' Her mouth tightened. Here was yet another instance of a man ruining a woman's life. Both her father and her uncle had been the cause of great unhappiness to a female in their orbit. It also explained her grandmother's cryptic remark about the trouble sons brought. A crease furrowed her brow, and she looked quizzically at Richard.

'But what does this have to do with the gentleman you met this morning?'

Crawford rapped his cane on the floor, startling everyone. 'Of course! You think it's Francis!'

'It seems obvious,' answered Richard flatly.

Crawford's face wrinkled in concentration. 'I suppose that could explain everything. He is about the right age.' He shook his head. 'Father must have known, but he never mentioned Francis when he told me about Frederick's death. I suppose he didn't want to spoil our friendship.' The major snorted. 'As if! I'm loyal to my friends. What a blockhead I am!' Crawford hauled himself up and started to awkwardly pace the floor. 'I still can't see Francis being behind all this. He told me he was illegitimate years ago, but his father was never mentioned. I doubt he even knows his father's identity.'

'Well,' said Richard, 'we must find out.'

Chapter 13

THE FOLLOWING MORNING, AN apprehensive Emma made her way to the breakfast parlour. She would have to tackle Richard about his plans. Make him see that she needed to be involved. The way that he and the major had huddled together after the revelations of the previous evening had infuriated her. How dare they exclude her from matters directly connected to her and her brother? It was indefensible. And if she provoked him, as she surely would, would his mask slip and reveal another side of him entirely? It'd be as well if it did, she thought ruefully. At least it would put to an end to this terrible attraction she felt towards him and prove she was correct to heed her mother's warning.

Steeling herself, she walked into the breakfast parlour. It was empty. Her shoulders slumped. He'd probably eaten and departed, and she'd not see him again till this evening. Why did that make her feel flat?

Emma went to the laden sideboard and helped herself to a slice of toast. After last night's sumptuous meal, she wasn't really hungry. The tempting aroma of coffee drifted past her nose. Yes, coffee might restore her. Spying the source of the smell, she stretched out her hand to grasp the handle of the elegant silver coffee pot.

'Stop!'

Emma froze where she stood at the sound of the harsh command.

Richard had entered the room silently. She turned her head. Goodness, he was right behind her. Her skin prickled as his hand grasped hers and nudged it away from the coffee pot. The warmth of his breath on the back of her neck sent delicious shivers down her spine. He smelt of soap and fresh linen.

'Sorry, didn't mean to startle you,' he said in a husky voice. 'Julia has burned herself before now doing just that. The handle gets too hot. I'll ensure it's replaced. Been meaning to tell Mrs Wilson.'

Emma turned her head to find herself inches away from his face. So close that she could see where his valet had nicked his chin with the razor. Just in time, she restrained herself from stroking it better. Drawing her gaze up past his mouth, she saw the gleam in his dark eyes, and she couldn't pull away. She heard him breathe and unconsciously licked her lips. His eyes flared wider.

A cry of "Fresh milk!" from the street outside broke the spell. Richard blinked as if coming out of a trance and took a step back. He was still holding her hand. Could he tell how fast her heart was racing?

'You gave me a shock, but thank you all the same.' She looked pointedly at his hand holding hers. He released it.

'Sorry,' he murmured, stepping further away. 'Let me pour your coffee.'

Emma sat down and tried to regain her equilibrium. Perhaps he hadn't noticed her racing pulse. She watched as Richard poured the coffee. The cup rattled in its saucer as he passed it to her. At last, he sat down to face her from across the small breakfast table.

Emma took a deep breath and started. 'As I've mentioned to you previously, I'd like to be a part of solving this mystery. I was just going…'

Richard's knuckles whitened around his knife and fork.

'I'm listening,' he said through gritted teeth.

Emma couldn't fail to notice the lines of tension on his brow. She swallowed and started again, keeping her voice emotionless.

'Please let me finish what I was about to say.'

'I apologise. Please continue.'

He sounded on the brink of exploding, and she hadn't even told him what she planned. She took another deep breath.

'Well, as you know, I managed to get back home to Minster Lovell with Jamie. I admit I had help for part of the way, that's true.'

Richard's eyes narrowed and his jaw clenched, but he remained silent.

'The very fact that I'm sitting with you now demonstrates that I overcame those dangers. Nothing too awful happened, and I wasn't injured in any way, apart from a few cuts and bruises…'

He opened his mouth to speak but closed it again as she held up her hand to silence him.

'We were running away from a situation, and I slipped and scraped my arm. Nothing serious at all.'

'You were lucky then.'

She ignored his growled words and continued.

'Ariadne, our housekeeper in Gytheion, ensured I was prepared. She arranged for me to have lessons… training, if you will, in defending myself. We lived in a coastal village that was in the past subject to attacks by pirates, and therefore the village girls had learned how to protect themselves. It was part of their lives, especially as their menfolk were often away and there was no-one else to defend them.' She chuckled. 'You'd be amazed at how resourceful they were and how many ways a slightly built woman can overpower a stronger man, leaving him incapacitated enough to make her escape.'

He was leaning forward now, absorbing her words. Different emotions flickered across his face. Some she recognised as shock and horror; others puzzled her. At one point, his intense gaze was somewhat reminiscent of the heated look his friend had given her the night before.

She decided to get to her point, keeping her voice firm so he would not suspect how nervous she felt.

'In short, I am no simpering miss who will faint at the first sign of trouble, and I *will* accompany you when you undertake any further investigations and when you visit the Duke of Wheatley.'

Richard's knife and fork clattered down on his plate, and his words came out with all the force of an exploding volcano.

'What? Are you serious? How on earth would we explain away your presence? You don't know the types of places I might be required to go.'

Her chin jutted out. 'There's no need to shout.'

He shook his head and muttered something that sounded like an apology. Emma spoke quickly before he could think of any more objections. 'I've thought of that. I propose to accompany you in my disguise as a young man.' Richard sucked in a breath, but she carried on. 'I've put on a little more weight, I know, but I'm still very slender and my hair is quite short. I'm sure I could pass for David. I understand he hasn't spent much time in London, so it's unlikely I will meet anyone who knows him.'

Richard rested clenched fists on the table and leaned forward. A nerve twitched in his cheek.

'No. No, it's too risky. What if you were discovered? Think what a scandal it would be.'

It was Emma's turn to explode.

'If that's all you're bothered about then I'm definitely coming. A little scandal like that is nothing if everything that's been said about Uncle Frederick is true.' She gave a scornful laugh. 'He's created more scandal for my family than anything I could do. And it's not as if I'm planning on looking for a husband, so there are no other parties to be concerned about.'

'What?' said Richard, an arrested expression on his face. 'But what if you get hurt? I'd never forgive myself.'

'That's a risk I'm prepared to take. And if I'm prepared, so should you be. I'm not one of your responsibilities, Richard. If anything happens, it will be because I chose to take a risk, and you'd have nothing to forgive yourself for. Besides, I've just explained that I can defend myself. I can use a knife or a pistol if necessary.'

Richard opened and closed his mouth but no sound came out, then he continued to stare at her in brooding silence.

She was on the point of getting up to check his pulse when he moved his hands to cup his face. He regarded her between his fingers with steady eyes.

'You'll be the death of me, I'm sure,' he said at last.

Emma knew she had won.

Richard sighed like a man who was resigned to his fate. 'I agree to your involvement, but only on certain conditions.' He gave her an unwavering look. 'And I won't be moved on those.'

Emma suppressed her excitement. 'Thank you, Richard. What are your conditions?'

She hoped they wouldn't be ridiculously stringent.

Jabbing his finger at her, he said sternly, 'You may accompany me on condition that you obey me while we are out. If I tell you to run, you must. No argument.' His eyes narrowed. 'Also, my second condition is that you do not speak. Not unless someone addresses you directly. Leave all the talking to me.'

'But what if we get to see the duke?' she asked impatiently. 'I must talk to him. Surely you can't object to that?'

He frowned as if considering. 'Well, that is the only exception. *If* we get to see Wheatley and *I* judge the circumstances to be safe enough, you may speak with him.'

Emma kept her elation hidden.

'Very well,' she answered meekly, 'I agree to your conditions. But if *I* judge that I can be of more use to you by remaining at your side, be sure that I'll ignore your instruction to run.' A determined gleam appeared in her eye, and she fixed him with a stare. 'I never left Jamie's side and, so help me, I'll not abandon you. Now, what have you arranged?'

Chapter 14

Later that morning, a missive arrived for Richard from the dowager informing him that she intended to pay him a call. He read it and pulled a face. He'd barely recovered from his bruising dealings with Emma, so he wasn't looking forward to an encounter with another termagant member of the Smythe family.

The day had started so innocuously when he'd entered the breakfast parlour and seen Emma about to injure her hand. Before he knew it, they were pressed up against each other and he was drowning in her limpid grey eyes. Luckily, he'd come to his senses before things had gone too far. Good Lord, he'd nearly kissed her! And what did she mean by saying she didn't want to get married? Wasn't that every female's ambition? He shook his head, trying to rid his mind of the scent of her and the feel of her body close to his and recalled instead how exasperated she'd made him feel with her unreasonable demands. His stomach churned. How had she contrived to get his agreement to her outlandish plans? Anxiety coiled his insides at the thought of what they were contemplating.

The clock struck the hour, and Richard hastened to join Emma in the drawing room before the dowager arrived.

Emma looked up from her book when he entered and gave him a bright smile. He couldn't help smiling back. She might be infuriating, but when she looked at him like that all his misgivings about her melted away.

He was feeling rather nervous about his first encounter with the dowager. Julia had warned him that, behind her fragile façade, the old lady was as spirited as her granddaughter. Richard paced up and down, straightening ornaments, rearranging cushions, and ensuring that the seating was perfectly aligned. Emma, meanwhile, sat reading her book, only occasionally looking up as he nudged yet again the Jasperware vase to a more perfect location on the mantelpiece.

At last the dowager's presence was announced by Grimes. After kissing her granddaughter and being formally introduced to Richard, the dowager allowed herself to be guided over to a seat near the fire. Attired in a simple robe of purple velvet with a matching Amazonian helmet adorned with a curled ostrich feather, she was the epitome of matronly elegance. Once they were all settled and served with tea, Richard braced himself. He was sure there was more to this visit than the social niceties. He was not mistaken.

The dowager scrutinised him with intelligent eyes, then, after what seemed like several minutes, she started to speak.

'Well, my granddaughter seems happy now she's back in England, and I only want her happiness.' The dowager cocked her head to one side, making her jet earrings sparkle in the light. 'I've met your sister, Mr Lacey. She speaks very highly of you... but, of course, she would. You *seem* to be an honourable man. However, I feel I must clear the air.'

Richard's insides coiled. What did she mean by "seem"? He *was* an honourable man! He glanced at Emma, whose hands were now clenched in her lap. If the dowager insisted on her removal to her own house, it would put paid to all her madcap schemes. Maybe not such a bad thing – but, then again, he wouldn't be able to keep her safe. His mouth twisted as the dowager continued.

'I took the liberty of looking into your background, Mr Lacey, once I was advised that you were the heir.' The dowager delicately sipped her tea, watching him with narrowed eyes above the rim of her cup.

He gave an outraged gasp. 'You suspected me of foul play?'

'Grandmamma, really!' uttered Emma.

'Of course! What else was I to think?' the dowager answered reasonably. 'There were too many coincidences. And then you were named as the heir. I didn't know who to trust. However...'

The dowager's cup rattled as she placed it back onto its saucer, a clue that she was not as composed as she wanted him to believe.

'Well, I realised when you wrote to me about Emma and James arriving at Easterby Hall that you couldn't possibly be involved.'

'Well, that's a relief,' muttered Richard.

The old lady continued, ignoring his pointed aside. 'You could have disposed of them easily and I'd be none the wiser.'

Richard quelled his seething fury at this outrageous remark, and the dowager cleared her throat.

'Erm, my solicitor also undertook some investigations into your background at my behest.'

His lip curled sardonically. 'And?'

He guessed she was going to bring up his lack of a title and connections with trade. Not many members of the *ton* involved themselves in the business of mining and engineering.

Her next words floored him.

'You're that rarity, Richard. A man of integrity. My man could find no-one with anything bad to say about you.'

For the second time that day, Richard could think of nothing to say.

'Furthermore,' the dowager blithely continued, 'you've taken on the responsibility of your siblings since the death of your father. You've maintained and improved his business holdings. Even your employees think highly of you – not something you tend to hear about mine owners.' Her blue eyes suddenly filled with uncertainty and she leaned forward. 'Will you forgive me, Richard, for not trusting you from the start?'

'What's to forgive?' he said, stretching out to take her hand in a reassuring grip. 'I'd have done the same in your place.'

The tense lines on the dowager's face relaxed.

'That's very generous of you, young man. I was half-afraid that you'd take umbrage at my confession.' Smoothing the skirt of her velvet robe, she added pointedly, 'Now, I'm sure I don't need to say it, but I trust you to behave honourably while my granddaughter resides here. It is only under the strongest pleadings from your sister that I have given my consent.'

'You can be sure of that, my lady,' he answered. No, he was more likely to throttle the headstrong miss than kiss her, if the truth were known.

The dowager beamed. 'Then I have only one more thing to say to you, Richard.'

Richard wondered what was coming.

'Welcome to the family, my dear boy.'

Richard soon decided he'd done his duty. Leaving Emma with her grandmother and Jamie, who'd also joined them, he set out for Manton's on Davies Street. He could certainly do with the practice; being too slow to even take a shot at the would-be assassin had demonstrated how rusty his reflexes were.

Deciding it would be safe enough to venture out on his own in broad daylight, he set off. Untroubled with thoughts of assassins, he concentrated on Emma and his confused feelings for her. What was he going to do? His body was telling him one thing while his more cautious mind was warning him off becoming entangled. He was definitely attracted to Emma, of that there was no doubt, but she would cause havoc in his life. Would he be able to deal with that? Besides, she'd declared that she would never marry... could he even change her mind? Whatever happened, he needed first to solve the mystery of who had a grudge against the family. He'd made a promise, and it was one he was going to keep.

After a pleasing hour or so practising his shots, Richard felt better. Returning his pistols to their box, he looked up to see Francis Heslop, also about to leave.

'Good day, Heslop. Fancy seeing you here.'

Francis hesitated, then smiled.

'Oh, it's you, Easterby. Good to see you.'

Richard, eager to make the most of the opportunity, strolled over.

'What luck that we should meet.' Richard's eyes rested inquiringly on the rather magnificent carved wooden case under Heslop's arm.

Heslop, seeing his look, answered, 'His Grace insisted I learn to shoot, so I thought I might as well try out these beauties.' He lifted the lid. Inside were two exquisite flintlock duelling pistols.

Richard sucked his cheeks in. 'They certainly are beauties. They look French. Such craftsmanship.'

'Yes, that's right, by Boutet. Wheatley gave them to me last year,' Heslop answered, his face flushed. 'I thought it was about time I learned how to fire them. Not that I'm expecting to be called out, you understand. No jealous husbands chasing me.' He slanted an amused eye up at Richard. 'They are rather nice, aren't they?'

'They are indeed. Wheatley must think very highly of you.'

Heslop's eyes slid away. 'Yes, erm… he's a very generous man.'

Richard, knowing he'd rattled Heslop, decided a change of subject was in order.

'What do you say to a bite to eat? I know somewhere close by that serves quite tolerable food.' Heslop seemed to waver, so Richard pushed a bit more. 'Go on, what do you say? I could do with some male company.' To his relief, Heslop nodded.

'Oh, all right then. Why not?'

The two men strolled the short distance from Manton's to Grosvenor Street and the Mount Coffee House and Tavern. Seated in a pleasant dining room, they ordered the soup, alamode beef, and salad, to be washed down with a bottle of claret.

Richard, wary of alerting suspicion, kept the conversation light, or as light as conversation could be in such troubled times. They discussed the war being waged on the continent and the disaster of the previous year's Walcheren expedition.

'Do you ever think about purchasing a commission?' Richard asked.

Heslop shook his head.

'No, that life is not for me. I don't think I could kill anyone, not even in anger.' He wiped his mouth with a napkin. 'It's true I sometimes feel guilty about not actively defending my country from the Corsican and his madness, but my work for Wheatley means I'm helping the war effort in a small way.'

'Really? How?' Richard couldn't disguise his disbelief.

Heslop reddened. 'Many of the crops grown on the duke's estates are sold at a low price to the army, and of course he employs vast numbers of people. Many are families of men who've gone away to fight.' There was a hint of fervour in his eyes. 'We've got to keep things running smoothly at home so that the men who do fight for king and country know they have something to come back to. Though I think the government could do more for the families left behind and invalided soldiers. Some of the stories one hears are quite shocking. Then of course there's the hidden war against Napoleon...' Heslop's mouth closed sharply.

Richard wondered what he'd been about to say.

Heslop cleared his throat. 'My apologies. I don't usually rant on, and I generally keep my opinions to myself.' He twirled the stem of his empty glass between his fingers, then looked directly at Richard. 'Look, Easterby, I'm not very brave and I generally prefer a quiet life. But I feel I can talk to you. You see, Nate's accusation is true. I do keep myself apart from society because I can't deal with the cut direct that I often get when Wheatley isn't with me. Apart from Nate, you and Mr Cullen are nearly the only individuals who do acknowledge me, and for that, I thank you.'

Richard waved his hand. 'No need for thanks.' This wasn't what he'd been expecting.

Heslop poured himself another glass and sipped it slowly. From the faraway look in his eyes, he seemed lost in his thoughts.

Richard, despite his initial suspicions, had been moved by Heslop's words. Here was no vindictive, vicious character. But to be certain… Richard smiled to himself. He had an idea. It would be risky and could get him into trouble with Emma. In fact, it would certainly get him into trouble, but he convinced himself that she'd agree to his subterfuge, particularly if it bore fruit.

Richard leaned forward and, in a confidential tone, said, 'Well, talking about a quiet life, may I share my news with you?'

Heslop looked up and met his eyes. 'Go on.'

'I'm hoping shortly to be betrothed. It's about time I settled down and established myself as a family man. You may wish me good luck.'

Heslop's mouth twitched into a smile. 'I say, that sounds serious. So, you haven't asked her yet? Who is the lady?'

Richard thought Heslop sounded genuinely pleased – or was he just a very good actor?

'The lady? Oh, she's a distant cousin.' Richard shrugged. 'We only met recently, but I think we'll rub along together pretty well.'

For some reason, the words were not far off the truth. There was no denying the physical effect she had on him. Could he learn to live with an independent-minded female? And could she be persuaded to change her mind about marriage?

'And what is her name, if I may inquire?'

'Emma Smith. Her family hails from Oxfordshire.'

Heslop shook his head. 'No, I don't know the family, but I'm sure she must be someone special to have attracted your interest.' Heslop raised his glass and smiled. 'I wish you success in your quest for the lady's hand.' Heslop shifted in his seat. 'As we're exchanging confidences, I think I ought to tell you something. Something that even Nate is not aware of.'

Richard's pulse quickened. Was he going to hear a confession?

'That sounds ominous. What is it?' Richard's light-hearted tone and pasted-on smile belied his tension.

Clasping his hands tightly together beneath his chin, Heslop started to speak. 'Well… you know I told you that I am illegitimate?'

Richard nodded. 'I told you before, Heslop, it makes no difference to me.'

'But what you don't know' – Heslop had the look of a man facing the scaffold – 'is that I'm related to you,' he blurted out at last. 'I… I realised when Nate introduced us, but… well, it's embarrassing.' His gaze dropped to the table.

Richard kept his tone neutral, but the blood was pounding in his ears. 'Do continue.'

There was now a bitter edge to Heslop's voice. 'My father was Frederick Smythe, son of your predecessor. When Nate said your name, well, it was a shock.' Heslop ran a hand through his hair. 'You see, my mother was innocent. Frederick Smythe ruined her. He denied he was my sire.'

'How can you be sure he was your father?'

Francis lifted his head and sent Richard a ferocious glare. 'My mother did not lie. *Ever.*'

The fury in Heslop's voice shook Richard. He held up his hand in a placatory gesture.

'I apologise. I've no reason to doubt your mother. But you must understand, I know nothing of her or indeed my predecessor's family.'

Inwardly, Richard was at first jubilant. Heslop's admission confirmed that if anyone had a motive for revenge it was he. Then doubts crept in. It didn't seem right. If Heslop was the culprit, he'd surely be trying to hide his relationship. Nothing was making sense.

Heslop was still speaking of his mother. 'She wouldn't have lied to me. She only told me this on her deathbed.' He grabbed Richard's arm. 'Who would tell untruths on their deathbed, about to meet their Maker, I ask you? Her uncle confirmed her story when I confronted him. The scandal sent her father to an early grave.' Heslop sighed. 'It seems lots of people had their suspicions but never said anything to me.' He lifted his dejected eyes to meet Richard's. 'I thought it only fair to let you know in case you wish now to cut the connection.'

'Now, why would I do that? Your quarrel is with Frederick Smythe, is it not?'

Heslop lifted his hands in a gesture of despair. 'Yes, my quarrel would have been with Frederick, that wretch, but it's too late now. I was too much of a coward to confront him. I've never forgiven myself.' He paused to take a sip from his glass. 'I failed my mother. I wanted so badly to hear Frederick Smythe admit his sin, to acknowledge me.' He swallowed hard. 'That's all I ever wanted.' Heslop slumped back into his seat, shoulders hunched and head lowered.

It was at that point that Richard knew for sure that the man across the table was no murderer.

'Courage, Heslop. You've not failed your mother. Look at the life you've made for yourself. She'd be proud of you, I'm sure,' he said bracingly.

Heslop roused himself and tried to chuckle. 'Sorry for that. Must be the wine talking. I don't usually blub.'

'Nonsense, my friend. You obviously still feel very deeply about the injustice. By the way, how old were you when you discovered the truth?'

'No more than sixteen years.'

'Well then, what could a mere boy of sixteen years have done?'

Heslop nodded. 'I know. That's what Wheatley said to me.' He smiled to himself.

Richard hesitated before asking, 'Wheatley knows of your background?'

'Yes, I told him some years ago.' Heslop had regained some of his composure now and answered easily. 'We'd become quite close, even though he is my employer, so it seemed natural to confide my past to him. He has been all that is kind to me.'

Richard guessed there was more to the story but decided to leave it there for now. He held his wine glass up to the light. 'Nice claret, don't you think? Westbrook seems to be able to get his hands on the finest French wines, despite our present troubles.'

'I daresay he has his contacts,' said Heslop. 'I understand that the War Office is concerned about the number of people who deal with the French, even when we are at war.'

Richard guessed that Heslop was rather more well acquainted with the War Office than he was letting on. So he let Heslop's comment pass and asked instead, 'What did Wheatley think to Frederick Smythe's unfortunate accident and the disappearance of the other Smythe brother and his family?'

Heslop sucked in a breath. 'When I brought it to his attention, he said, "It couldn't have happened to a more deserving fellow." I assumed he only knew of him because of what I'd disclosed about my parentage, but I suppose he could have known Frederick at Eton. When I later told him of the viscount's death, he told me not to concern myself, even though he knew the man was my grandfather.'

Heslop paused to take a drink, then wiped his mouth before speaking again.

'Anyway, you're Viscount Easterby now, so you've gained something by their deaths, have you not?' His mouth snapped shut and he bit his lip. 'My apologies... I didn't mean to imply anything. Frederick's death was a riding accident. And the other son – he was killed by bandits in Greece. They were accidents, misfortune.' Heslop's face clouded. 'Weren't they?'

Richard glared back at him. It took a moment to subdue his urge to land Heslop a facer. 'Just to be clear, Heslop, I was unaware of my connection to the Smythe family until my solicitor informed me of the fact a very short time ago.' Richard spoke through clenched teeth. 'However, I'm very much of the mind that Frederick's death was not an accident, nor was the disappearance of the younger brother and his family.' Heslop's face paled as Richard continued talking. 'In fact, I strongly believe that someone has a grudge against the family. Since it was announced that I'd succeeded to the title, there have been several attempts on my life.' Richard smiled grimly. 'Fortunately, as you can see, all unsuccessful.'

Comprehension dawned in Heslop's eyes. 'My God, you think it's me. Is that why you've taken the trouble to befriend me? Good Lord, I don't believe it.' Heslop rose out of his seat, his face a mixture of horror and disappointment.

Richard, out of patience, leaned over and grasped Heslop's arm, tugging him back down.

'Sit down, man,' he hissed. 'For what it's worth, I don't believe you're behind the attacks.' He cocked his head to one side. 'But you have to admit, you have a motive. You have told me as much.'

Heslop slumped in his seat and put his head in his hands. 'I swear. It's not me. I left off being angry with my father a long time ago. I failed my mother, I know that. But I've learned to live with it.' Heslop took a deep breath and raised his head, his chin jutting out defiantly. 'I saw how Frederick Smythe's actions destroyed my mother's life. I wasn't going to let him destroy mine by clinging on to thoughts of revenge.' He gave a rueful chuckle. 'I've enough problems without that, God knows.'

'What problems?' Richard was intrigued. 'I might be able to help. Does Wheatley know?'

Heslop nodded. 'Of course he does.' He smiled weakly. 'And no. You can't help. But thank you for the offer, in any case. Forget I said anything, I beg you.' Checking his pocket watch, he stood up and stretched out his hand. 'I have to go. Farewell.'

Richard gripped Heslop's hand. 'I meant what I said. If there's anything I can help you with, let me know.' He sent him a meaningful look. 'But you can also help me.'

Heslop arched his eyebrow. 'What do you mean?'

'Just keep your ears open. Someone's taking shots at me, and I don't like it.'

There was a brief pause as Heslop seemed to consider Richard's words. 'I will, you can be sure. Keep safe.'

With that, he turned and left the dining room, leaving Richard alone to ponder the day's developments. His instincts told him that Francis Heslop was no ruthless killer. The chap was grateful for his friendship and had been open about his connections to the Smythe family. For a man who admitted that he lacked bravery, it had been a morally courageous thing to do.

Richard checked his own pocket watch. It was time to return home and share his discoveries with Emma. With a sinking feeling, he remembered that Heslop now believed that Emma and he were about to be betrothed. Would she go along with the deception? Or would she ring a peal over his head for taking matters into his own hands? He'd soon find out. Lord save him from headstrong women!

Chapter 15

'What have you got there?'

Startled, Emma looked up to see Richard leaning over the sofa trying to peer at the volume in her lap. She'd been alone in the library, ostensibly to read, but more often than not, her mind had wandered, thinking about how he was spending his day. So far away in her thoughts, she'd not heard him approach.

'This?' she said, reddening. 'It's the first volume of *Belinda*, the novel you recommended. I thought I'd purchase my own copy.' Feeling rather flustered, she gabbled on. 'It's the most recent edition according to the gentleman in Hatchards. Apparently, there are some plot changes because something in the first two editions gave offence. He didn't give me any details, so I wonder what it was that was so objectionable. Anyway, I've just spent the last quarter hour cutting the pages, and now I'm not sure I want to continue reading it.' She looked up to see him staring at her, his gaze intense and unsettling. She got the strong impression that he wanted to devour her. 'What are you staring at? Have I got a smudge on my face?' She brought a trembling hand up to her cheek. It was getting difficult to breathe.

'No, you haven't. Your face is quite… perfect.' His voice had a husky tone.

'Pardon?'

Had her ears deceived her? Had he just said her face was perfect? Surely not.

Richard stepped back, turning his face away from her. His voice became gruff.

'I meant that your face is perfectly clear, of course. No smudges.' He cleared his throat and moved towards one of the bookcases to straighten a set of volumes that the maid had not replaced correctly when dusting. 'But… we do need to talk, Emma.' There was a pause. 'I'm afraid I have a confession to make.'

Emma spun round.

'Gracious. What do you mean?'

Richard came to sit next to her. Her heart fluttered as his thigh fleetingly brushed against hers. She drew her skirts together and moved ever so slightly away. To be this close to him was far too unsettling for her nerves. Goodness, it really was getting hot in here.

'Don't worry,' he said, chuckling. 'I've left the door ajar, so we are entirely respectable. And we are cousins, so I think the rules are a little more relaxed. But what we discuss should be private.'

Emma subdued her almost overwhelming desire to lean into him and rest her head on his shoulder. It would be nice to have someone one could rely on, especially a gentleman as steady as Richard. Instead, she pulled herself together and waited for him to speak. Had he discovered who was behind the attacks? She wanted to get on with her life, take back her own identity, be independent. Didn't she?

'I met Francis Heslop today – quite unplanned, as it happens,' he began. 'I'd gone to Manton's to practise, and…'

'Practise what?' she cut in. 'Sorry, I didn't mean to interrupt.' At his raised eyebrow, she coloured and sent him an apologetic smile. 'Well, yes, I suppose I did. What is Manton's?'

He grinned back at her, his brown eyes twinkling.

'Sorry, I should explain. Manton's is a shooting parlour, where gentlemen practise their skills with pistols. I had thought to brush up on my aim, seeing as I was so slow when I was attacked on the way back from Oxford.'

His words jolted her. How could she have forgotten how close he'd come to being killed? Richard took her hand and gave it a squeeze, making her skin tingle and her pulse race. 'Now don't worry, I'm being very careful. But you see how dangerous it has been and why I am anxious that you may get hurt.'

Emma pulled her hand away.

'You don't need to worry for my safety. The attacks have all been directed on the male members of the family, so there is no risk to me.' She sent him a hard stare. 'You're not going to wriggle out of your promise to allow me to take part? If you insist on doing so, Jamie and I will leave for Grandmamma's immediately.'

His face hardened. 'No, I'm not trying to wriggle out of anything, as you so charmingly put it,' he shot back. 'Merely pointing out the necessity of care. I'm a man of my word, Emma. I agreed to your demands, and I will honour my promise, but it would be remiss of me if I underplayed some of the risks.' In a more reasonable tone, he added, 'There will be no need for you to go to your grandmother's.'

Emma's anger faded. She'd misjudged him again. The least she could do was apologise.

'I'm sorry. I thought you were trying to persuade me to let you carry on alone.'

The lines about his face softened. 'Apology accepted.' Richard tapped his chin with a finger. 'I admit that I have anxieties, but I know your mind is made up.' His head turned towards her. 'You're a very determined woman, Emma Smythe.' He settled back into the sofa, crossing one leg over the other, and sent her a wry smile. 'Now, shall I continue?'

'Of course, please do,' she said faintly.

'Where was I? Yes, as I was leaving Manton's, who should I see but Francis Heslop. He had a beautiful pair of pistols, a gift from Wheatley, he said. They looked to have cost a pretty penny.' Emma wondered where all this was leading. She watched as Richard's brow furrowed.

'Wheatley must think very highly of him,' he muttered almost to himself. He lapsed into thought for a moment before continuing. 'Well, I invited him to join me for a bite to eat. Thought I could use the opportunity to find out a bit more about him. As it happens, it paid off.' Richard stopped abruptly and began to fiddle with his neckcloth. A flush rose from his neck to his cheeks.

Emma couldn't hide her impatience. 'Do go on.'

Richard shifted on the sofa and cleared his throat.

'Well… it seems I was correct. Francis Heslop is your uncle's by-blow, if you'll pardon my bluntness.' He flicked a glance towards her. No doubt to check she hadn't fainted, Emma thought.

Seemingly satisfied that she wasn't about to have a fit of the vapours, Richard continued. 'Heslop's mother disclosed everything on her deathbed. His uncle also confirmed the story to him in later years. Sadly, the whole affair brought his maternal grandfather to an early death.'

'Oh, the poor lady. And how despicable of Uncle Frederick!' It was not the fact that she had an illegitimate cousin that shocked Emma but the vile treatment Francis Heslop and his mother had received at the hands of her uncle. It was a good thing Frederick was dead; she would certainly have given him a piece of her mind.

Richard nodded in agreement. 'Despicable indeed. Most importantly, I don't believe Heslop is behind the attacks. He seems quite a mild chap, very open, and I'd swear that he's without guile.' Looking thoughtful, he added, 'In my opinion, if he is involved, it would not have been in his interest to disclose the facts of his parentage to me.' Richard steepled his fingers beneath his chin. 'To be honest, although Heslop has the patronage and indeed what looks like the friendship of a duke, he seems to be lonely and in need of friends. I formed the impression that although his mother's family do support him, he doesn't see too much of them.'

Emma came to a rapid decision. 'I must meet him. He's my cousin, after all.' Seeing Richard's raised eyebrows, she added, 'It is because of my uncle that he's had such a poor start in life. I should try and make amends, or don't you agree?'

'Y-e-e-s.' Richard did not meet her eyes. 'There's just one more thing I need to tell you,' he said.

'What is that?'

Richard toyed with his cuffs.

'I, er… gave Heslop the impression that you and I were to be betrothed.'

'I beg your pardon?' Her tone was icy. Inside, she was a mass of confused emotions – anger, shock, and… disappointment. Was he like all the rest, a man who wanted to control?

Richard kept his eyes averted from her gaze.

'Yes, well… I thought he would open up to me more if I shared some intimate family news. And it worked, don't you see? He told me all about his background…' Richard trailed off. A pulse twitched in his cheek. For a man normally in control, he looked and sounded curiously adrift to Emma. Very puzzling.

Emma stood up, the better to confront him.

'How dare you! Are you trying to force me into marriage? How like a man! You're more like my father than I guessed.' Emma's words came through gritted teeth and pulsed with anger.

Richard leapt up and grasped her hands.

'Please, hear me out. Heslop is the only person I have told.'

'Yes, but it will be all over London when he divulges it to someone at his club, or shares it with the duke,' she spat out. Men gossiped just as much as women, she was sure.

'Heslop told me that he doesn't go out much in society and Wheatley doesn't socialise at all.' Richard clung to her hands as she tried to pull them away. There was a hint of desperation in his voice. 'Please, listen to me, Emma. If no-one else hears of this, it doesn't matter and no harm done.'

'No harm indeed!' she snorted.

'He's not likely to tell anyone before I've asked you. I only told him that I was considering settling down and that I hadn't actually asked you as yet. No gentleman would break a friend's confidence, and I believe Heslop to be a gentleman.'

Emma's initial shock and anger were dissipating, but she was still unhappy.

'Well, let's hope so,' she said bitterly. 'I'll not be bounced into marriage, not to you, not to anyone. Is that clear?' She folded her arms. Why did a female always struggle to be taken seriously? Why did it always seem necessary to be repetitive, forceful, and even loud in order to get one's point of view across? And then, of course, she thought wryly, you'd be accused of being emotional and told to calm down. It was so unfair.

She jumped at the touch of Richard's hand on her shoulder.

'You've made yourself absolutely clear, my dear,' he said, a hint of sadness in his eyes. 'Believe me, Emma, I've no wish to be married to someone who doesn't love me heart and soul. I respect you and will only ask that you try and trust me. And' – his grasp on her shoulder became firmer as if to emphasise his words – 'I am not like your father.'

Richard's considered words dispelled her anger. He was not one of those who coldly and efficiently chose a wife on the basis of breeding and suitability. He was looking for love. She swallowed. Guilt replaced anger.

'I'm sorry for accusing you of being like my father,' she said haltingly. 'I know you're not. I was just upset that you'd spoken to Heslop.'

Richard gave a dismissive shrug and stalked to the fireplace where he gave the glowing coals a prod with the irons, sending a shower of sparks up the chimney.

'I can see why you would be upset,' he said, turning round to face her. 'In fact, I did think twice before saying anything to him, believe it or not.' He gave a wry smile. 'However, I decided that if I mentioned I was thinking of settling down and starting a family, it might prompt him to react if he was the person intent on ending the Smythe line.' He propped his elbow on the mantelpiece. 'I am convinced that Heslop most definitely is not the culprit.'

The words "starting a family" caused Emma to blush. Could she really live the rest of her life without knowing what went on between a husband and wife? Julia positively radiated with happiness, so it couldn't be anything awful. And Mama had never discussed such matters. Lost in her thoughts, Emma jumped at the touch of Richard's hand on her arm.

'Y-you don't believe Francis Heslop is responsible for our current troubles, though?' she stuttered, hoping he hadn't noticed her blushes.

'Correct,' he answered. 'I'm more convinced than ever that Wheatley is our man. I'll let you know if there are any further developments. Blake said he thought he might have something for me today.' He turned to leave.

An idea occurred to her and impulsively she grasped his arm.

'I'll inform Grandmamma. I'm certain she'll want to know she has another grandson.'

'Do you think she'll acknowledge the connection?' he asked, glancing down at her hand still gripping his sleeve. She heard him swallow and immediately released her grip.

'I think so. She's not such a high stickler, you know. She was aware of Frederick's poor reputation despite Grandfather trying to shield her from the worst. I'll send her a note and arrange to see her.'

Chapter 16

IT WAS SEVERAL DAYS later, and Emma was pacing her bedchamber, uncertain as to whether she was doing the right thing. She glanced at the clothes laid out on the bed. Boy's clothes. Richard, true to his word, had raided David's wardrobe and supplied her with all she needed to accompany him in the guise of his young brother. When he'd brought them, he'd been terse.

'Are you still set on this?'

At her nod, his face remained grim, and he thrust the bundle into her hands. His words were curt. 'I'll meet you later in my study. Please ensure that Julia and George have no suspicion of what you're about to do.'

'Of course.'

She'd barely been able to meet his eyes. But why should she feel guilty? she asked herself. True, she didn't like deceiving Julia, or Richard's involvement in her subterfuge, but that was at his own insistence. There was nothing to be ashamed of in her desire to resolve the situation her family found itself in.

The proposed plan for the evening was to attend a small private musicale at the home of one of Julia's married friends. Julia had thought it the perfect opportunity to introduce Emma to a select gathering. Emma judged that Julia would find it difficult to cancel the engagement because the hostess was one of her closest friends. But even so, she'd need to play it carefully, only crying off at the very last moment in case Julia insisted on staying to look after her.

Taking a final look in the mirror, she brushed a stray hair into place. Polly had purposely been given the night off, so any adjustments to her costume would have to be made by herself alone. Trusting that she would be able to negotiate the intricacies of the fastenings on her dress and her underclothes, Emma took a deep breath and went downstairs.

While Emma was pacing her room, Richard could be found in his study, deep in thought. Seated at his desk, he now toyed with one of the seal fobs in his writing tray, turning it over and over in his fingers. He'd already straightened every last item and book lining the shelves and moved the armchair so that it aligned with the corner of the mantelpiece, not to mention adjusting the rug before the fire so that its edges were equidistant from each corner of the hearth.

Sadly, he was unable to exert the same order on his thoughts. He'd again made a complete fool of himself by disclosing that he would only marry for love. Had he revealed too much? Richard distractedly ran a hand through his hair, wondering if he was about to do something even more foolhardy.

Why had he agreed to her demands? How could he allow her to risk at best a scandal and at worst her life by accompanying him to his arranged assignation with an informer? He'd managed to stop her from coming to the tavern with him, but this was ten times worse, and he'd agreed, for God's sake! How had that happened?

The fob rolled out of his hands and across the desk. He didn't bother to retrieve it but put his head in his hands as the questions kept coming. How could he ensure no-one would recognise her or discover her sex? How to explain her presence to Phil Cullen, who was also coming along? Richard's mind continued in circles. There was only one small glimmer of hope. With luck, Emma's plan to avoid the social event to which Julia was intending to take her would fail and she'd be obliged to go, or perhaps Julia would smell a rat and decide to stay at home too. He could only hope.

Richard tutted. The infuriating minx was determined to assert her independence. An inner voice reminded him that it was the same independent streak that had enabled her and Jamie to return home safely, and he ruefully acknowledged that it was what made her so damnably attractive. Drat it. If she'd not been so determined, he never would have met her. So he shouldn't, in all conscience, complain about that aspect of her character.

His brow furrowed as he considered how his existence had changed. Before Emma had come into his life, evenings were normally spent conversing with like-minded engineering friends at his club, poring over the reports from his Cornish estate manager, or checking the accounts for his mining interests.

Tonight, however, was different. He was planning an excursion to a brothel and taking a lady with him. The very thought made him shiver. Emma was like a whirlwind, bringing mayhem to his settled way of life.

There were just the four of them for dinner. Jamie was having a tray in his room, and David was spending a couple of days away with friends. The meal itself was uneventful. Julia and George were so engrossed in their world of connubial bliss that they didn't notice the covert looks Richard kept sending Emma's way or her state of general unease.

Richard was already pacing the hallway just as the coach was brought round. He hoped it was too late for Emma to call off now. Perhaps she'd have a change of heart and leave him to deal with things. He heard a step on the stairs and looked up… and felt the air leave his lungs. Emma's evening dress of brocaded sarsnet was in a shade of blue that suited her colouring to perfection. The square neckline was not too low, he was pleased to note. He didn't want every other male leering at her. Long sleeves in Mechlin lace reached to her wrists, making her seem so demure that even he found it difficult to believe what she'd planned. Richard stepped forward to take the three-quarter-length velvet cloak out of Grimes' hands and arrange it around her shoulders. He breathed a sigh of relief. It seemed that she'd changed her mind about coming with him. Just when he thought all was well, as she reached the bottom stair, Emma lurched sideways and fell against the bannister.

Richard's heart sank.

'Oh, oh… oh dear, I think I've turned my ankle,' Emma whimpered convincingly. Richard masked his scowl and bit his cheek when she winked at him. She really was going to go through with her audacious plan. The woman was incorrigible.

'Emma, you do seem to have trouble with your feet, don't you?' he said through gritted teeth as he grasped her by the elbow and hauled her up.

'What's going on? Emma, are you all right, my dear?' Julia's voice wafted down the stairs, soon followed by the lady herself. His sister sounded concerned, and Richard hoped Emma was feeling guilty at her deception. He certainly was.

'It's nothing, Julia. I just went over on my ankle. I think they're still a little weak from my recent problems.' Emma fluttered her eyelashes. 'I'm sure I'll recover with a little bit of rest.' Her act was so convincing that if it hadn't been for the cheeky wink, he'd have been fooled himself. 'I think I should stay home and rest,' she said. 'You and George go on without me. I'm sure I'll be fine enough to join you for another outing soon.'

She at least had the grace to blush, Richard noted, as she drew out her fan and began to waft it in front of her flushed face.

Julia was having none of it. 'Oh, we can't leave you like this. I'll stay.' She turned to her brother. 'Richard, you go with George. I'm sure you'll enjoy it.'

Richard, despite his misgivings, decided to step in. He couldn't permit Julia to organise them all and ruin everything.

'Nonsense, Julia. You and George deserve a night out together seeing your friends. I'll ensure Emma rests. A musicale is not my thing at all, as well you know.' He caught sight of George, who was hovering uncertainly halfway down the staircase. 'Don't you agree, George? You and Julia should go on together? Just the two of you.' He hoped George would take the hint implied in his final words.

George's bemused expression turned to one of understanding.

'Yes, of course. I'm sure Emma is in safe hands, Julia. Come on, we'll be late. Emma, my dear, I hope your injury is not too severe, and we'll see you up and about in the morning?'

'Yes, of course, thank you, George. Now do go on, Julia, and have a lovely time,' Emma answered, waving them away.

Julia sent her husband a suspicious look but allowed herself to be wrapped in her evening cloak. Richard noted with approval how George expertly manoeuvred Julia towards the door. The devil! Well, his brother-in-law's evening was beginning to look more promising after all, the lucky chap.

The door finally closed behind them.

'Right, I'll change, then join you in your study. I'll be but a moment,' Emma called as she skipped back up the stairs. Richard stood open-mouthed and shook his head. What was he letting himself in for?

Standing silently by the door, Grimes' impassive features gave no sign of what he'd witnessed.

Richard found Phil in the dimly lit study, hunched in one of the leather armchairs close to the fire. He appeared deep in thought, staring into the glowing coals. Richard decided they could both do with some fortification.

'Let's have a brandy before setting off.' At Phil's surprised expression, he added, 'Only a small one. I know to keep a clear head.'

Richard checked his pockets as Phil went over to the side table for the decanter. There was a knife secreted in his dress coat, and he intended to carry a pistol in his greatcoat.

'Here you are,' said Phil, handing him a glass. Richard arched his eyebrow at the small amount, but Phil shook his head. Richard couldn't blame him for his caution, and Phil only knew part of it.

After knocking back his brandy in one gulp, he allowed Phil to act as valet and help him on with his greatcoat. The weight of the pistol in his pocket was reassuring, but he prayed he would not be called upon to use it. It was one thing to discuss and plan things. It was something else entirely to carry them out. He wasn't cut out for a life of danger.

He watched as Phil drained his glass and wordlessly shrugged on his own coat. Normally a quiet man, tonight Phil was exceptionally taciturn, for which Richard was grateful. Conversation was the last thing he needed.

There was a light tap on the door, and without waiting to be told, a diminutive figure entered. Richard had to look twice before he realised it was indeed Emma, dressed in David's breeches, shirt, and waistcoat beneath an unfastened, caped overcoat. A muffler covered the lower part of her face, and a hat was pulled down over her forehead.

Phil turned his head and frowned. 'You didn't mention David was coming with us this night, Richard.'

'Hmm… no. It was a last-minute decision. Thought he needed to see the seedier side of London, you know, to put him on his guard,' answered Richard, hoping Phil would accept his explanation. 'I can't be with him all the time, and he needs to discover what dangerous characters there are out there to snare innocent young, erm, men.'

The muffled figure nodded and coughed. For good measure, Richard quickly added, 'Forgot to mention. Poor chap's got a bit of a raw throat, not able to talk very much.'

Phil grunted, and after giving the muffled figure a swift, searching glance, silently headed off through the door. Richard let out his breath. Had they got away with it? As Emma started to follow Phil, Richard grabbed her arm and hissed in her ear, 'Don't forget. No talking, and run if I say so.'

He was almost sure she rolled her eyes, not that he could see for certain in the dim light of the passageway, but she tipped her head as if in agreement.

Some time later, having been dropped off by the hackney they'd hired, the three made their way to the address given by Blake's informant. It was in one of the streets off St James's, Bury Street, in fact. Home to several high-class brothels, or so Richard had heard. His eyes darted apprehensively up and down the cobbled street. Fortunately, there weren't too many birds of paradise parading around for Emma to see. He dreaded what they might find once they entered the intended establishment. At last, he spotted the house he'd been directed to.

'This is it.'

With Emma close behind him and Phil bringing up the rear, Richard led the way up the steps and pushed at the door. It opened easily on silent hinges, and a large, lumbering figure came towards them. Built like an ox, Richard guessed the fellow had once been a prize fighter, if his squashed nose and cauliflower ears were anything to go by.

'Evenin' gents. Can I take your coats?' the large figure rasped. His ham-like arms stretched out to relieve them of their outer garments.

Richard mentally kicked himself for not thinking to put his pistol in an inner pocket. There was no way he was going to relinquish his coat, and he certainly didn't want Emma to remove her outer garments. Slightly built as she was, she could easily pass for a youth, but Phil would surely recognise her without the muffler and hat.

'No, I don't believe we'll be staying long,' said Richard in haughty tones. 'We're meeting with Mr Downing.'

The ox tilted his head and stared uncertainly at them. It was apparent that he'd not encountered many customers who didn't intend to linger awhile. After several gut-churning seconds, he nodded. 'Go through to the parlour. Mrs Newbody will be with you shortly.' He pointed to a polished door at one side of the candlelit hall.

Grateful that they'd passed the first hurdle, Richard sauntered towards the indicated doorway, affecting nonchalance even though his insides were churning. He turned the handle and entered, Emma and Phil on his heels.

Richard's eyes took in the sumptuous but gaudily furnished room, a contrast to the austere hallway. Red-velvet sofas and brocaded armchairs were placed around the impressive parlour. Matching swagged curtains adorned the windows, and silver mirrors reflected the subtle light of strategically placed candles. A uniformed maid came forward from one of the darker corners. She'd been almost invisible at her station near a well-stocked sideboard.

'What would you like to drink, gentlemen? First drink is on the house.' Her eyes flickered over them assessingly. From her relatively demure dress, Richard judged that she was not one who offered her services.

'Claret for me,' Richard answered. Avoiding strong spirit seemed the wise course.

'Me too, thanks,' muttered Phil, his eyes appreciatively raking the portraits of scantily clad young women above the fireplace.

Emma shook her head. Her eyes were wide as she gazed around. Now that she'd lowered the muffler, Richard could see that her lips were pursed. He prayed that she wouldn't have the vapours. He should have saved his prayers for something more important. She caught his glance and her eyes narrowed in scorn. It hit him. Good Lord, she thought he was in the habit of patronising these sorts of places.

Before he could tell Emma that she was mistaken, the door opened and a sharp-featured, expensively dressed woman of about fifty years of age swept into the room. She paused at the door for a moment, her keen, dark eyes sweeping over them before her thin lips curved upwards in a parody of a smile. Richard was reminded of a malevolent bird.

'Gentlemen, I don't believe you've patronised my establishment before. I'm Ruth Newbody. I take it you've heard of me?'

Her voice was husky, no doubt a product of nights spent in smoke-filled rooms. Richard judged that her faux-friendly look meant she'd weighed them up and decided they were worth expending some charm on. He stepped forward to answer.

'I'm afraid not, ma'am,' he said, sending her what he hoped was a winning smile. 'Though I'm certain we should have done before long. We were directed to your establishment by an acquaintance. He said he would meet us here.'

Mrs Newbody frowned. 'Ah, who would that be?' A speculative look passed over her face as she swept her gaze once more over them, her scrutiny lingering on Emma. 'Are you planning a… party?'

Newbody put Richard in mind of a cat about to pounce on an unsuspecting bird.

'No, nothing like that. The gentleman we are meeting is Mr William Downing,' answered Richard.

The woman's aspect and demeanour changed in an instant. Her smile became broader, and there was a hint of calculation in her eyes.

'Billy, eh? I wasn't sure you looked the type, but you never can tell, can you?' The woman chuckled and leaned towards Richard to add in a stage whisper, 'Don't worry. Your secret is safe with me.' She winked. 'Wouldn't be good for my business, otherwise, would it? Everyone knows I'm discreet. I'm privy to many a gentleman's indiscretions.'

What on earth was the woman talking about? Richard had no idea, although he was certain that she did indeed know many a gentleman's indiscretions. It was rumoured that all sorts of underhand matters could be dealt with quietly at particular establishments like this. Richard decided silence was the best option, so he smiled back at Mrs Newbody and nodded his head as if in agreement.

She gestured to them. 'Follow me, gentlemen.'

From the parlour, Ruth Newbody took them across the entrance hall and started to lead them down a passageway to the rear of the house. As they trooped behind her, a door in the passageway was flung open and a young woman in a state of agitation came charging out. With her shabby dress, tumbled hair, and red-rimmed eyes, it looked as if she'd been crying. The girl halted at the sight of Mrs Newbody, who fixed her with a glare.

'Get yourself upstairs and ready, my girl, like I told you. You've had long enough. Customers will be arriving soon, and they won't want to see you looking like that.'

Mrs Newbody paused, as if recalling her visitors. She snapped round, wiped the scowl from her face, and addressed them in far gentler tones. 'A moment, gentlemen, if you don't mind.'

Signalling for them to wait where they were, she took the girl none too gently by the arm and walked her a few paces away from the three companions.

Richard, filled with foreboding, made use of the time by examining his surroundings, noting which way they'd come. They might need a quick exit, after all. Keeping an eye on his hostess, his ears caught the words "spent a lot of money on you… ungrateful... owe me… been patient for now… you'll have to do it".

The cowed girl eventually nodded and, with slumped shoulders, started to climb the stairs at the end of the corridor. Phil, who all the while had kept his eyes trained on the harridan and her reluctant charge, watched as the young woman slipped off, a thoughtful expression on his face.

Phil was definitely not his usual self, thought Richard, putting his friend's unusually subdued behaviour down to nerves. He turned to Emma and was overcome with a sense of growing unease. With her clenched jaw, narrowed eyes, and twisted mouth, he would swear that she was ready to plant their hostess a facer. Fearing she would actually do so, he gripped her arm and shot her a warning glance. Emma at once assumed a more neutral expression, though her hands were still fisted at her sides and Richard could have sworn he heard her growl. Richard sympathised with her sentiments, but he knew that if they did anything to upset Ruth Newbody, their chance of meeting William Downing would be lost.

Ruth Newbody bustled back, her expensive silk skirts rustling as she moved. She shrugged apologetically.

'Sorry about that, gentlemen. She's new, daughter of a… friend. I said I'd give her a chance at working as a maid before she joins the rest of my young ladies.' She smirked before adding, 'But you're not interested in young ladies, are you?'

Her words jolted Richard. With a sinking feeling, he understood what the old witch thought they were there for.

Without waiting for a reply, Ruth Newbody continued down the passageway, gesturing for them to follow. Emma forged ahead, but Richard almost had to tug Phil along with him. Oblivious to the bawd's words, he'd been gazing distractedly in the direction the girl had gone. Richard wondered what was wrong with him and was becoming rather inclined to give him a shake.

At last, their hostess stopped in front of a large, polished oak door at the end of the corridor and tapped gently.

'Billy. Billy, are you there? There's some gents to see you.'

Ruth's attempt at a whisper grated on Richard's nerves. He wondered how she'd started in this business – surely ladybirds were expected to entice with dulcet tones? He turned to the other female in their group. Emma was still glaring daggers at the woman's back. If she had one on her person, he would wager that it wouldn't take much for it to be embedded between Ruth's shoulder blades. In fact, it was becoming increasingly difficult for him to recognise the fragile young female who'd turned up at Easterby Hall such a short time ago; she'd transformed into a veritable warrior. Viscount Wellington could use her on his staff. The war with France would surely be speedily dispatched with a few like Emma on the English side. His face softened as he looked at her, then he brought himself up with a jolt. What was he thinking? He preferred docile, submissive females, didn't he?

Richard's thoughts were interrupted by the sound of the door creaking open. Over Ruth's shoulder, he espied a large, bald head appear in the gap.

'Ruth, what's that you say?' a male voice rasped.

Richard edged forward. 'My friend Mr Blake sent me, Mr Downing. Said you had some information for me.'

The door opened wider and the bald head's owner retreated. 'You'd better come in then. Thanks, Ruth. I'll see you later.'

'I'll leave you gentlemen to it then, shall I?' said Ruth with a knowing leer.

Suppressing his revulsion, Richard strolled past the smirking Ruth into the room, tugging Emma firmly by the hand.

As Phil closed the door behind them, the clicking of Ruth's heels could be heard as she returned up the corridor. Richard shook off his feeling of disgust and turned his attention to William Downing, who was now seated in a rustic wooden chair at a small, round table. A single lamp suspended from the ceiling illuminated the room with a gloomy glow.

Without looking up, William Downing gestured for them to sit down. Richard took the chair across the table from him, while Emma sat a little behind in the shadows. Phil pulled up a chair near the door. Billy, as Mrs Newbody had called him, looked to have been going through his account books. A tankard of ale stood at his elbow on the table and a smoking clay pipe rested near a jar of tobacco. Several thick ledgers lay on the table in front of him, and he swiftly closed the topmost one before Richard could catch a closer look at the lines and columns of figures they contained.

'So,' said Billy, his eyes darting round nervously, 'you weren't followed? And who are your friends? I was only expecting you, my lord.'

Richard was strongly reminded of a ferret. His gamekeeper used ferrets to keep the rabbit population down on his estate in Cornwall. Ferrets could be nasty, vicious creatures.

Adopting a haughty tone, Richard answered, 'Nobody followed us, Mr Downing.' He crossed his fingers and prayed that was true. 'These are close friends helping me to sort this matter out. No need for you to be concerned.' He hoped his clipped explanation would satisfy the man's suspicious nature. No need to let the man know their identities, assumed or otherwise. He was paying enough for the information, God knows.

Downing seemed to consider for a moment, then spoke. 'I told Mr Blake that it was dangerous to talk in my line of business. I make my living by being discreet.' He squinted at Richard. 'Rogers talked, didn't he? And now he's gone into hiding. Haven't heard from him in a while – used to bring me a lot of good custom.'

Downing hawked and cleared his throat, an unpleasant sound. Richard wondered what line of business the man was in – smuggling, perhaps? Goodness knows, there were enough people at it these days. But unwilling to spend any more time than necessary in Downing's company, he decided to come to the point.

'Mr Downing, let's be quick. What do you know about the Duke of Wheatley?'

Downing's eyebrows shot up, and his mouth curved in a vicious grin.

'You mean you really don't know? Took you for an intelligent cove an' all.' He leered at Emma. 'You seem to share some of his interests, if I'm not mistaken.'

Richard felt slightly sick, wondering if her disguise had been rumbled. He pretended exasperation.

'Come on, man. I wouldn't be here otherwise.' He thumped his fist down on the table. 'Tell me what you know.'

On his own, he would have grabbed the man by the throat and throttled the information out of him, but even with Phil at his back, it would be unwise to do so with Emma present.

Downing, looking less sure of himself, shrugged. 'Just thought with the young gentleman there, you and your friend were going on somewhere else, private like.' He sent Richard an ingratiating smile. 'If you wish, I can have a word with

Ruth. She doesn't mind letting a room out for a few hours to gentlemen who share your interests when I'm unable to oblige.' He nodded to himself. 'Always ready to do a favour, is Ruth.'

The bile rose in Richard's throat.

'This young man is my friend only, and we do not require a room,' he answered through gritted teeth. 'You seem to have misunderstood.' Behind him, Phil cleared his throat, stifling what seemed to have been an expletive. Emma remained silent. Richard prayed that she was ignorant of what Downing had implied.

Downing started to speak again, his bulbous, thread-veined nose and stained teeth testament to his love of brandy and tobacco.

'Wheatley used to attend my parties, but I haven't seen him now for several years. Must have found somewhere else to indulge his fancies.' Downing pulled a face. 'Now Rogers has disappeared, I thought I'd better tell, seeing as your man was looking for information.'

Richard leaned forward. 'What sort of parties?' He lowered his voice. 'You mean orgies?'

He cast a quick sideways glance at Emma. Why had he been foolish enough to permit her to accompany him? This was all getting far too near the knuckle for his liking. But what *did* Downing mean by parties?

Downing was grinning again, making it obvious that he considered Richard a bit of a slowtop.

'Orgies? Yes, you could call them that. But these were for men only, no women.'

'I see,' said Richard. He'd guessed as much, but now Downing was confirming it.

Sodomy was a capital offence, even, in theory, for a peer of the realm, though executions were rare and usually only for those of the lower orders. If convicted, Wheatley might be forced into exile. But what did this have to do with the attacks on the Smythe family? Frederick had definitely been in the petticoat line, so Richard struggled to see what bearing it had on things.

'When exactly was the last time the duke attended one of your, er… parties, Mr Downing?' asked Phil, who so far had been silent.

Downing scratched his head thoughtfully. 'Let me think. Oh, it must be nigh on four years ago.' His eyes gleamed at the memory. 'I'd lay a monkey it was when we were celebrating the victory of Trafalgar. Had a right good time of it. Enough gin, brandy, and ale to float one of His Majesty's ships.' His lips pursed. 'Never saw Wheatley after that. But a man doesn't change his nature like that, does he?'

Richard racked his brains. There had been attempts by the authorities to clamp down on molly houses, lots of prosecutions. Some even reckoned there'd been more hangings for buggery than for murder one year. Was that why Wheatley had decided to withdraw from his usual haunts? Had he been blackmailed? Was he trying to protect himself or someone else? How did this fit in with Frederick Smythe's murder and the attacks on himself? Richard shook his head. It was no good. It still didn't make sense.

Downing's smirk reappeared. Richard longed to wipe it off, preferably with his fist. The man was a parasite who preyed on men's weaknesses. Richard didn't understand the men who preferred other men, but as far as he was concerned, so long as no-one was being coerced or harmed, it was no-one else's business, least of all that of the courts.

'Thank you for the information, Mr Downing,' he said tersely, pushing a purse of coins across the table. 'If you think of anything else, contact Mr Blake.'

Downing snatched the purse, a greedy look on his face. He weighed it in his hand and gave a satisfied grunt.

Richard rose to his feet, his chair scraping on the floor as he pushed it away from him. Downing jumped at the sound, his eyes darting towards the door. Richard sent him a puzzled look.

'I'm a bit jumpy, see?' explained Downing. 'My place got closed down last week, so I'm lying low. Ruth's letting me stay here for now. She's very kind.'

Richard had the impression that Ruth Newbody didn't have a kind bone in her body, but he refrained from contradicting. There was something in it for her, of that he had no doubt. He strongly suspected blackmail.

Leaving Downing to his accounts, the three of them headed back down the hallway. Now all that was needed was to get clear of this unsavoury establishment and get Emma home safely. Richard glanced at Phil who was lagging behind. He gestured for him to hurry up, but Phil ignored him. There was something in his face that told Richard his friend was concerned. Richard whispered for Emma to wait for him and stalked back towards Phil.

'What's the matter? Shouldn't we get out of here?'

Phil hesitated before answering. 'You and erm... David go on without me. There's something I need to do.'

'But what about...?' Richard started.

'Don't worry about me, Richard.' Phil jerked his thumb towards Emma who was now scrutinising a particularly explicit framed engraving on the wall. 'Get her home.' Without waiting for an answer, Phil spun on his heels and darted up the same stairs the young woman had disappeared up earlier.

Richard stood open-mouthed for a second before coming to his senses. So Phil had guessed their secret. He swept back up the hall, tugging Emma away from the engraving and marching her back to the front hall where the doorman was occupied in greeting a party of gentlemen who'd just arrived. Fortunately, no recognisable faces were in the boisterous crowd. If their luck held, he'd get Emma home safely.

Outside, Richard paused and looked around. There were plenty of people about, men certainly, and a certain class of woman. Gripping Emma's arm, he walked briskly to the end of the road where a hackney had just pulled up. Two passengers stumbled out. Gentlemen on a spree and definitely a little the worse for wear. One staggered towards them, waving his arm to encourage his companion to keep up.

'Come on, Chivers. All the best ones will be taken if you don't get a move on.'

The second gentleman swayed about on the pavement, then grabbed on to some nearby railings for support. As Richard and Emma came abreast, the fellow bent over and commenced casting up his accounts. Grimacing, Richard deftly slid sideways, pulling Emma with him. How he wished she didn't have to see that. It wouldn't improve her opinion of the male sex, and he was pretty sure it wasn't very high to begin with.

Richard caught the attention of the hackney's jarvey, who'd been watching this performance from his lofty perch, a wry sneer on his face. At the sound of Richard's voice, the sneer disappeared, and the man was all attention.

'Where to, my lords?'

Richard gave him their direction, pushed Emma unceremoniously into the hackney, then jumped in after. At last he might be able to regain control of his nerves and breathe normally once more.

'Don't worry, Emma. I'll soon get you home,' he said soothingly.

'Well that was exciting.'

He slowly turned his head, not quite believing his ears, and watched as she calmly removed her hat and smoothed her hair. One might almost think it was normal for her to be dressed as a boy and alone in a cab with a gentleman. Indeed, a casual observer might well conclude that she was returning from a particularly enthralling theatre performance.

'Wasn't that amazing?' Emma said, her eyes sparkling. 'I've never been anywhere like that before. Is that where gentlemen go when they say they're going to their club?' Her questions came tumbling out. Before he could answer, she carried on. 'But that woman. She was awful, and she made my skin creep. That poor girl. What do you think is going to happen to her? Mrs Newbody didn't look very pleased.' Emma grinned at him. 'Do you think she's the reason why Mr Cullen stayed behind? I do hope so! She looked as if she needed help.'

There was a pause as Emma glanced out of the hackney window.

'Are you all right, Richard? You look a trifle pale. Perhaps you're starting with a cold?'

Richard slumped against the squabs. He was dazed; the whole situation was unreal. He was almost sure he'd wake up in a moment to find the entire episode had been some sort of nightmare. He hadn't just experienced an adventure, had he? He was steady, always in control. Adventures didn't happen to him.

Richard felt Emma's fingers on his arm as she repeated her question. Her voice penetrated his thoughts and he jerked himself upright.

'I don't believe it. I'm the one suffering with palpitations at the risks we've just taken, and you are… you are treating it like a trip to Vauxhall.' He knew he sounded like a maiden aunt, but he couldn't stop himself. 'Did you truly not feel any fear at all? I've been shaking in my boots that you'd be discovered or that it might all be a trap. We've been subjected to some of the most unsavoury talk, which I fervently hope you did not understand.'

In the gloomy light, Richard thought he saw her cheeks redden but couldn't be entirely sure. 'Please tell me you shared some of my anxieties, Emma. Am I really such a coward that I wanted to scoop you up and run before we entered that awful place? I was terrified something dreadful was going to happen and that I'd be unable to protect you.'

Emma grasped the hand that he'd been about to rake through his hair. The feel of her fingers stroking his skin sent delicious tingles up his arm.

'Richard, you're not a coward, believe me,' she said. 'I thought you handled Ruth Newbody and that horrible, shifty Mr Downing admirably. I confess, I had my hand on my knife the whole time we were in that room.'

Richard's head whipped round.

'Knife? You have a knife with you?' He groaned.

Emma gave him a look of incomprehension. 'Of course I had a knife. It was one of the first rules that Ariadne drummed into me. Always have a weapon to hand.'

Richard closed his eyes and emitted another groan. What was he going to do with her? She was incorrigible.

'Anyway,' she continued, 'what I was going to say before you interrupted me was that I was nervous. Of course I was.' She squeezed his hand. 'But I was with you. I knew I'd be safe.' Richard heard her swallow and opened his eyes to meet her intense gaze. Emma's voice became a whisper. 'You've looked after me since we first met. I've never felt so safe with anyone else.'

He was beginning to feel almost normal again when she added crushingly, 'I wouldn't have liked to have gone there on my own, I can assure you.'

Richard pulled himself together. It was time for him to assert himself and make it clear that she shouldn't take such risks and certainly not on her own.

'Please tell me you will never attempt to do anything like that by yourself.'

Emma giggled. 'Of course not. I'm not a complete widgeon. I'd insist that you accompany me.'

Richard shook his head despairingly.

'But we've discovered more about Wheatley, haven't we?' she continued, ignoring his disapproval. 'And we've done it together. Thank you for trusting me and taking me with you. I didn't realise how much I craved excitement.' Emma's eyes were shining. 'And it was exciting, wasn't it, Richard?'

Richard's heart skipped a beat. Emma spoke the truth. Now that they were out of danger, he could admit to himself that it had been exciting. Overcome with a sudden urge, he threw caution to the wind and scooped Emma onto his lap. It registered somewhere at the back of his mind that she did not put up any resistance.

His lips swooped down on hers and he revelled in their yielding warmth. Emma was warm and soft, with her fingers tangled in his hair, holding him close. Her skin felt smooth next to his as he breathed in her scent. After several intense, intoxicating moments, they drew apart, both breathing heavily.

'Do you suppose,' Richard gasped, 'that if I come up with other exciting things we can do together, I can persuade you to marry me, Emma?'

Had he just said that? Had he just proposed marriage to the most unpredictable, headstrong woman of his acquaintance? Richard couldn't quite believe it. But he had, and he meant it. He held his breath, waiting for her answer.

Emma stiffened in his arms. She arched away from him and struggled back to her side of the cab.

'I'm sorry, Richard. I don't know if I want to get married at all. Not to you, not to anyone.'

The demented beating of his heart slowed to a more regular beat at these dampening words. Richard felt cheated. He'd done what she'd asked, despite his strong misgivings, and they'd somehow come out of it in one piece. Overcome with the euphoria of the moment, he'd made the momentous decision to risk his entire future happiness on this wild, headstrong female, and she was turning him down. It was enough to send a fellow to Bedlam.

Emma was still speaking. 'I don't want to be like my mother, downtrodden and subject to a man's authority, even though it was obvious that my father did not have much common sense.' Her mouth twisted. 'She warned me that marriage was a prison for a female.'

Richard couldn't argue. Emma's father had not been the most sensible of men. But surely she didn't think he was like that? He quelled his annoyance and tried to keep his voice steady and emotionless.

'I'm not like your father, Emma.'

'I know,' she answered flatly. 'But would you permit me to have opinions of my own, to speak up when I think you're wrong… and to be listened to?'

She sat back against the squabs, her eyes earnestly searching his face. Then it struck him. Emma's concerns were genuine.

'Of course. Have I not proved that?' he asked. 'We wouldn't be here tonight if I hadn't done so.'

Richard knew he was no authoritarian, no domestic despot. Good grief, Julia would testify to that. Seeing Emma's troubled expression in the gloomy light of the carriage lamp, he resolved to prove her anxieties were baseless. Hell, even if it cost him more heart-stopping moments like tonight, it would be worth it to reassure her. Richard didn't know how it had happened, but he'd fallen headlong in love with this totally unsuitable woman, and the thought of losing her was unbearable.

They both started to speak at the same time.

'Will you…'

'I agree that…'

Emma held up her hand. 'You go first.'

Richard took a deep breath, determined to convince her. 'I realise your experiences so far in life have given you a poor opinion of the male sex, but please allow me to demonstrate that, although I have faults, being overbearing towards the females in my family is not one of them. While I cannot pretend that I'm entirely happy with you putting yourself at risk by continuing to take part in the investigations, I'm willing for you to do so nevertheless.' He sent her a pleading look. 'Will that prove to you I'm not and never will be a despotic husband?' Richard held his breath.

Emma's lips curved into a smile.

'I never said you were a despot.'

He raised an eyebrow.

'I didn't,' she repeated. 'And I know you are not... not now. But after marriage, men can change,' she added sadly.

'Pardon?' Richard didn't understand at all. Why would she think he would change?

'My mother,' Emma replied. 'She warned me. The last evening we spent together. She told me how she'd fallen for my father's charm. But after marrying her, his charm disappeared.' Emma swept a hand across her brow. 'She was so unhappy. And I'm frightened that the same will happen to me.' Her chin jutted out defiantly and she sent him a challenging look. 'Besides, my journey back taught me that I can think and act for myself. What's more, I've enjoyed it. I don't want to retire into a life of domesticity and boredom.' She paused. 'There. Have I shocked you?'

Richard reached out for her hand. 'No, I'm not shocked, Emma. Your mother was rightly unhappy with the circumstances she found herself in. I promise I will never do anything like that to you.' Before he could speak further, the hackney drew to a sudden halt. They were home.

'We'll finish this conversation at another time, I think,' he said resignedly. Richard helped Emma down, paid the jarvey, and led her up the steps. Grimes, who was on duty, didn't bat an eyelid as the pair tiptoed up the stairs and to their separate rooms.

Chapter 17

EMMA CLOSED THE DOOR behind her softly and stepped into her darkened chamber, illuminated only by the dying embers of the fire. She drew in a sharp breath when she caught sight of a huddled figure under the bedcovers and almost screamed.

Just in time, she recalled that she'd left the bedcovers bundled in case Julia decided to check on her when she returned. She gave herself a mental shake. Her nerves were more shredded than she'd thought. Throwing off her borrowed clothes and stuffing them into one of the drawers of the armoire, she pulled on a nightdress and climbed into bed.

But sleep eluded her, and she lay restless and confused. How was she going to arrange to see Wheatley, and was he really as dangerous as everyone claimed? How could she keep her brother safe? And Richard… yes, what about Richard? What should she do? Was her mother's warning about marriage and men truly meant, or were her words the result of an accumulation of sorrows, a product of her fatigue and frustration?

Emma's thoughts turned again to Richard. What would life be like married to him… or even worse, what would her life be without him? Her stomach lurched. She'd grown accustomed in the short time she'd known him to enjoy his company. He was intelligent, amusing, and cared deeply for his family. A careful man who, despite his strong misgivings, had been brave enough to allow her to accompany him tonight. An inner voice nagged at her – but would he flout society's conventions by continuing to treat her as a sensible human being if they married? She wanted so much to trust him, and he'd given her no cause to believe he was a tyrant. But if she was wrong, she'd have a lifetime to regret it. What should she do?

Early the next morning, Emma rose and padded down to the deserted library. She hadn't slept well and wondered if Richard had suffered an equally disturbed night. She was anxious to know whether her words on the journey home had given him a disgust of her. She flushed, recalling the kiss they'd enjoyed. She smiled to herself. Well, she'd certainly enjoyed it. She was also desperate to know what their next steps should be with regard to Wheatley. This matter needed to be settled as soon as possible, as far as she was concerned.

Stepping to the window, she rubbed the glass and peered down to the garden below where frost glittered on the lawn and silvery webs bedecked the shrubs. A fanciful person might imagine that a demented lacemaker had been busy throughout the night. She sighed. How different it all was to sunny Gytheion.

A copy of the *Quarterly Review* lying on the table caught Emma's eye. She picked it up and settled on the sofa, hoping it might while away the time until breakfast.

'Ah, Grimes said you were in here.'

She looked up and saw Richard's head poking round the door. Her spirits lifted, for he was smiling.

'Have you breakfasted yet?' he asked.

'Never mind breakfast,' she answered. 'We need to talk.' At his puzzled expression, she added, 'About what we're going to do about Wheatley.' How could he contemplate food at a time like this?

Richard scratched his head.

'What? I'm not sure, to be honest. We learned only that Wheatley used to keep rather dubious company up to about five years ago. That was about the time he met Heslop, I think. I don't know where that takes us.' Cocking his head to one side, he scrutinised her through narrowed eyes. 'How much of what Downing said did you understand exactly?'

She frowned. Did he think her a slowtop?

'Why, everything, of course. What do you think I didn't understand?'

Richard grunted non-committally and moved towards one of the bookshelves. He plucked a volume, glanced at the cover, then replaced it on the shelf, carefully aligning it with its neighbours.

Emma got the strong impression that he didn't want to answer. She stood up and moved towards him. 'I've spent nearly all night awake puzzling and turning things over in my mind. Tell me if you think I've missed something.'

There was a nerve twitching in his cheek as he faced her.

'Well, I suppose I'd better, though I have to say, I don't know what bearing it has on our current situation,' he muttered.

'I'm not going to have hysterics or faint, if that's what is troubling you.' Emma guessed by his guilty expression that he wished to avoid explanations.

'No, I know you won't.' Richard cleared his throat. 'It seems that what Wheatley was involved in…' Richard ran a finger round his neckcloth and shook his head. 'Good Lord, you shouldn't know about these things.' His mouth clammed shut.

'Nonsense. I'm a grown woman.' Emma pulled herself up to her full height and glared at his chin. 'I saw and heard some terrible things on the way back from Greece, so don't think I'll be shocked by anything you can tell me.'

Richard winced and his face turned grim. It was a few seconds before he spoke.

'Have you heard of men who prefer the company of other men… in the biblical sense, I mean?' Beads of sweat appeared on Richard's brow.

'Yes, of course,' she answered matter of factly.

Richard's eyes widened.

Ignoring his reaction, Emma carried on. 'It's mentioned all the time in the classical texts. My father, for all his other faults, did not censor what I read. I understood from Mr Downing's words that Wheatley is of that persuasion. It's a capital offence, is it not? Well, for ordinary folk, not peers of the realm like Wheatley.' Emma frowned up at him. Was that what had bothered him? Had he truly thought she had no knowledge of such things?

Looking considerably more at ease, Richard answered, 'Yes, you have it correct. I've come to the conclusion that Downing only wanted to cause trouble for Wheatley. He heard of my inquiries and thought he'd make some money.' Richard sucked his cheeks in. 'I'll have to think carefully about how we engineer a meeting with His Grace.' Emma looked up as he suddenly tapped his head. 'I know, I'll send a note off to Heslop inviting him to pay a call tomorrow.' Smiling now, he asked, 'You plan on visiting your grandmother this morning?'

'Yes, that's right.' Emma took his proffered arm and they walked through to the breakfast room.

'If you have no plans for the afternoon, I thought you might enjoy an excursion to Montagu House to see the Townley Marbles and the Rosetta Stone.'

She beamed back at him. 'I'd love to. Thank you.' How thoughtful of him to recall her interest in ancient artefacts.

Richard looked pleased with himself. 'Why, we might even find time to stop at Gunter's,' he added. 'I've noticed you have a fondness for sweet things, Emma.' His eyes were twinkling.

Emma caught her breath. Goodness, he was teasing her.

'You've noticed far too much, my dear sir.'

'You'd be surprised just how much I notice,' he replied with a wink.

Later that morning, Emma paid the promised call on her grandmother and tentatively broke the news about her newly discovered grandson.

'I knew it!' her grandmother cried. 'I suspected at the time, of course. I heard rumours of Frederick's misdeeds, but your grandfather, God bless him, wanted to spare me the heart-ache.' The old lady shook her head, making the Mechlin lace on her elaborate cottage cap quiver. 'If only he'd told me, I could have done something, forced Freddie to marry or at least made sure the young woman and the child had a comfortable life.'

The dowager retrieved a handkerchief from her reticule and blew her nose forcefully. Emma hadn't the heart to tell her that, in her opinion, the young woman had probably been better off not married to Uncle Frederick, if the stories about his character were all true. After some sniffing and dabbing at eyes, the dowager composed herself, tucked her handkerchief away, and smoothed down the silk of her skirts. She turned her piercing blue eyes on her granddaughter.

'So, you know who this young man is? What does he look like? Will he meet me?' Her face held the determined look that was becoming familiar to Emma. 'Well, I must meet him whatever.'

Emma ventured to advise a little caution. 'Do you think that wise, Grandmamma? What will your friends say? It might be thought a little scandalous.'

'Stuff and nonsense. I don't care what others think. He's my grandson, and I will acknowledge him as such.' The dowager sighed. 'Goodness knows, I've lost too many of my family to wilfully ignore those I have left.'

A dangerous smile hovered on the dowager's lips. Emma wondered what outrageous scheme her grandmother had in mind. It wasn't long before she found out.

'In fact,' announced the dowager in decisive tones, 'once I've made his acquaintance, I'll take great pleasure in introducing him to society as my grandson. That will give some of these high sticklers something to think about.' She tapped Emma's arm with her fan. 'From what you've said, Richard's opinion is that he is a personable young man?'

'Yes, Grandmamma,' answered Emma. 'Richard is inviting him to call tomorrow, when I shall meet him for the first time. I think I should disclose my true identity and acknowledge the fact that we are cousins.'

The dowager nodded her agreement, so Emma added, 'We have told no-one else apart from the immediate family and one of Richard's closest and most trusted friends. Only if all goes well will I tell him that you wish to meet him.'

Her grandmother frowned. 'Of course, I'd nearly forgotten about this other awful business.' She waved her hand dismissively. 'He can't possibly have anything to do with it.'

On what she based this assessment, Emma had no idea. Her grandmother hadn't even met Heslop yet but was obviously prepared to think the best of him. She hoped Grandmamma was correct.

'Yes, do as you propose, Emma dear, and let me know how things go.' The dowager wagged her heavily beringed finger. 'As soon as may be, mind. I shall be all at sixes and sevens until I hear from you.'

Emma decided to broach the subject that had been troubling her.

'Grandmamma, was Mama and Papa's marriage a happy one, do you think?'

'Why, my dear! Whatever has prompted you to ask?' Her grandmother gave her a shrewd look. 'Were matters strained between them on your travels, my dear? Is that why you ask?'

Emma shifted uncomfortably. She didn't enjoy discussing these things, but she needed to know.

'Somewhat, Grandmamma. Papa took no account of Mama's wishes, especially when she advised him to return home. Things settled after we reached Gytheion safely, but when we were about to return…' Emma brushed away a tear.

'Oh, my poor darling. There, there.' The dowager's arms wrapped around her. 'Theirs was indeed a love match, I can assure you, Emma. And most unusually, it remained one. In fact, I tried to talk your mama out of accompanying Charles on his ventures abroad, but she would have none of it. Said they couldn't bear to be apart.'

Emma looked up at her grandmother, startled by this revelation.

'I had no idea.'

'Well, you were only seventeen when you left. How could you understand? It sounds as if the troubles you encountered caused problems. I know Charles could be obsessive about his work, and I suppose being without the support of friends and family…' Seeing Emma's look of denial, her grandmother added hastily, 'I mean older females, Emma darling. I'm sure you were Marie's greatest support, my dear.' The dowager sent Emma a questioning look. 'Were matters very bad?'

'The last night we spent together, Mama bade me never to marry. Said no husband valued his wife and, if I wanted to be happy, to live independently.'

'Oh dear. And I suppose that because it was the last time you spoke, you took it very seriously, did you not?' The dowager shook her head. 'I'm sure it was only said in the heat of the moment. I can't believe that your mother truly wanted you to live the life of a spinster and never know the happiness that marriage to the right man can bring.'

Gently taking hold of Emma's head so they were both facing each other, her grandmother looked her in the eye. 'Now listen, Emma. I loved your grandfather, God bless him, and there is not a day when I do not miss his company. But we had our disagreements.'

Emma remembered the novels and smiled.

'I know.'

'Some days I was so angry with him I could barely acknowledge him. But we sorted our differences out. If that dreadful accident had not occurred, I think your mama would have retracted her warning. But she did not get the chance. Don't, I beg you, let this blight your life. By all means, choose a husband wisely. And be sure I will want to know all about any prospective suitors before I grant my permission.' The dowager's eyes twinkled as she kissed her granddaughter on the forehead before releasing her. 'I think I require a calming cup of tea. Will you join me, my dear?'

Emma smiled. 'I'd love to, Grandmamma.'

Richard stared at the note on his study desk. It was from Phil, who'd left a rather cryptic message. In a scrawling hand, Phil stated that he had urgent business and it might be some time before he returned. Richard smiled grimly, guessing that the urgent business in question had something to do with the War Office. But at least he had the satisfaction of knowing that Phil had made it out of Ruth Newbody's establishment in one piece. There'd been times the previous evening when

Richard had feared for their lives. There was something very dangerous about Ruth Newbody.

Richard looked at the pile of account books on his desk and sighed. At least they'd been left in reasonably good order before Phil had abandoned them. He picked up the topmost of the volumes. Perhaps immersing himself in numbers might take his mind off Emma for a while.

Emma arrived back from her grandmother's in time for luncheon, brimming with news of what the dowager intended to do once she'd met Francis Heslop. Richard chuckled at the thought of how the poor chap would be taken in hand and marched round all the social events of the *ton*, whether he wanted to or not.

After lunch, despite the work on his desk, Richard kept his word and escorted Emma to Montagu House. He'd been quite looking forward to spending more time with her, especially now she wasn't dressed as a boy and he wasn't in fear for their lives. He was also quite keen to resume the conversation that had so abruptly been curtailed the other night.

Now he'd made his mind up about marriage, the thought of spending the rest of his life with this unusual and spirited woman filled him with excitement. Why had he ever thought he could settle for a docile wife? The adventure of their trip to meet with Downing had made him feel alive. It was something he hadn't felt in quite a while, weighed down as he'd been with all the responsibilities of a family and a business since his father's untimely death. All he had to do, he told himself, was convince Emma that marriage to him would not mean she'd be under his thumb or that he'd expect her to change. Remembering how determined she'd looked when she'd said she didn't want a life of domesticity and boredom, he wondered what he'd need to do to change her mind.

To his surprise, he was enjoying Montagu House much more than he'd expected. For someone who'd only ever been interested in engineering, Richard was finding Emma's enthusiasm infectious.

'Oh look, that's very like something Papa found last year,' she said, marching over to a glass case containing a marble bust. The elderly gentleman who'd been peering at the same object, his eyes screwed up in concentration, turned to glare disapprovingly.

'What would you know about these, young lady?' He pushed the spectacles balanced on the edge of his nose up to his eyes and scowled at her.

Richard hurried forward.

'I don't believe we've been introduced, sir,' Richard said with considerable hauteur.

'My apologies, young man. I was just taken aback by this young lady's words. These items are very rare, and I'm surprised anyone but a scholar would understand their importance.' The gentleman peered myopically through his spectacles at Richard and held out his hand. 'I'm sorry, I'm forgetting myself. I'm Dr Shaw, keeper of the Natural History Department here at the museum.'

Richard shook the gentleman's hand. 'Pleased to make your acquaintance, Dr Shaw. I'm Richard Lacey, Viscount Easterby. May I present Dr Shaw, my dear? Dr Shaw, this is my cousin, Miss Emma Smith.'

Dr Shaw bowed stiffly, and Emma made a nervous curtsey in return. Richard guessed that she'd realised her careless words had very nearly exposed her true identity. He wondered what she would do to allay suspicion.

Dr Shaw leaned towards her, a mixture of curiosity and excitement in his eyes. 'Now, Miss Smith, did I hear you say your father discovered a similar bust only last year?'

A vacant smile appeared on Emma's face, and she looked guilelessly at Dr Shaw.

'Oh, silly me. I'm always getting muddled, aren't I, my lord?' She giggled in a way that Richard had never heard before.

Richard bit his cheek. Somehow his intelligent and eloquent companion had turned into a silly miss in the blink of an eye. Emma continued to simper and explain at some length that her father had bought a similar bust that he'd discovered *in a shop* last year and it was in the hall of their house, together with lots of other busts. She proceeded to describe not only the busts but also the particular rooms in which they were located in meticulous detail. Dr Shaw's eyes took on a glazed look. Richard squeezed her arm in warning. There was no need to do it too brown.

Emma smoothly brought her recitation to a close and bestowed a brilliant smile on the now-bemused Dr Shaw.

'Well, it was nice to make your acquaintances, Miss Smith, Lord Easterby.' With another bow and smiling uncertainly, Dr Shaw wiped his brow with a large white handkerchief and retreated surprisingly quickly for such an elderly gent. Richard sympathised with the old chap – Emma had the same effect on him.

Richard looked down at Emma, who was gazing up at him, a finger to her lips.

'Well, that was a close call,' she said, rather unnecessarily. 'How did I do?'

Richard, barely able to contain his laughter, shook his head. 'You were quite magnificent. You almost had me convinced you were a feather-brained miss. But before you get totally carried away and decide to take to the stage in earnest, let's go and treat ourselves at Gunter's.'

Chapter 18

As the mantel clock chimed four the following afternoon, the sound of wheels on the cobbles drew Richard to the window of his study. Outside, a smart curricle drawn by matching bays pulled up at the front door. A familiar figure in a many-caped coat sprang down from the vehicle, and the groom took over the reins. Minutes later, Grimes knocked on the study door to announce that Francis Heslop had arrived.

'Thank you, Grimes. Please show Mr Heslop into the drawing room and tell him I'll join him shortly. Advise his groom that he may take his vehicle round to the mews if he is to wait for his master.'

Richard swiftly gathered his paperwork into a neat pile and placed it carefully in the top drawer of his desk, then locked it and put the key in his waistcoat pocket. Before leaving, he glanced at the mantelpiece and tutted. Somebody, probably the new maid, had disturbed the alignment of his ormolu clock. He'd have to have a word with Grimes to explain to her that he preferred things just so. Twitching the clock back into place, he cast a last glance round the room. His desk was clear, the bookshelves were tidy, and not a speck of dust could be seen. Just as he liked it. His nerves were stretched, and when they were, he needed order around him. His stomach coiled with tension. Was he doing the right thing by introducing Heslop to Emma?

Richard headed for the library first before joining Heslop. Emma was chatting with Julia. They'd been sketching when Richard had seen them earlier. Emma put her pencil down.

'Has he arrived?'

'Yes, just now,' said Richard. 'Come, we'll go in together.' Setting her sketchbook aside, Emma rose to take his arm.

'Don't tell him anything if you have any misgivings about his character,' warned Julia.

'We'll be careful,' answered Richard. Though, now the man was in his house, he knew it was far too late to be having misgivings.

Emma stared at the pale young man who stood up as she entered the room on Richard's arm. It was almost like meeting a younger version of her father.

There was no doubting that Heslop belonged to the Smythe family. An attractive gentleman, he possessed the same regular features, blond hair, and piercing blue eyes as all her close male relatives. She'd always considered herself the unlucky one to inherit her mother's unfashionable darker colouring.

Richard made the introductions.

'Cousin Emma, may I introduce Francis Heslop, the gentleman I told you about? Mr Heslop, this is my cousin, Miss Emma Smith.'

Emma smiled and held out her hand. Heslop smiled shyly back at her and bowed gracefully, taking her hand and holding it for a brief moment.

'How nice to make your acquaintance, Mr Heslop,' she said. 'My cousin has only had good things to say about you, as does Major Crawford.'

Heslop reddened. 'The pleasure is all mine, Miss Smith, but you embarrass me. I'm sure I don't merit any more praise than the next man.'

Emma couldn't drag her eyes from Heslop; the resemblance to her father was uncanny. It had taken all her control not to display her shock. Fortunately, a diversion came in the form of a maid, accompanied by Grimes, bringing in trays of refreshments. Though Emma became even more unsettled as she caught sight of the delicate gilded Sèvres tea set and wondered how she'd manage to pour the tea without doing some damage to the dainty cups, as her hands were trembling uncontrollably. Richard, meanwhile, was making small talk with Heslop and gestured for him to sit down. Richard took up his usual stance at the fireplace. Emma knew that, for all Richard's affected nonchalance, he was tense with nerves. Richard wasn't the only one who noticed things.

'Tea, Mr Heslop?'

'Yes please, with milk, but I don't take sugar.'

'Do help yourself to a cake or two.' She turned to Richard. 'Tea for you, Richard?'

'Yes please, my dear.'

Emma finished serving the drinks and picked up her own cup and saucer. They rattled loudly in her hand. Good grief, she might as well be waving a banner to declare the state of her nerves.

Emma asked Heslop about his life in London. He told her shyly that he did not socialise much, as his employer led a quiet life when in town and only attended court and parliament when absolutely necessary.

'But surely you are not required to be with His Grace all the time?' she inquired with a questioning smile.

'Not required, no, but His Grace is very good company, and we both enjoy discussing all sorts of subjects.' Heslop's countenance became animated. 'Wheatley spent several years on his Grand Tour and enjoys looking at the artwork and sculptures he brought back. One of my more pleasurable tasks is to research the artists and ancient sculptors whose work forms part of his collection. I'm in the process of cataloguing the contents of His Grace's many houses.'

Heslop's fervour when speaking about his work resonated with Emma. She shared the same passion for scholarly research and art, yet another Smythe family trait. Heslop told her how he spent his time when he wasn't in London, helping the duke to reorganise some of the agricultural working practices on his rural estates.

'Wheatley sounds to be a very paragon and an expert in every field,' said Richard cuttingly.

'Yes, he is a very talented person,' agreed Heslop. Emma was pleased that he'd missed Richard's sarcasm. 'I'm incredibly fortunate to have his patronage.'

Just then, the door burst open and Jamie bowled in, eyes brimming with excitement.

'I say, Cousin Richard, there's a top-of-the-trees pair of matched bays in the mews. Do you think I could...' Jamie stopped dead at the sight of Heslop.

Heslop, who'd turned sharply at Jamie's noisy entrance, paled. He leapt to his feet, dropping his teacup onto the table and splashing most of its contents on his pristine pantaloons. Emma's eyes swivelled between Heslop and Jamie, and she sucked in her breath. Seeing them together, it was obvious they were related.

'I think we all need to sit down,' said Richard, taking control of the awkward situation. 'Jamie, come in for goodness' sake. Heslop, here, take this napkin and dry yourself. I'll call for my valet shortly. I'm sure he has a remedy for tea stains.'

To Emma's relief, Richard's matter-of-fact tones brought the two other males to their senses. Heslop slowly sat back down but watched transfixed as she led her shaken brother to a seat beside her on the sofa.

'Who is he?' hissed Jamie. 'He looks like Papa, only younger.'

Emma patted her brother's hand. 'I'll explain in a minute.'

Heslop regarded her coldly. 'Yes, please do explain,' he said in a clipped tone.

'Mr Heslop... Francis,' she started. 'We three are related. We're your cousins.'

She almost quailed under Heslop's disdainful look. 'How can that be, Miss Smith? I'm sure Viscount Easterby' – he paused and glared at Richard before continuing – 'has told you about my parentage. I'm illegitimate. My father was Frederick Smythe, the oldest son and heir of the previous Viscount Easterby. How can I possibly be related to you and this young man? Though I admit, he looks very like me when I was younger. I was quite taken aback.'

'Believe me, you are our cousin. Our surname is Smythe, not Smith. Forgive us for our deception.' Filled with remorse, she desperately wanted him to understand that their ploy had not been malicious. She watched as Heslop frowned. Then his eyes widened.

'My brother Jamie,' she continued rapidly, wrapping an arm protectively round Jamie's shoulder, 'is the real Viscount Easterby.'

Heslop sent a questioning look to Richard.

'I'm afraid it's true,' Richard answered. 'I've been masquerading as Viscount Easterby in order to protect this young man from whoever it is who's been trying to rid the world of all the legitimate male members of the family.'

Heslop finally found his tongue.

'What? I don't understand. You said the other day that someone was trying to kill you...' He paused, Richard's words finally sinking in. 'Wait, you said "legitimate". Does that mean? Oh my God! Is that why you invited me here? You still think it's me, don't you?' Heslop's mouth twisted. 'Lord, how stupid I am to think you were offering friendship.'

Heslop slumped and cupped his head in his hands. The elegant and composed young man who'd entered the room earlier was now the picture of despair. Emma sprang up and laid a comforting hand on his arm.

'No, that's not it at all. You misunderstand completely. We wanted to tell you, and we were about to when my brother came in. The likeness between you is astonishing, is it not?' Emma gave Heslop's arm a squeeze. 'Please, Mr Heslop – or may I call you Cousin Francis? – we don't think the culprit is you. You must believe me.'

Something in the earnestness of her tone must have convinced Heslop of her sincerity. He slowly turned his eyes towards her.

'Are you sure? I don't understand. Why would you acknowledge the connection to me in any case? My father never did.'

It almost broke Emma's heart to hear the bitterness and despair in his tone. She grasped his hand.

'Uncle Frederick's actions towards your mother were dastardly. I intend to try and make some sort of amends.' At Heslop's look of disbelief, she added, 'You also ought to know that the dowager is very keen to make your acquaintance.'

'What? The dowager viscountess is willing to acknowledge me?' Heslop sounded incredulous.

'Yes, indeed.' Emma smiled. 'When I told her about you, she was in alt to learn that she had another grandson. She'd apparently suspected something of the sort, knowing what a scoundrel Frederick was, but I'm afraid he kept it from her, and Grandfather never did discover the truth.' Emma looked directly into Heslop's eyes, noting that his face had now regained some of its colour. 'The dowager instructed me to tell you that she expects you to call on her at the earliest opportunity.' She smiled crookedly. 'And I'd advise you not to disappoint her. Grandmamma can be very formidable when she chooses.'

Jamie came over and nudged his sister. 'Emma, are you saying this gentleman is our cousin? I don't understand. And he is Uncle Frederick's son? But Uncle Frederick wasn't married, was he?'

His innocent question took Emma aback. That wasn't a subject she wished to deal with at that moment. Fortunately, Richard had heard and stepped in.

'I'll explain, Jamie,' he said, drawing Jamie apart. 'It's true, your uncle Frederick wasn't married. However, he did a great wrong and caused a young lady to become pregnant. He ruined her life and his child's by not admitting he was the father. Mr Heslop is her child. He cannot inherit your grandfather's title, being illegitimate, so that is why, when your uncle died, the title was to go to your father and then, on his death, to you. However, that does not alter the fact that Francis Heslop is your cousin.'

Jamie turned towards Heslop and looked at him thoughtfully. After a few seconds, Jamie extended his hand.

'Cousin Francis, I'm very pleased to make your acquaintance.'

There was a moment's hesitation, then Heslop grasped the boy's hand and smiled.

'The pleasure's all mine, Lord Easterby.'

Jamie grinned. 'No, you must call me Jamie. And I will call you Francis. We are family, after all.' He smiled mischievously. 'This is wonderful. Since I returned home, I've acquired several new cousins. But the best thing is' – Jamie's eyes lit up – 'you and Richard are both top sawyers!' He cocked his head to one side. 'Might I take a closer look at your bays, Cousin Francis?'

Emma chuckled. Trust her horse-mad little brother to break the tension. Richard good-naturedly cuffed Jamie on the shoulder and ruffled his hair.

'You are incorrigible, young man.'

Jamie's face was all innocence. 'What did I say?'

Richard laughed. 'I'm sure Cousin Francis will let you examine his horses. Why don't you go down to the stables and ask Mr Dawkins to show them to you?' He cocked an eye at Heslop. 'That is if you agree, Cousin Francis?'

Francis, who was still looking slightly dazed, nodded. Jamie, needing no further encouragement, raced out of the room to find Richard's head groom.

Emma looked at the two gentlemen. 'Shall I send for more tea? Or would you prefer brandy?'

'I think brandy is called for, don't you, Heslop?' said Richard. 'Though I suppose I should call you Francis as we are cousins, and if you've no objection? And, of course, you must call me Richard.'

Francis was smiling as he took the glass Richard handed him. 'I have to say, I feel thoroughly thrown. This morning, I left home believing I was almost alone in the world, apart from my distant connection to you, and this afternoon I discover a whole family.' His eyes twinkled. 'Gracious, even a grandmother. How one's life can change in an instant. Wheatley will be amazed when I tell him.'

Emma and Richard exchanged glances.

'Is something wrong?' asked Francis. 'You both seem a little anxious.'

'Well, that's the thing, Francis,' said Richard.

'We've been doing some digging,' said Emma, cutting in. 'And I'm afraid that the information we have leads us to believe that, for whatever reason, Wheatley is behind my uncle's death and the attempts on Richard's life.'

Francis leapt to his feet, banging his glass of brandy down hard on the small occasional table. Its polished surface glistened with droplets of spilt liquor.

His voice was harsh, unbelieving.

'No, no, I don't believe it, not His Grace. Your information must be wrong, cousin, or malicious. Wheatley would never stoop so low. He has been everything to me. He has given me not only employment and a home but also his friendship, and…' Francis crossed his arms about his chest and waved Emma away as she moved towards him.

'I'm sorry. I can't accept your friendship if you continue to make such accusations. Wheatley is not guilty of these crimes. The man is ill.' Francis swallowed. 'I believe… I believe he may not have a great deal of time left. Why would he do such a thing?' His emotions getting the better of him, Francis stopped speaking.

Emma tried approaching him again. 'Francis, I know this is difficult for you. I don't understand the reasons for it myself. Richard has employed the best investigators to try and discover who is behind it all, and each time it has come back to Wheatley. I'm sorry, I truly am. I can see you think highly of him.' Francis ignored her, his face expressionless.

Richard coughed.

'May I make a suggestion?' Twirling his now-empty glass in his fingers, Richard looked at Francis.

'Francis, would you be able to get me a private audience with Wheatley? I think I need to meet him face to face. It's the only way to clear this matter for everyone's sakes. Suspicions need to be cleared or confirmed.'

Emma cut in, all bristling indignation.

'My connection to this matter is far closer than yours, Richard. If any meeting is arranged, I'd wish to be present.' She raised her chin and looked from one to the other. Francis was staring at her as if he'd never heard a female speak out in such a fashion. He probably hadn't, she thought.

Richard waved a dismissive hand. 'We'll discuss this later, Emma. Let me sort out the details.' He repeated his request to Francis. 'Do you think you could arrange a meeting, Francis?'

Francis gave a scornful laugh. 'Of course I can. But he'll ridicule your absurd accusations. Nevertheless, if this is what it takes to silence this nonsense, I'll certainly request that he grant you an interview.'

Francis sat down and absentmindedly rubbed the table with a handkerchief where the brandy had spilt. After a few seconds, he looked up at Emma. 'I apologise for my outburst of temper. Please forgive me.'

'It's no matter,' she said. 'We've all been rather overwrought this afternoon, I think. Now, you will go and pay a call on the dowager, won't you, Francis? She's been through such a lot. She truly does want to get to know you, and it would be terribly sad if this matter with Wheatley stopped that.'

Francis' features softened, and with a smile that warmed his eyes, he replied, 'Of course I'll call on her. You don't know what this means to me, to be accepted by my father's family. I never hoped before, you see.' His eyes flicked to Richard. 'But I want this matter settled too. I'm sure when you get to meet Wheatley you'll realise that somebody has been telling you Banbury tales. One other thing, cousin.' Francis looked Emma in the eye. 'I'm not one for holding grudges. My experience in life has shown me that bitterness does no good. It destroyed my mother. I won't allow it to destroy me.'

Emma gave Francis a hug, pleased that at last things seemed to be settled between them.

Francis went on to explain that while he was happy to arrange a meeting between Richard and Wheatley, Richard shouldn't expect it to take place very soon. Wheatley was suffering one of his periodic bouts of ill health, rarely leaving his bedchamber, never mind venturing out. Francis' voice was sad when he spoke of his employer's illness, and it struck Emma that there might be something more to the relationship than that of employer and employee.

'Well, what did you think?' asked Richard as he and Emma watched Francis drive away.

'About Francis, you mean? I'm convinced that your instincts are correct. He is no more a villain than I am.' Her brow creased in a frown. 'I think he might be mistaken about his employer's innocence though. Understandably so when you consider their friendship. In fact, I believe his feelings for Wheatley go quite deep.'

'Mmm, yes,' Richard answered non-committally, almost wishing that Emma wasn't quite so perceptive. Francis' relationship with Wheatley wasn't a subject he wished to discuss, and certainly not with her.

'I think Grandmamma will take to him. His resemblance to my father is uncanny.'

'I take it that your father and Frederick were both blessed with blond hair?'

'That's right. But as to character, well, Francis reminds me much more of Grandfather with his openness and gentle humour. I must confess I like him, Richard. I truly can't believe he's behind any of this awful business.'

'Unless he's an exceptional actor and is fooling both of us,' Richard said, not really wanting to consider that possibility.

Emma's eyes widened, then an expression of disbelief settled on her face. She waved a dismissive hand in the air.

'No, I can't believe I would so easily be fooled. And neither would you.'

'Nate Crawford also vouches for his good character, so that is something else in his favour. He's known Francis since he was a boy. But I'm not so sure about Wheatley, however much Francis trumpets his virtues.'

A dangerous glint appeared in Emma's eyes. 'Ah yes, about this proposed meeting with the duke. I am coming too. I insist.'

Richard's stomach lurched. He must have windmills in his head, but if agreeing to Emma's madcap scheme was the only way to convince her that he wasn't a tyrant, so be it.

'Yes. I think I might have a way we can manage it,' he heard himself saying. 'Let me think about it for now. I'll soon have everything in hand,' he added glibly. 'Believe me, I know how important this is to you.'

To him too – his whole future happiness depended on it.

Chapter 19

EMMA WAS SITTING WITH her grandmother a day or so later, perusing the latest edition of *La Belle Assemblée*. They were seeking inspiration for the new wardrobe that the dowager insisted her newly returned granddaughter required when they were interrupted by the appearance of Dent, the dowager's butler.

'My lady, sorry for the intrusion, but a gentleman has called and wishes to know whether you are at home.'

Dent proffered a silver tray on which lay a visiting card with its upper right corner turned down. It was a nicely engraved card with gold lettering in a simple but elegant design. Emma couldn't quite read the name and didn't want to peer too closely. Her grandmother arranged her pince-nez and bent her head to read it.

'It's him. He's come at last.' The dowager excitedly thrust the calling card at Emma. 'See? Francis Heslop Esquire. Please show him up, Dent.'

The butler, face implacable at this unusual outburst from his mistress, bowed and departed to fetch the visitor. *La Belle Assemblée* was abandoned as the dowager started to pace the room, her black silks rustling and jet earrings bobbing as she twirled from the window to the fireplace and back again.

'Grandmamma, calm yourself, I beg you.'

'I'm perfectly calm, Emma. I'm just a little impatient to meet my grandson. Don't treat me as if I'm made of glass.' The smile on the dowager's face smoothed the reproof of her words. Halting her pacing to check her appearance in the large mirror above the mantelpiece, the old lady pushed a stray silver hair back under her satin-and-lace cap. Satisfied, she turned to face the door.

The door opened, and Dent announced with all pomp, 'Mr Francis Heslop, Your Ladyship.'

Francis entered rather hesitantly. His gaze flicked briefly round the room before it settled on the dowager, who was advancing towards him, her eyes overly bright. Dressed in a smart, navy-coloured morning coat, white Marcella waistcoat, and drab pantaloons, he cut an elegant but not over-showy figure. Bowing low, he addressed the dowager.

'I'm grateful that you have agreed to receive me, Lady Easterby.'

Disregarding all pretence at politeness, the dowager grasped the startled Francis by the arm and tugged him towards the light of the window.

'My dear boy, come here and let me see you,' she ordered. 'Oh my goodness, you are so like my Charles when he was your age.' Her face crinkled with joy. 'And Freddie too. That wretched boy, why did he not tell me about you? Why did he abandon you? I can't find it in my heart to forgive him, God help me.'

The face that had been smiling up at him now crumpled, and a tear rolled down the dowager's cheek. Emma watched as Francis, putting a tentative arm round her grandmother's shoulder, guided her to the sofa. From his expression, it was apparent that he'd been deeply moved by her words.

Dabbing at her eyes, the dowager composed herself.

'I'll be all right in a minute, my boy. Emma, don't you think he looks just like your dear papa?'

'He does indeed, Grandmamma. Let me ring for some tea, and then you and Francis may get to know one another better.'

The dowager grasped Francis' hand.

'I want to hear all about you, my boy, and then we must make plans to introduce you into society as my grandson.'

Francis, who'd barely uttered a word since his arrival, stammered, 'Are you s-s-sure, Lady Easterby? I'm q-q-quite happy for just you and Cousin Emma to acknowledge me. I don't expect anything further. I understand how it would cause embarrassment.'

The dowager snorted.

'Nonsense, my boy. I had enough embarrassment thanks to Freddie's antics when he was alive. His misdeeds are not going to dictate what I can or cannot do now he's dead, the wretched boy. Goodness knows, as his mother, it is left to me to try and make some amends for his despicable treatment of you.' She prodded his chest with a beringed finger. 'You're my grandson, and I will treat you as such. Anyone who feels affronted, well, they can take themselves off. And I insist you call me Grandmamma, young man.'

'As you wish… Grandmamma.'

'Now, Francis, tell me about your mother. I'm told that she was of gentle birth.'

Francis' face softened. 'Indeed she was, Grandmamma.' Faced with a barrage of questions not only about his mother and her family but his schooling and life at university, Francis answered them all patiently, his voice emotion-filled whenever he spoke about his mother.

Every so often, the dowager tutted and shook her head. 'Dear me, to think I never knew.'

When Francis eventually explained that he was employed by the Duke of Wheatley, the dowager's expression became thoughtful.

'Let me think, yes, I'm sure it was Wheatley who contacted my solicitor to inquire if Easterby Hall was entailed. He was thinking of purchasing it, apparently. Now isn't that a coincidence?'

'When was this, Grandmamma?' Emma's instincts were telling her that this was another piece in the puzzle of Wheatley's involvement. Francis looked bemused.

'He didn't mention anything to me. How strange. I'm normally privy to all his business dealings.'

'It was some time after my dear husband's death.' The dowager sighed. 'Word had got out that Charles and his family had disappeared and were feared dead. But of course we were unable to do anything until the courts had made their decision regarding that. It was thought the title was going to die out, that is until Mr Lacey's solicitor discovered his connection to the family and it became known he would inherit. As it happens, the estate is entailed, so it could not have been sold.'

Emma watched as her grandmother sipped her tea. Despite her animated demeanour, she looked tired. Her cheeks were pale beneath their discreet application of Circassian Bloom, and her eyes were beginning to look heavy.

'I think it's time for me to go now, Grandmamma,' said Emma. 'I promised Julia that I'd go shopping with her this afternoon.'

'I, too, must leave,' said Francis. 'I'm obliged to attend His Grace.' He turned with a smile to Emma. 'May I offer you my escort home, cousin?' With a twinkle, he added, 'If it would induce you to accept, I should let you know that I've brought the curricle that so impressed your brother.'

Emma giggled. 'Well, how can I refuse?'

The dowager slowly rose to her feet and took each of them by the arm.

'I think I'll retire to my room for a few hours' rest. It's been a very exciting day. You will call again soon, won't you, my boy? We must plan for your launch into society, and yours too, Emma, my dear.' The old lady's face beamed despite her tiredness. 'This is so exciting. I never thought I'd be happy again, but now I'm blessed beyond all expectations –three grandchildren indeed!' She gave Emma's hand one final squeeze before releasing it. 'And we must do more about your wardrobe, Emma dear. I know your cousin Julia has been uncommonly helpful, but I insist that it is a grandmother's duty to spend on her favourite granddaughter, and I intend to do so.'

Emma was still chuckling at her grandmother's words as she and Francis proceeded down the stairs to the hallway where a footman and a maid were waiting to help them on with their outdoor clothes. Emma was feeling a little guilty that the maid who'd accompanied her would have to walk, but to her pleased surprise, Francis, who'd spotted the girl hovering uncertainly in the hallway, gave her some coins to get herself a hackney.

'I'm much obliged to you, Francis. I'm afraid I don't have any coins with me, so I was unable to give her the fare myself.'

'Don't mention it,' said Francis. 'I've had such a wonderful morning, meeting Grandmamma and also spending time with you.' He leaned in confidentially. 'You know, I never dreamed that I'd have a real family. It never seemed possible.'

'Well, you have family now, like it or not,' Emma said, laughing, 'though I daresay there may be times when you'll wish us all to Jericho, especially when Jamie pesters you about your horses.'

On the short drive back to Richard's townhouse, the two chatted easily, Emma finding Francis to be both a genial companion and a competent horseman. He advised her that Wheatley was graciously willing to grant Richard an audience the following evening.

'He would not prefer a morning appointment?' she inquired as Francis negotiated his way between a lumbering coal cart and a young dandy driving his high-perch phaeton in the opposite direction at breakneck speed.

'His Grace normally feels a little better at the end of the day during these bouts of illness,' explained Francis after the two obstacles had been cleared. 'It's the time he sets aside for inspecting his estate books or dealing with any other business.'

'And what do *you* do when you are free of an evening, Francis? Do you attend many social functions?' Emma was curious to know what interested her cousin.

'No, I don't go out much in society. His Grace and I usually spend time together. We play chess or read. His Grace is also teaching me to play the piano.'

Emma knew she was being too inquisitive, but she couldn't stop herself. 'You're very close to him, are you not? And from what you have said, he values you highly.'

Francis' features hardened. 'Yes, he does. His Grace is a very kind and generous man.' By the set of his mouth, she knew more questions would not be welcomed.

Some minutes later, they pulled up outside the front door of the townhouse. Francis leapt from the curricle and came round to help her down. The groom, who'd been perched on the back of the vehicle throughout the journey, sprang off to take the reins.

As he took her hand, Francis sent her an apologetic smile.

'Please forgive my bad mood, Emma. I'm all at sixes and sevens. I'm not accustomed to sharing the details of my life with anyone.' There was a hint of anxiety in his eyes.

'No wonder you're a trifle out of sorts; you've had the ordeal of Grandmamma's interrogation earlier.' Francis chuckled at her choice of words. 'Will you forgive my prying?' Emma continued. 'Jamie always says I ask too many questions, but it's usually when he doesn't want me to find out about something.'

Francis nodded, a wry smile on his face.

'Yes, we all like to think we have our secrets, I'm afraid.'

Divesting herself of her bonnet and pelisse and handing them over to the waiting footman, Emma was still puzzling at Francis' cryptic remark when she heard Grimes telling her something about Richard being in his study and wishing to see her.

'I'm sorry, Mr Grimes, I was wool-gathering. Cousin Richard is in his study, you say?'

'Yes, miss.'

She hurried off to discover what Richard wanted.

Richard didn't hear the tap on the study door. Lost in his thoughts, he sat smiling to himself, his feet propped up on the desk and hands clasped behind his head. He was remembering the kiss he'd enjoyed with Emma in the carriage on the way back from the meeting with Downing. He'd been thinking about it all morning, in fact, and hadn't been able to settle to any work. Papers littered his desk, and every time his eyes alighted on them he knew Phil would have a fit if he saw it in such an untidy state.

A discreet cough brought him to his senses, and he saw Emma staring at him from the door. Richard sprang to his feet.

'I'm sorry, Emma. I was miles away. Do come in. I think we need to talk.' He started to gather up the scattered papers. 'Not usually this untidy. I don't know what has come over me this morning.' He reddened at his blatant lie.

'Shall I come back later?' she answered, a slight frown on her face as she surveyed the chaos.

'No. Not at all. Please sit here.' He hurriedly pulled out a chair. 'It won't take a moment for me to sort these out.' He gathered the papers and shoved them to one side. 'There. All tidy now.' Even he didn't believe the two tottering piles of notes and correspondence constituted anyone's idea of tidy. Never mind, it would do for now, he told himself. He leaned against his desk and crossed his legs. He hadn't felt this nervous in ages.

They both spoke at the same time.

'Ladies first.' Richard gave a weak smile, bracing himself for a tongue-lashing.

Emma kept her eyes downcast as she spoke in a low voice. 'I wanted to say how sorry I am for my forward behaviour the other evening on the way back from our meeting with Downing. It's been playing on my mind, you see. I think I was overcome with the excitement of it all and forgot how a true lady should behave.'

For one moment, he thought he was imagining things. He gaped at her. Why was she apologising to him? This wasn't right at all.

'No, no. It is I who must apologise to you. I don't think you were in any way to blame. I don't know what came over me. You must think me a veritable animal. I can assure you I don't normally treat young ladies in such a fashion. My offer of marriage still stands if you think you can overlook my poor behaviour.'

'Pardon?'

'Would you still consider my offer of marriage, Emma? I've never known anyone like you. You don't know what you do to me.' By this time he was on one knee, clasping her hands. He prayed that he hadn't really burned his bridges with his rakish behaviour.

She bit her lip. 'I was concerned you would think me forward, but it seems I'm wrong. Like you, I don't know what came over me the other day. I only meant to give you a chaste kiss but' – she cast her eyes down – 'I don't know what happened.'

Richard started to feel optimistic. Would she say yes? His pulse began to race.

'I'm still unsure about marriage,' she whispered.

'What? With me? There is no need, I can assure you.'

'No, you don't understand. Even though Grandmamma has explained that all marriages have their ups and downs and that she was sure Mama and Papa really loved each other, how can I be sure that what we feel for each other is love and not just a fleeting infatuation?' Before he could answer, she went on. 'We were both in a state of high emotion. How do I know that you won't grow tired of a woman who speaks her mind?'

Richard ventured a smile. 'I've decided I would much prefer a wife with a mind and opinions of her own than a milk-and-water miss. I've lived a life up to now that has been laden with responsibilities. When Julia left to get married, I thought I'd enjoy a peaceful existence. I thought I needed only a quiet little mouse of a wife who'd run my household and fill my nursery.' He grasped her hand. 'But that's not what I want, Emma. I want someone like you. From the moment you arrived at Easterby Hall, I've never known a minute's peace.' He grinned at her dismayed expression. 'But I've never felt so alive! And this is no passing fancy. I'm sure we'll have our ups and downs, but I know that in the end, I can rely on you, Emma, and I promise that you can rely on me. Please say you'll be my wife and make me the happiest of men.'

Richard held his breath and waited for her answer.

Emma stood up and paced to the window. The silence grew. His insides coiled. This wasn't looking good. At last, Emma turned.

'Not yet. I cannot give you an answer yet.' She sounded upset. He allowed a glimmer of hope to kindle.

'When?' For some reason, his throat and mouth were dry.

'When we've met with Wheatley. I promise to give you my answer then.'

Richard forced a smile. 'Very well.' He'd do anything to prove himself. But how was he going to protect her? It was unlikely to go as smoothly as their visit to Mrs Newbody's. Phil was still absent, so who could he trust to offer assistance? Dear Lord, what a fix. With any luck, Wheatley would be unable to see him for some days. Francis had explained that Wheatley was ill. Richard brightened. Given time, he was sure he would think of something.

'Come,' he said, crooking his elbow. 'I believe there are some refreshments awaiting us in the dining room. Cook will be most disappointed if we don't try them.'

'By the way, I forgot to mention,' Emma said as she took his arm, 'Francis told me that Wheatley is willing to meet with us tomorrow evening.'

Ice formed in the pit of his stomach. Hell and damnation! What should he do? He looked down at Emma's glowing face. Infuriating witch.

'You'll be the death of me, Emma Smythe,' he growled. He knew he'd do anything she asked, risk everything for her sake.

Chapter 20

Emma woke up the next morning, something nagging at the back of her mind. Wiping the sleep from her bleary eyes, she slowly sat up and peered around. The clock on the mantelpiece showed it was nearly eight o'clock; Polly would be up soon with her hot water. Then it hit her. She and Richard were to meet with Wheatley that evening. Emma swung her legs out of bed. There was no time to be lost. She needed to speak to Richard and discover what he'd come up with to get her inside Wheatley's townhouse.

Richard had spoken to her briefly after dinner the previous evening, giving only the bare details of the arrangements for the planned meeting with the duke. They'd both felt rather awkward with each other after the emotional revelations of the afternoon. She'd hoped the usually perceptive Julia hadn't noticed. Julia hadn't commented, but Emma knew nothing much got past her. Emma suspected that she was going to be subjected to some sort of inquisition as soon as Julia got her on her own.

Emma's stomach clenched when she saw Julia was already in the breakfast parlour. She'd hoped to avoid a tête-à-tête with her friend for as long as possible.

Smiling brightly, she said cheerily, 'Good morning, Julia.

You look well. No sickness this morning?' Sometimes attack was the best form of defence.

Julia smiled back at her, a shrewd look in her eye.

'Good morning, my dear. I'm not feeling too bad at all, thank goodness. I even fancy a small piece of bread with my egg today.' Julia set down the knife that she'd been using to butter her bread and regarded Emma from under lowered lashes. 'You're looking very, erm, buoyant. Or do I mean excited?' She gave a little laugh. 'How are things between you and Richard? I must say, I thought you two were very cool towards one another at dinner.' She smiled archly before taking a bite from her bread.

'That's enough, Julia.'

Richard gave his sister a hard stare as he stalked across to where Emma was standing near the sideboard, about to help herself to some coddled eggs. She'd been struggling to find a suitable retort when the sound of Richard's voice caused her to freeze. His face softened as he took the plate out of her hand, squeezing her fingers briefly.

'Allow me. You sit down, and I will see to your plate.'

Emma took a seat across the table from Julia who, unabashed by Richard's reprimand, was looking smug. 'I see things are back to normal now between you two.'

Emma watched as Richard busied himself filling two plates. As usual, he was dressed impeccably with tight-fitting riding breeches and a dark-blue riding jacket. When he'd finished, he came and took the chair next to Emma. She thought how nice it might be to sit this close to him every morning.

'I see you're dressed for riding, Richard,' said Julia, her face all innocence. 'Do you have any plans for the day, Emma?'

Emma flashed a quick glance at Richard.

'Erm, no, not at the moment. I thought perhaps to spend some time catching up on some reading. I can't visit Grandmamma today, as she's occupied with one of her ladies' committees.'

Richard cleared his throat.

'Emma, if you don't mind, might I have a word with you later when I return? I don't expect to be out longer than an hour, so shall we say eleven o'clock in my study?'

Before Emma could reply, Julia giggled.

'Honestly, Richard. That sounded like a summons to the headmaster's office, not a romantic assignation!'

Emma coloured up, and Richard set down his cutlery and frowned at his sister.

'I'll thank you for not making impertinent remarks, Julia. It's not an assignation, as you call it, romantic or otherwise. I merely wish to discuss with Emma some matters appertaining to the investigations.' Perhaps realising that he'd been a little harsh, he added with a smile, 'Why don't you and Emma plan an outing for this afternoon? Hopefully, I'll be free to escort you. Just promise me that it will not involve shopping.'

Julia, who'd initially looked as if she'd wanted to box his ears, brightened.

'I say, that's very handsome of you, Richard.' She looked at Emma. 'And I apologise if I made you feel uncomfortable, Emma. That wasn't my intention.' She smiled contritely.

Emma couldn't help but smile back. She knew Julia meant well. As for Richard… In her opinion, he'd missed his calling as a diplomat. She felt a light touch on her arm and looked round to see Richard gazing at her intently.

'Eleven o'clock. Is that all right with you? You didn't say.'

She nodded, her arm tingling from the touch of his fingers and her heart hammering at the intensity of his gaze.

'Y-yes, of course. I'll see you at eleven o'clock.' By then, she hoped she'd have a better grip on her nerves. He'd change his mind about her going with him to see Wheatley if he discovered what a quivering mass of emotion she became in his presence.

They all looked up as the door opened and George strode into the room. With a sudden loud scraping of her chair, Julia got to her feet. Richard, being the gentleman that he was, abandoned the sausage he was about to place on his fork and got up too, a puzzled look on his face. His sister hadn't finished her breakfast.

Julia smiled at her husband.

'Ah, there you are, George dear. A word, if you please.' It was not a request. With a swish of her skirts, Julia swept round the table and pulled a bemused George back out of the room. The look of longing that George cast over the food laid out on the sideboard would have melted the heart of a lesser woman, but not Julia, apparently. Richard and Emma exchanged looks, and they both suddenly broke into laughter.

'I think he's in for a scolding. Poor George.' Richard wiped a tear of laughter from his eye. 'Wonder what he's done.'

Emma smiled back at him. Julia was a prime example of a woman not under her husband's thumb. She surely wasn't the only one. Perhaps marriage to Richard would not be so awful after all.

At the appointed hour, Emma tapped on Richard's study door and went in. He was slumped at his desk, as if the weight of the world were on his shoulders. At the sound of her footsteps, he looked up.

'Oh Lord, how long have you been there, Emma?' he said, leaping to his feet. 'I didn't hear you come in. Forgive me.'

Yes, he'd been agonising over how to get her in and out of Wheatley's townhouse without it being bruited all over town. He had to do it. If he didn't, no matter the outcome, she'd never trust him again. He'd made a promise, and he never broke a promise – though keeping this one would surely kill him one way or another.

'Only just this moment,' she answered, frowning. 'I could see you were deep in thought. What are you worrying about?' As he shook his head, she added, 'Don't deny it. I can see the stress on your face.'

Richard shrugged.

'Oh, all right. I admit I'm concerned about how to get you into Wheatley's house. Or rather, how to get you in and out without anyone else discovering. I'm not sure how we can do it.' He absentmindedly picked up the ruler on his desk and began to tap it rhythmically on the wooden surface. If only he could come up with a magic solution. He looked up to see her pacing towards him, recognising the determined look in her eyes and the set of her chin and wondering what outlandish scheme she'd come up with next.

'Why can't I disguise myself again? Pretend to be David? Wheatley has never met him, has he?'

Richard rolled his eyes. Here we go again.

He kept his voice steady. 'No, he's never met David. And I did consider that option, but now I'm having second thoughts.' At her questioning look, he continued. 'You see, I asked George and Crawford to accompany us. Safety in numbers and all that. They both know you. Haven't told them you're coming with us; thought I'd leave that to the last.' Richard screwed up his face in concentration. 'Crawford is discreet, I'd guarantee, but George?' He shrugged. 'He's bound to tell Julia, and she will flay me alive for risking your safety.' He sent her a look that he hoped conveyed his concerns. 'It's pretty unfair to ask the chaps to look out for you as well as me.' Richard could think of dozens more reasons that he could mention – someone could see them arriving or the servants might talk. If Wheatley himself discovered the deception, he could easily ruin her reputation. And so it went on.

He sighed. Were those reasons sufficient to give her pause for thought?

But she surprised him again.

'Blow the consequences,' she said forcefully. 'I'll be the only one to suffer. As a man, your reputation wouldn't even be dented. Besides,' she added, eyes gleaming, 'I want to get this matter sorted once and for all.'

Richard shook his head. She was infuriating. Infuriating but wonderful. He knew then that he wouldn't be able to stop her, and if he tried, he'd lose her forever. She was now pacing backwards and forwards from the desk to the fireplace, talking almost to herself.

'If George and Major Crawford see through my disguise, then we can ask them to be discreet. And if they want to cry off because of my presence, then so be it, but I'm coming, no matter what.' She paused, her brow creased in a thoughtful frown. 'Or... I could go on my own.' Richard's blood ran cold. He was about to remonstrate with her when she suddenly banged her fist into her hand. 'I've had enough of hiding and pretending to be someone I'm not. If I can drag myself and my brother out of the continent and back to safety' – she glanced up at him – 'well, all right, I know I did it only by the skin of my teeth, but I'm certainly capable of confronting Wheatley in his den.' She took in a breath, her chest heaving with suppressed anger, then looked him square in the eye. 'If all this makes you want to withdraw your offer of marriage, I'll understand.'

Richard gaped at her, completely taken by surprise. She'd actually been considering accepting his offer. Exultant, his nerves about the coming night's exploits vanished. He could do this.

'Do you really think this will make me change my mind? Don't be a ninnyhammer.' He grabbed her hand. 'Since I met you my life has changed. I've never felt so alive. I was getting stuck in my ways and becoming old before my time. I don't care whether George and Crawford come with us or not. You and I shall go together and take the consequences.'

By God, he meant those words. It was time to stop worrying about what others would think. He'd worried for years about doing the right thing, what with the responsibility of his brother and sister, not to mention the estate, the mines, and all his tenants and employees. He'd been sober and serious, dutiful.

Well, he would still be all those things, Richard told himself. But he could also afford to take risks. He had to help

Emma, and doing it her way would not be boring. If she was strong enough to go it alone then so was he. He and Emma would do it together – a team, partners. Hopefully, partners for life… if she would have him.

Emma was gaping at him, shocked into silence by his outburst. At last he saw her mouth move. 'Oh, thank you, Richard,' she whispered. 'You don't know what this means to me.'

'I do, my love. Believe me, I do.'

The rest of the day raced by. Richard, buoyed up by new-found feelings of exhilaration and the realisation that he didn't always have to be a model of propriety, retreated to his study to review all the paperwork and written evidence he'd amassed concerning Wheatley. He wanted to go over everything to ensure he'd not missed anything crucial. It all had to be watertight. If Wheatley decided to take him to court or, heaven forfend, issue a challenge, he wanted to be certain his evidence would stand up to scrutiny. He might feel more carefree, but he was certainly not going to be careless, especially over the details. Blake had taken sworn statements from the two informers prior to Richard personally interviewing them. Even though Bill Rogers had disappeared, his statement should still carry weight with a court.

The thought that kept nagging at him, though, was the possible involvement of Francis. Not that he believed Francis had anything to do with the murder attempts, more the fact that, if matters became public, his relationship with Wheatley would become food for scandal. Richard was pretty certain that the relationship between Francis and Wheatley went beyond what were considered normal bounds.

He feared that Francis would likely be punished if it all came out. Francis didn't deserve that, and neither Emma nor her grandmother deserved the heartbreak it would bring. Richard knew that as a member of the peerage, Wheatley would not be prosecuted. The same could not be said of Francis. Francis would be the one to suffer any penalties that the law decided to dish out. Richard pushed these worrying thoughts out of his mind and returned to the task in hand, familiarising himself with every detail.

Emma spent the afternoon with Julia and George, who'd apparently been forgiven for whatever transgression he'd committed and was back in his wife's good books. Julia had prevailed upon him to escort them to Ackermann's on Bond Street. Richard, with his sister's blessing, had finally decided to remain at home. Emma wondered if she, too, ought to stay, but he persuaded her that by accompanying his sister she could allay any suspicions about their intended outing that evening.

Emma, distracted by fears of what the evening might bring, listened with only one ear as Julia chattered on about choosing some prints for her drawing room.

'It would be so much easier if I could create my own, but I was hopeless at drawing and watercolours. I never could quite get things to look as they ought,' said Julia with a laugh. 'Ask Richard; he'll tell you. He and David used to laugh themselves silly trying to guess what I'd drawn. In the end, Papa decided to save himself the expense of an art master and allowed me to get on with what I really enjoyed.'

'What was that, Julia?' asked Emma, wondering what she'd missed by her inattention.

'Numbers. I loved going over the business accounts. Papa capitulated when he realised I was picking up mistakes that he'd missed and I was actually saving him money.'

George's face was proud as he smiled at his wife. 'Yes, you're a clever puss, aren't you? And now you look after our accounts.'

That gave Emma something to think about. Here was another man who respected his wife's abilities. Perhaps she'd been wrong about all men being the same. It seemed Richard wasn't alone in treating the females in his life as rational beings.

After Ackermann's, they made a brief visit to Hatchards to pick up some books before returning to the carriage for the journey home. Julia slumped back into the squabs, stretching her feet out on the seat opposite. Removing her bonnet, then stifling a yawn with the back of one gloved hand, Julia said, 'I think I've probably overdone things today. Would you mind very much if I don't join you for dinner, George? Emma, do you mind? I'll take a tray in my room and have an early night.'

George shot his wife an anxious look. 'Are you sure you're all right, my love? I must say, you don't look to be in prime twig; you look a little tallow-faced. Do you need to see the doctor? I'll send for him if you wish.'

Julia batted him away with her hat. 'Oh, George, don't be a gudgeon. I'm fagged, that's all. I'm sure after an early night I'll be as fine as ninepence tomorrow.'

'If you're sure, my love,' said George, then he frowned. 'I forgot to mention I may have to slip out for an hour or so with Richard. He has a meeting he wants me to attend with him, but he assures me it won't last above a couple of hours.' He sent Julia another anxious look. 'I'll tell him he'll have to go on his own.'

Julia leaned forward and grasped her husband's hand.

'Dear George. Stop worrying, I'm just a bit fatigued. I've been on my feet all afternoon, and I've been advised that fatigue is normal at this stage, in any case. You go with Richard.' She sent him an impish smile. 'Just make sure you come in to see me when you return.'

Emma felt superfluous to the moment and wished she could magically disappear and leave husband and wife alone. Blushing furiously, she answered, 'Of course I don't mind, Julia. You need your rest. As you know, I'm accustomed to entertaining myself. I've got lots of things to keep me occupied.'

Thank goodness Julia had no inkling of what she had planned for that evening.

Chapter 21

Emma paced back and forth in her bedchamber. She'd been doing it for at least the last half hour and was sure that if the clock fingers refused to move any faster she'd wear a path in the Turkey rug. At last, the clock chimed the hour, and without wasting a moment to check her appearance one last time, she slipped out of her room and glided down the stairs to join Richard in his study.

Tapping lightly on the study door, she didn't wait for a reply before she entered. She was confronted by the sight of an open-mouthed George, who gaped at the figure she presented.

'I say! What are you doing dressed like that, Emma?'

She looked down and smiled, as if seeing her costume for the first time – a smartly cut coat with a high collar, striped toilinette waistcoat, kerseymere breeches, and a finely starched neckcloth. Over her arm, she carried a greatcoat.

'What, don't you like it, George? I'm told it's all the first stare,' she answered.

George's eyes swung to Richard, who'd remained seated. Richard took a sip from the glass in his hand and looked her up and down with approval.

'Why don't you take a seat, Emma,' Richard said at last, 'and I'll pour you a drink before we depart?'

'What? Surely you don't mean...?' George blustered. 'You can't possibly... You don't intend her to be one of our party, do you? Do you, Richard? Tell her she can't.'

George's eyes were fairly bulging out of his head, his mouth opening and closing like a fish even though he'd stopped speaking. Emma struggled not to laugh.

'Calm down, George. Yes, she is coming with us.' Richard finished pouring the glass of port and turned to his brother-in-law. 'Or just me if you now don't wish to be one of the party. I must say, I didn't expect you to be so lily-livered, George. Has my little sister really stolen all your backbone?'

George bristled. 'Now look here, Richard. I wouldn't take that from any other man. Julia hasn't taken my backbone, as you so nicely phrase it. She and I work well together. But... but this is something else entirely. Surely you're not allowing Emma to put herself at risk? We don't know what Wheatley is capable of – or rather, we suspect we do, and that is even worse.'

Emma decided to intervene. 'George, I understand your concerns, but first, I should remind you that Richard is in no position to dictate what I do. Second, I am of age and quite capable of making my own decisions, thank you very much. Third, this problem is my responsibility. I've taken care of my brother since the death of our parents, and I'll not abrogate that care until I'm sure all danger to him has passed.' She waved a hand. 'Richard has kindly offered to accompany me to this appointment with the duke, but if he decides he doesn't wish to come, and if you decide not to accompany me, please be assured, I will go on my own.'

She took a sip from her glass and added, 'Have I made myself clear?'

George looked at her. He then turned to Richard, who only shrugged. George looked back at Emma. Emma stared impassively at him, her mouth set. Richard continued to sip his drink. Throwing his arms in the air, George blew out a loud breath.

'I give in. You're both incorrigible. I have to say, I'm surprised at you, Richard. You used to be such a sobersides. And you, Emma, well, you remind me of my lovely wife. No wonder you two get on so well together. It's almost a pity she can't join us. She'd love all this.'

Richard chuckled. 'It's a good thing Julia is your responsibility now, George. I don't think I could deal with two such females.' Grinning at Emma, he stood up. 'Well, what are we waiting for? Let's be off.'

That was one hurdle cleared, thought Emma with relief. It only remained to be seen whether Richard could convince Crawford to keep to his agreement. They were due to pick him up outside his lodgings at half past the hour.

Some twenty minutes later, their carriage pulled up outside the Albany as Crawford was slowly descending the steps from the front door. The carriage door opened, and the major heaved himself in and settled in the corner seat next to George. Emma huddled in the opposite corner, half-hidden by Richard's body. Neither of them were sure what Crawford's reaction to her presence would be.

Crawford's eyes sparkled with anticipation. 'Evening, Lacey. Evening, George. I'm quite looking forward to this. I've been lacking excitement in my life lately.'

Crawford frowned, suddenly noticing the extra figure in the corner.

'And who is this?' he asked in a mock stern tone. 'I thought it was just to be the three of us. Don't say you thought we'd need reinforcements, Richard? I'm mortified you think George and I are weaklings.' There was a chuckle in his voice as he said this. Crawford's eyes narrowed as he peered at Emma's half-hidden face. George coughed and turned an I-told-you-so expression towards Richard. Crawford, noticing, asked, 'Well, are you going to tell me?' He stretched out his hand to remove the hat covering Emma's face.

Richard's arm streaked out and grabbed him.

'Don't.'

Crawford sat back in his seat with a look of amusement.

'Well, this is interesting… Let me guess.'

Emma spoke up.

'Major Crawford… it is I, Emma Smythe. I'm coming with you to see Wheatley. You can't stop me, so if you wish to leave now, please do so.'

Crawford chuckled.

'Well, Lacey, I see you've finally met someone to shake you out of your steady life.' He grinned at Emma. 'Miss Smythe, I'm delighted to accompany you. The prospects for this evening seem to be getting better and better. I haven't had this much fun since… Well, I'd better not say in mixed company.' He folded his hands behind his head and stretched out, careful not to knock his bad leg in the cramped space. A relieved Richard felt fortunate to have such loyal friends.

It didn't take long to get to Grosvenor Square. The coach drew up outside the duke's imposing property, which was set back behind iron railings. Richard alighted first, studiously avoiding assisting Emma. For her disguise to work, she needed to pass as a male until they were safely back home. He perused the impressive façade of Wheatley House. George sidled up to him, craning his head to gaze up at the windows. They were all ablaze. Emma loitered in the shadows.

George gave Richard a nudge.

'Wheatley mustn't be bothered about the cost of illuminating all those rooms when he isn't entertaining. I've heard he's very plump in the pocket.'

'Not bothered at all by the looks of things,' agreed Richard.

All three turned at the sound of Crawford's groan as he finally alighted from the coach. The poor chap had landed heavily on his bad leg.

'Sorry about that, lads. Damned leg is playing up again.'

Richard read the frustration in his friend's face and heard the suppressed anger in his voice. Crawford had seemed a trifle ungainly clambering into the coach when they'd picked him up.

'Seems to happen from time to time. Blasted thing just stiffens up when the weather turns cold,' Crawford muttered, his voice gruff.

'Oh, stop whining, man. Don't play the sympathy card with me; you're not getting out of this now,' Richard shot back. He knew Crawford would hate to be pitied.

His friend straightened up, cast a quick glance at Emma, and snarled back, 'Not a chance.' His sardonic smile indicated that he understood Richard's tactics.

'Right, gentlemen, this is it.' Richard led the way up the steps.

Two lanterns, one either side of the door, illuminated the large brass door knocker in the shape of a lion's head. Richard grasped it and knocked twice. The sound reverberated round them in the dark and deserted square. Richard shivered. Only because of the cold night air, he told himself. He angled himself so that no light would fall on Emma when the door opened.

A stately butler waved them into the foyer.

'Good evening, gentlemen. I believe you are expected.'

Richard looked around, taking in the impressive hallway. The walls glowed in the flickering light of the central chandelier suspended from the ornately plastered ceiling. Black-and-white marble tiles made up the floor, and a fireplace to one side sent out welcome heat into the large space. Above the mantelpiece hung a full-length portrait of a gentleman dressed in what Richard surmised was fashionable court dress during the reign of Charles II. No doubt one of Wheatley's illustrious forbears. Richard kept an eye on Emma, who was keeping to the shadows, hovering at the edge of the hallway away from the light cast by the chandelier and the fire. Clever girl.

'Your cards, gentlemen.'

The butler held out a tray.

A jolt of horror ran up Richard's spine. Why hadn't he remembered to pick up one of David's cards?

'I'm afraid my brother doesn't have a card as yet. He's only just down from Oxford and the printers have not completed the order. I do apologise.'

The butler nodded, and once the three cards were placed on his tray, he left the four companions standing in the hall. Richard turned and winked at Emma. She looked shaken but had kept her nerve.

'Talkative chap, isn't he?' grinned George as he went over to the fireplace, stretching his hands out towards the warmth cast off by the glowing coals.

'I think it's meant to keep us in our proper place,' answered Richard.

Crawford sat down on one of the austere wooden chairs that stood at each side of the fireplace. He stretched his right leg out, kneading it where his breeches met the top of his immaculately polished boot.

'Playing up still?' Richard asked him.

Crawford gave him a hard look.

'Don't worry. I can still manage if you need some muscle.'

Richard grinned at him.

'Well, I wasn't intending to come to fisticuffs with Wheatley, but it's good to know you'll have my back.'

Crawford looked speculatively at Emma, who was now pacing up and down.

'Don't worry about her, Richard,' he said in lowered tones. 'We'll see you both home safe and sound. For what it's worth, I think Miss Smythe is more than a match for a mere duke. You're a lucky man, my friend.'

Richard silently agreed.

Despite his air of levity, Richard's nerves were as taut as viola strings. He didn't expect Wheatley to physically attack him – as he'd told Emma, that was not Wheatley's style. Besides, Francis had warned him how the duke's health had deteriorated. No, he was more concerned about accusing a man of murder to his face. How would Wheatley react? He had a good idea how he'd respond to such an accusation, and it wouldn't be pretty. He wasn't expecting much different from Wheatley and wondered how Emma would deal with it.

Richard caught the sound of footsteps coming down the polished stairs. Turning, he saw a nervous-looking Francis descending, followed by the butler. Francis, as usual, was dressed in an impeccable but understated style, with close-fitting black trousers that finished just above the ankle and shining buckled slippers. Beneath his beautifully embroidered waistcoat, whose green and yellow silk threads glistened in the candlelight, was a fine linen shirt. The whole was topped off with an exquisitely folded cravat. Richard reckoned his own valet would be green with envy to see such elegance.

'Good evening, Richard. You're very punctual,' Francis said, before nodding to Crawford, who acknowledged him with a bow of the head, and then George, who was lounging near the fire. Francis then spotted the third figure, and Richard heard his gasp of surprise. It was apparent that Francis hadn't believed Emma when she'd said she was coming along.

'I didn't realise you'd be bringing company, Richard,' Francis said in strained tones.

'Yes, it was a last-minute decision to accompany my friends,' interrupted Crawford in a jovial manner. 'We're planning on going to White's later.'

Good old Crawford, thought Richard. He made it sound as if he and George were just tagging along, not that they were in fact acting as bodyguards.

'Francis, allow me to introduce my brother-in-law, George Morton. George, this is Francis Heslop, Emma's cousin, and mine too.'

He thought it worth mentioning that fact to impress on Francis that he wasn't going to be cut adrift from the family, regardless of what was to be learned tonight. Francis extended a hand to George.

'Good to make your acquaintance, Morton. You must be married to Richard's sister, Julia. Is that right?'

George grasped his hand in return. 'I have that honour, yes. Pleased to meet you.'

Richard continued the introductions for the benefit of the butler who was hovering nearby. 'And this is David, my younger brother. You don't mind if he accompanies me, do you, old chap?'

Francis peered at Emma as she lifted her head and slowly removed her hat. Richard hoped the butler was not standing close enough to get a good look at her facial features. He held his breath until Francis slowly extended his hand.

'Good evening, David. I'm very pleased to make your acquaintance.' He turned to Richard. 'His Grace was only expecting to meet with you, Richard, but I think he'll not object to your… erm, brother being present. But, if you don't mind, gentlemen' – he waved to George and Crawford – 'I think it best if you wait in the drawing room. Too many people upset him when he's indisposed. The fire is lit in there, is it not, Smith?'

'Indeed, sir.'

'And, Smith, if you would bring the gentlemen some refreshments while they wait.'

'Certainly, Mr Heslop. Please follow me, gentlemen.'

George and Crawford trailed after the butler, Crawford making a long job of the stairs on account of his bad leg. At last they reached the first landing where they turned right towards the public rooms. Coming behind them, Francis led Richard and Emma in the opposite direction towards Wheatley's private apartments.

'His Grace's health is not too bad this evening, but please don't tire him,' whispered Francis.

'I promise we won't stay overlong, but I do mean to have this matter out,' replied Richard. He hadn't come here with Emma just to make a social call. Francis sent him a sidelong look and opened his mouth as if about to say something, but then he seemed to think better of it.

Through a pair of polished wooden doors, Richard found himself in a sumptuously appointed chamber. It was quite an effort for him not to gawk like a complete bumpkin. The rooms in his own house in Cornwall he'd considered very well appointed, but this room was truly special. This was Wheatley's famed library, an indicator, if one was needed, that said that Wheatley was a cultured and educated man. Richard knew it held an impressive collection of rare manuscripts and incunabula. Book presses lined the walls. Fires blazed in two large marble fireplaces, one at each end of the room. He glanced at Emma. Her eyes were wide, taking everything in. Knowing her love of manuscripts, Richard guessed that this must be her idea of heaven.

In addition to the glow cast by the fires, the room was illuminated by several large candelabra placed on tables arranged around the room, their flickering light glancing off the gold lettering embossed on the spines of the volumes lining the shelves. A lion's head picked out in gold adorned the base of each spine. Silk brocade sofas in shades of yellow and green were placed near each of the full-length windows. Francis pointed to the lion's head carved into the centre of each mantelpiece.

'That's the Wheatley heraldic beast. You'll find it all over the house.'

Francis led them across the room towards the matching set of doors at the far end. He tapped softly and, without waiting for a reply, opened the door and ushered them both in.

Here was a room of a totally different ambience to the one through which they'd just passed. Dimly lit as it was, Richard saw it was more comfortable, masculine in character, and conveying the feeling that this was a place where one could relax. It was furnished in shades of red and cream, with silk crimson wallpaper covering the walls and matching heavy velvet curtains draped across the windows to muffle the sounds of tradesmen's carts and carriage wheels on the cobblestones in the square below.

'I see you are admiring my private retreat, Viscount Easterby... or should I call you by your real name, Mr Lacey?'

Wheatley's purring voice took Richard by surprise. The duke, dressed in a dark-blue brocade banyan embossed with silver thread, was reclining in a high-backed wing chair near the fire. His slippered feet rested on a footstool and a *cashemire* rug covered his legs. Richard's eyes widened. The figure before him was the shadow of the man he'd seen mere days before, with gaunt, hollow-cheeked features and dark circles round his eyes. He wondered how someone looking so ill managed to draw breath and almost considered making his excuses and departing.

'You're quite correct, Your Grace. I'm Richard Lacey.' Richard gestured to Emma who was standing several paces behind. 'And this is my brother David. I hope you don't mind that he's accompanied me this evening?'

Emma bowed.

'David, eh?' Wheatley arched a sardonic eyebrow. 'I see. Not at all. Forgive me for not rising to greet you. As you can see, I'm not in the best of health at the moment.' Wheatley gestured to the table at his elbow on which stood various bottles and glasses.

'I think my doctors have decided to kill me slowly with their potions and poisons, haven't they, Francis?' Wheatley smiled up at Francis who stepped towards him, his face filled with concern.

'No, you're not dying. You will recover, Henry, erm, I mean, Your Grace.' Francis looked stricken and Richard felt a pang of sympathy. Wheatley reached out and took hold of Francis' hand. The depth of feeling between the two men was obvious.

Richard inwardly squirmed. He shouldn't be intruding when plainly the man did not have long to live. He cleared his throat.

'Thank you for agreeing to see me, Your Grace. I understood you were not in the best of health but hadn't realised… that is to say, would you prefer me to call back when you're feeling better?' Privately, he decided a miracle would be required before Wheatley recovered his health.

Wheatley chuckled.

'I've had several of these bouts since I turned forty, and each time I've recovered, apparently spontaneously. I've consulted different doctors, and I've taken the potions they give me, but as none of them know what my condition is, I don't think they help. Bleeding and cupping only make me feel worse.' Wheatley pointed to the bottles on the table beside him. 'These will be the next to go, I've decided.' He held his hand up as Francis opened his mouth. 'No, don't interrupt, Francis.' Wheatley sighed and shook his head. 'I think my chances of complete recovery are extremely remote, whatever dear Francis chooses to believe. I've reluctantly accepted that I may suffer these episodes until I end my days.' He shrugged. 'It's a trifle inconvenient for someone with my responsibilities.'

Richard nodded. This illness, whatever it was, was indeed a heavy burden for a man with ducal responsibilities.

Wheatley shifted in his chair. 'So we must talk now, Mr Lacey. I don't think this bout of illness will end soon, and as my fatigue lessens slightly in the evenings, this is the best time to discuss what we must.' Wheatley pointed to the chair matching his own at the other side of the fireplace. 'Please be seated. You are making me uncomfortable.'

Richard reluctantly sat down. Emma took a seat a short distance further back. Richard was grateful that the room wasn't ablaze with candles – at that distance, Wheatley would be unlikely to see her clearly. He was still uneasy about raising the subject he'd come to discuss, having no desire to increase Wheatley's suffering. These could be Wheatley's last few days on earth for all he knew. Then he turned and saw Emma's face, and his resolve hardened. She, her brother, and the dowager had all been through hell and back, and they deserved to know the reason. The truth, however unpalatable, should be disclosed. He mustn't allow pity to cloud his judgement. Was the man sitting opposite really behind the attempts on his own life and the death of Frederick Smythe? Had he also arranged for Emma's parents to be wrongly advised in Greece? If the answer was yes to all of these, then the next question would be *why*. What triggered a campaign of vengeance against one particular family?

However, before Richard could formulate his first question, Wheatley pulled Francis to one side. 'Leave us to speak privately, there's a good fellow. I'll call if I need you.'

Francis looked distraught. 'But, Henry…'

'No buts, if you please, Francis. I'm fine for now, and this is not for your ears. Now go.'

Francis didn't argue, and with shoulders slumped he left the room.

Chapter 22

Wheatley looked at Richard over slender, steepled fingers, his silver eyes glittering.

'I know why you've come, Mr Lacey. It's about Frederick Smythe, is it not?'

There was a sharp intake of breath from Emma. Richard decided to be equally blunt.

'Yes it is, Wheatley. I've reason to believe that you were somehow involved in his untimely death and possibly also those of his brother Charles and his family.' Richard's eyes narrowed. 'Not to mention the subsequent attempts on my life.'

Tension crackled in the air.

'Well, you don't mince your words, do you, Lacey?' drawled Wheatley. 'I admire you for that. Therefore I will not mince mine. I did have a hand in helping that despicable worm Frederick to meet his Maker rather earlier than he anticipated. He was completely foxed and shouldn't have been riding in that state in any case. My man just ensured that his horse was a little friskier than he should have been.' He paused and gazed thoughtfully into the fire.

Richard fidgeted, waiting for Wheatley to give a reason.

At last the duke's eyes turned back to him. 'I hear you're assisting one of our agents, Mr Lacey… a Mr Cullen, I believe?'

Richard frowned. What did that have to do with anything? And how did Wheatley know?

'I see you're puzzled, Mr Lacey,' said Wheatley with a chuckle. 'I have fingers in many pies, and one of them is the War Office. It is through that work that I learned about Frederick Smythe's treachery.'

There was a gasp from Emma. Wheatley's eyes flickered, but he continued speaking.

'Yes, Frederick was discovered to be intimately connected with a certain establishment we've been keeping under observation. You may know it; it's run by a woman called Ruth Newbody.'

It was Richard's turn to gasp.

Wheatley smiled. 'Yes, we know about your visit there.' He waved a hand. 'Anyway, as I was saying, Frederick had to be disposed of. He was about to pass on a list of government agents to a French spy. If he hadn't been killed and the list retrieved, the war against Napoleon would go badly for us.'

Richard found his voice. 'But I still don't understand. Why the attacks on me? Why was Charles Smythe cut off from his family?'

'Ah yes. I must admit to having additional motives for ordering Frederick's "accident".' Wheatley sighed. 'It's something I'm not very proud of, but at least this meeting gives me the opportunity to clear my conscience.' He smirked. 'Despite rumours to the contrary, I do have one.' Wheatley took a deep, rasping breath. 'That cheat-gallows Frederick all but ruined Francis' life; in fact, the only good thing he did was to sire Francis. For that alone, I concede I owe him thanks.'

Wheatley was suddenly caught up in a fit of coughing. He pointed with a shaking hand to a half-filled glass on the side table. Richard moved quickly to place the pungent-smelling medication to Wheatley's mouth and helped him take a draught. The coughing subsided and Wheatley drew a deep breath 'Laudanum. My current doctor thinks it might help, but I'm not sure. It just makes me feel even more damned sleepy.' The words wheezed out of his chest, and it was plain that it was an effort for him to speak.

Richard glanced at Emma before speaking.

'I'll come back when you've rested, Wheatley.'

'I've told you. I want to say this now. There may not be time later.' Wheatley's eyes were closing as he spoke, his fingers gripping the arms of his chair. Richard resumed his seat and waited.

'Francis means a lot to me,' said Wheatley in a weaker tone. 'He's been a good friend. We met some years ago and I employed him as my secretary. He proved his worth over and over and I was impressed by his diligence, his attention to detail, and above all his integrity.'

After a few more laboured breaths, Wheatley continued. 'It's not often one meets with integrity. Not when you're a duke. But Francis wasn't afraid to let me know when he thought something wasn't right. I respected him for it, and we became friends. He confided in me, told me about his childhood, and how his mother struggled to bring him up without the support of a husband. Needless to say, I eventually prised out of him the name of his father.'

Wheatley took another sip of his tincture, and Richard's insides clenched with fear. Would the drug render Wheatley senseless before he finished his story?

'Where was I?' Wheatley said at last. 'Ah yes. I knew Frederick at Eton.' Wheatley snorted. 'He was some years older than me, but his reputation as a degenerate with pockets constantly to let was well known even then. Pestering the maidservants for favours, taking favours whether they were granted or not. Borrowing and never paying back. Apart from a few cronies, he was disliked and avoided by everyone. So yes, when Francis told me his father's name, I wasn't surprised. I knew Frederick was entirely capable of getting a gently born woman with child, denying it all, and leaving her to bear the consequences.' Wheatley cleared his throat. 'By this time, Francis and I were… how shall I put it? Somewhat closer than friends. I wanted to do something for him, do you understand? To make amends for the failings of his father. I know that when I die, I can't leave him much from my estate or there will be talk.' He shook his head. 'There will be talk.'

Richard flinched as Wheatley stretched out a claw-like hand and grasped his arm to emphasise his point. 'Do you understand what I'm saying, Lacey?'

Richard nodded. He understood all right. Francis would be prey to accusations of unnatural practices once Wheatley died and he was left unprotected. If Wheatley made the mistake of leaving him a substantial bequest from his unentailed estates, society would take it as proof that they had enjoyed an "unnatural" relationship. Francis' life in society would be untenable. The poor chap would be a pariah.

Wheatley continued, his voice getting weaker. 'As for the other brother, we had word at the War Office that he, too, might be involved in passing information to the French.'

There was an infuriated hiss from Emma, which Wheatley appeared not to hear, for he kept on speaking. 'Lord, what a fool that man was. Who in his right mind would take his family down to the wild Ottoman lands? All that was needed was to intercept his letters. Bedworth at the consulate in Patras was well paid for his services. It was from him that I heard they were killed by bandits. But that was a lie, I discovered. So too was the information about Charles Smythe being a traitor. Bedworth was a troublemaker who had an eye to some money that Smythe had left in his care. He expected Smythe and his family to perish on their expedition, and so it proved, but in the end, Charles Smythe was the author of his own misfortune.' Wheatley gave a humourless chuckle. 'Bedworth, however, will pay for his lies.'

Wheatley's head lolled back for a moment, and Richard thought it was all over, but the man was stronger than he thought.

'It was decided that exposing the scandal of Frederick's treachery would not work in our favour. It would alert the French to our knowledge of their spy ring. Besides, there was only the dowager viscountess left, and she was above suspicion. It only took a few words in the right ears to persuade the courts to declare them all dead before the seven years were up. I planned to buy the estate and gift it to Francis. It should have belonged to him in any case if Frederick had been an honourable man.'

Wheatley's words were becoming more slurred. It was difficult to stand by and listen to a dying man's last confession, but Richard desperately wanted Wheatley to complete it. Would a man lie if he thought he might soon meet his

Maker? Richard didn't think so. He glanced at Emma. Her face had drained of colour. He didn't wonder at it. Here was Wheatley telling of treachery and scandal, and it was all about her family. Richard's stomach lurched. It was his family too.

Wheatley's fingers clutched Richard's arm. 'I must also confess to arranging the attempts on your life, I'm afraid, Lacey.' Wheatley gave a lopsided grin. 'You rather upset my plans for Francis when you emerged as the heir. There were signs that my illness was returning, returning more rapidly than I'd anticipated, and I was getting desperate to sort matters out for him. I apologise most sincerely, although I don't presume your forgiveness.' Wheatley smiled wryly. 'I'm sure I would not be very forgiving if someone admitted to trying to do away with me. Although at this moment it might be a blessing.' He sighed deeply. 'You're a very patient man, Lacey. You've listened to my ramblings without interruption.'

'Wheatley, I wanted to understand, and now I do. For what it's worth, I'll forgive you for the attacks on myself, provided they cease.'

Wheatley nodded. 'Thank you. You have my word.' Wheatley closed his eyes for a moment, and Richard thought he'd fallen asleep, but then Wheatley stirred and spoke again.

'Let me tell you something, Lacey. Something astonishing. Francis told me that, against all odds, Charles Smythe's children survived and have returned home. Is that correct? What's more, he says they wish to make amends for Frederick's misdeeds and will acknowledge him as a member of the family. I fear that Francis might be spinning me a line so that my remaining days of suffering aren't plagued with worry for him.'

Richard smiled. 'It's true, Wheatley. Emma Smythe and her brother are safely returned. James is the viscount now. They were delighted to acknowledge Francis as a cousin. As am I. The dowager viscountess is keen to introduce Francis to society as her grandson. You can be assured that Francis has a family now, one that will love and support him.'

Wheatley closed his eyes and smiled. 'That is indeed good news.' There was silence for a moment, and Richard was on the point of leaving when Wheatley spoke. 'Miss Smythe, you may come out of the shadows now. You've heard my confession. I'm sorry I was unable to spare you the details of your uncle's treachery, but they will go no further. You have my word. There will be no taint of scandal for you or your brother. But I beg you, please don't allow your opinion of me to affect the way you treat Francis. There is nothing I want more than for Francis to be happy.'

Emma stood up and stepped nearer. 'You knew it was I? Why didn't you say?'

'No matter, Miss Smythe. Your presence here shall be kept secret. But tell me, please, I implore you. Will you be kind to Francis?' Wheatley's ducal arrogance had disappeared. He was just another human being, pleading for his friend… his lover.

Richard knew what her answer would be before she spoke.

'I promise, Your Grace,' she said, taking Wheatley's hand. 'Francis will never lack for family again. Thank you for your discretion; I can assure you that I, too, will be discreet.'

'You both must understand' – Wheatley's rapidly unfocussing eyes flicked wildly between Richard and Emma – 'Francis means the world to me. I wanted to make things right for him. God help me, I do love him. It was done for love of him.' Wheatley's eyes closed.

The sound of a sob broke the stunned silence, and Richard and Emma turned to see Francis silhouetted in the doorway where he'd been listening. Striding over to where Wheatley lay slumped, Francis knelt down and took the unconscious duke in his arms, sobbing uncontrollably.

'My darling Henry. Why? Why? Don't leave me now. Not yet. I can't live without you.'

Emma swiped at her eyes while Richard stood motionless, awkward and embarrassed at this display of raw emotion. It reminded him all too much of his own helplessness when faced with the death of loved ones. Taking refuge in practicalities, he felt for a pulse in Wheatley's wrist. There was a faint beat.

'Francis, he's still breathing. He hasn't gone. I think it's just the effect of the laudanum.'

Francis looked up. 'What? He's breathing? He's still alive? Oh God, please let him live.'

'Let me help you get him into bed,' said Richard, tugging Francis to his feet. 'He'll be more comfortable there. Do you want me to call for his doctor?'

Francis wiped his tear-stained face with his sleeve. 'Yes, help me to move him, please. The bedchamber is through there.' He pointed to the door through which he'd entered. 'He won't want the doctor again. I'll see to him, don't worry.'

The two men easily lifted Wheatley between them and carried him through to the bedchamber, with Emma following closely behind.

Once they'd placed Wheatley on the bed, Francis said, 'I'll manage now, Richard. Thank you too, Emma. I'll get him into his night things and see him settled.'

'Only if you're sure you'll be all right on your own. We can stay, and I'll tell Crawford and George to go home, if you prefer.' Richard felt uncomfortable making the offer, but compassion ensured he made it anyway.

Emma echoed his words. 'Richard and I are happy to stay with you for as long as you need us.'

Richard smiled at her. Trust his kind-hearted, generous Emma. How he loved her.

Francis glanced at the figure on the bed. Wheatley was now breathing faintly but steadily. 'No, you go home. I'll manage. Thank you for your help.' His red-rimmed eyes searched both their faces. 'Will you still really want to know me after all this? Will anyone? What will you tell everyone?' His mouth twisted, and he turned his head away.

Emma put her arms round Francis as Richard spoke for the two of them.

'We won't disclose anything about tonight, you can be sure about that. And of course we'll still want to see you; you're part of our family. Isn't that right, Emma?'

'Yes, you must believe that, Francis,' she said. 'Wheatley was just a little too zealous in his wish to look after you, but love can drive one to mad actions. I, of all people, understand that. It got me back home to England, after all.' She smiled and gave Francis a final squeeze before moving back to stand next to Richard.

Richard coughed. 'Francis, I just wanted to say also, about your relationship with Wheatley...'

Francis tensed as if expecting a blow.

'Y-yes?' he faltered.

'It's of no matter to us. We'll disclose nothing. Neither of us believes that your relationship with Wheatley should be a matter for the courts, despite what the law says. Look after your friend and come and see us when you're ready. And if you need any help in the meantime, let me know.' Richard gripped Francis' hand. 'Do you understand that, Francis? We'll always be here for you.'

A tear ran down Francis' cheek.

'Thank you, my friends.'

Chapter 23

Recalling that they were supposed to be passing for brothers, Richard relinquished Emma's hand as they retraced their steps back through the library, down the corridor, and across the landing. Richard tried several doors before he found the drawing room where his friends were ensconced.

Crawford was lounging in an armchair, his leg propped up on a footstool, while George, with head bent and hands clasped behind his back, paced up and down. George's head spun round at the sound of the door.

'How did it go? Don't say he's issued a challenge? I'll be your second, of course.'

Emma giggled as Richard shook his head and grinned.

'Calm down, George. No challenge has been issued. If you're up to moving, Crawford, we'll be on our way. I'll tell you everything once we're in the coach.'

Crawford nodded and eased himself out of his seat. A look of relief spread over George's face.

'Thank God. Julia would've had my guts for garters if we'd got involved in a duel.'

'She wouldn't be very happy with me either,' quipped Richard, thanking the heavens that it had not come to that. The four of them returned downstairs, Emma, seemingly lost in her own thoughts, trailing behind. Richard decided that the true import of Wheatley's words were only just beginning to register with her, and of course, there had been the high emotion of her cousin's despair.

Once they were all back in the coach, Emma remained silent, leaving it to Richard to explain to the two men what had transpired. He omitted the details of the relationship between Wheatley and Francis and skirted around the subject of Frederick's treachery. That was for him and Emma alone. All the same, he suspected that Crawford understood how things stood between Wheatley and Francis. Richard explained to George that Wheatley had acted purely out of compassion at the injustice done to Francis and his mother.

'Damned rum do though, ain't it? What are you going to do now, Richard?' asked George.

George's question at last roused Emma from her introspection.

'Apart from telling my grandmother that there is no longer a threat, we shall do absolutely nothing.'

'Oh!' George shrugged, then smiled, evidently relieved at the prospect of returning to a quiet life.

Richard agreed with Emma. It was pointless to take matters further; all sorts of unsavoury secrets concerning Frederick and his dealings with French spies might come out. Wheatley had confessed and begged forgiveness, and he was possibly near death. By pure good fortune, neither he nor Jamie had been seriously harmed, and Emma's parents' deaths had been a tragic accident, nothing more. Richard didn't want to think about the punishment Wheatley had planned for Bedworth. Doing and saying nothing was the wisest course. Richard hoped the dowager would agree.

After first taking Crawford back to the Albany, the coach arrived in front of the Bedford Square townhouse. They were greeted by Grimes, who cast only a cursory glance at Emma's appearance before informing them that Mrs Morton had retired to bed.

George turned to Richard and Emma.

'I'll leave you to it. I must go and see Julia. I'll wager she is tired out. All the excitement of shopping can't be good for her in her condition.' He ran a hand through his hair. 'I'm considering taking her back to Cornwall if she's up to the journey.' George waved to them as he sprinted up the stairs. 'See you in the morning.'

Richard chuckled. 'Well, good luck with that, George.' He couldn't see his sister submitting to being cloistered in the country, not when the Season was on. He'd wager that George's plans to remove to Cornwall would soon be abandoned.

Richard led Emma into the small drawing room. He'd decided they both needed a drink before retiring. If Emma's nerves weren't stretched, his certainly were.

Emma flopped down on the sofa in front of the fire while Richard made for the decanter. He poured two drinks and came back to sit beside her. She was gazing into the flames as they licked and curled around the coals.

Leaning back, he stretched his legs out in front of him, feeling the tension of the previous hours leave his body. Had he really been that person who'd confronted a duke with an accusation of murder? It seemed he was turning into a different person.

Emma shifted slightly. Her legs, encased in breeches, brushed against his thigh, causing his pulse to quicken. It was all due to her, he thought. He'd led an uneventful, steady life until she'd arrived. Now he could do anything – travel, have adventures. If only he could be sure she would remain in his life. He'd climb mountains, tackle dukes, fight Napoleon himself if it meant Emma stayed with him.

Richard smiled to himself. How cosy this was, the two of them together, sharing the fireside. It reminded him of their first evening together at Easterby Hall.

Emma, too, was again lost in her thoughts. She'd been tossing and turning in her mind all the things that Wheatley had told them. To think her uncle had been a traitor! Thank goodness Wheatley had given his word to keep it a secret. Her grandmother must never know.

Emma sighed. At least he'd confirmed that her parents' death had been an accident. She was still sad, especially at the loss of her mother. But thanks to her grandmother, she now also knew that her parents had loved one another. It had been her mother's choice to accompany her husband on his travels.

Emma decided she would tell Jamie the truth of their parents' death on the morrow. It would not bring them back, but it should ease the pain of thinking that they'd been murdered. Emma smiled at the thought of Jamie, who was now back to his normal, boisterous self. He'd thrown himself into learning all about horses, spending all his time lurking about the stables and trying to help the grooms, but more often, she suspected, getting in their way. He also got on well with Richard, treating him as he would a respected elder brother.

She glanced at Richard next to her on the sofa. What was she going to do about him? She knew in her heart that she had come to a decision. All her doubts had been wiped away by what had taken place that evening. He only needed to ask again, and she would give him her final answer.

Richard let out a deep sigh. A sigh of contentment.

'Penny for them.'

He turned to see the warmth in Emma's eyes. He'd been miles away, wool-gathering.

'I was thinking of the first night you and I spent together talking after dinner. You remember, don't you? At Easterby Hall.'

'Yes, I remember,' she whispered, her cheeks turning pink.

'I was also wondering if we'd enjoy more evenings like this.' Richard's pulse quickened as he heard her quick intake of breath. Was now the right time to ask his question again? Was it unfair of him to press for an answer when she was probably tired and her mind occupied with dealing with Wheatley's revelations? Emma's reply took him by surprise.

'I was wondering that too.' She took a sip from her glass, and he watched as her tongue flicked out to lick her lips. Such pretty lips. 'I've never felt about anyone the way I feel about you,' she said, her eyelashes fluttering.

Richard's heart thundered in his ears. Had he heard her right?

He set his glass down with a shaking hand and turned towards her. 'Do you mean if I ask you to marry me again you'll not refuse me, Emma, my love?' He held his breath.

A smile played about Emma's mouth. 'I'll not refuse you, Richard.'

He knelt in front of her and took both her hands in his. Her pulse was racing. She smiled at him, her eyes sparkling.

'Darling Emma, would you do me the greatest honour and consent to be my wife? I can't conceive of a life without you, my love. Please make my life complete and say yes.'

At last, Richard heard the words he'd been praying to hear.

'Yes, Richard. I'd be happy and honoured to be your wife.'

He kissed her hands, then stood, pulling Emma up with him and wrapping his arms around her. She gazed up at him, lips slightly parted. He couldn't resist. His mouth swooped down on hers, and for several moments they were lost in a whirlwind of sensation.

Several long minutes later and they were seated again, this time Emma curled next to him, his arm about her shoulder, keeping her close. Soon they would be able to spend every night like this, he told himself, as he rested his head against hers. Emma stifled a yawn, and he started to yawn too. Fatigue was creeping up on both of them, but he didn't want this enchanted part of the evening to end.

'Who would have thought that actions committed by Uncle Frederick so many years ago would have such long-reaching and devastating effects?' Emma's sleepy voice broke the silence. 'Wheatley, so desperately ill. Despite all his money and possessions, it cannot buy him what he wants. And what he tried to do, trying to get rid of you too, he did it all for love of Francis. Love had deranged him.'

'Yes, indeed,' answered Richard, rubbing his eyes. 'Not to be able to declare one's love openly. To be forced to keep it a secret. And concern for what his death would mean for Francis. Well, I think Wheatley was temporarily out of his wits.'

'Love can force us to do all sorts of things. It was my love for Jamie that kept me going when things were at their worst. You've no idea how often I was on the brink of giving up.'

Richard pulled her closer and tipped her chin gently with his finger so that they were gazing into each other's eyes. 'I'm so glad you didn't, my love. But you've got me now. We'll weather life's joys and trials together. Together we'll be strong.'

'Yes we will,' she agreed, then a shadow crossed her face. 'I feel sorry for Wheatley and Francis. They share a love I'd wager is as deep as ours, but they're having to risk their lives because of it. It all seems so unfair.'

'Society is very hard on people who do not fit the pattern card of respectability. Perhaps someday things will change.'

'Anyway, I shall tell Grandmamma that the matter has been resolved without giving away too many of the facts. I certainly won't be disclosing that Frederick was a traitor. Grandmamma has suffered enough scandal in the family without introducing any more. With luck, she'll be so excited about being able to introduce Jamie and me back into society that she won't pry any further.' Emma suddenly pulled away from Richard's arms.

It struck him for one awful moment that she'd changed her mind again about marriage.

'Oh goodness! When I tell her that we are to marry, there'll be such a to-do.' Emma turned a panic-stricken face towards him. 'I'm not sure I can deal with all the fuss that will entail. Shopping for clothes last week was trying enough.'

Richard looked at her in astonishment. Was this the woman who'd trekked across the continent accompanied only by her young brother, visited a brothel in disguise, and just this evening been present when a duke was accused of murder? And she was balking at shopping for clothes? Richard burst out laughing.

'What's so amusing?' she said, eyes flashing. 'You've no idea how tiresome it is, standing still for hours, being poked, prodded, and measured.' She dug Richard in the ribs before bursting into laughter herself.

Chapter 24

One afternoon, some weeks later, a visitor was announced at the Lacey townhouse. Francis, for it was he, was shown into the family drawing room, where the newlywed couple (they'd been married for all of a week) were planning a trip. Maps were spread around on tables, chairs, and even the floor.

'I'm sorry. I didn't mean to disturb you,' said Francis, hesitating at the door. 'Your butler showed me in. I see he was mistaken.' He turned as if to go.

Richard leapt to his feet.

'Stay, Francis. We don't stand on ceremony with family. You should know that.'

'Come in, Francis. I'll ring for tea,' added Emma, stepping gingerly over the map-strewn floor to pull the bell for the maid.

'If you're absolutely sure? I can't stay for long, though, so don't worry about tea.'

'Of course we're sure, old man,' grinned Richard. 'Come in and sit down. Rescue me from my wife. I think she wants to travel everywhere. You'd think after her experiences she'd have had enough of travelling.' He ducked as a cushion, thrown by his wife, caught him on the shoulder.

'I may have done some travelling, but that was in Europe and in most uncomfortable circumstances,' Emma said, laughing. 'I want to see something of my own country, and, besides, your travelling coach is very well appointed, so I don't think it will be too arduous.' Emma cleared the sofa of maps so that Francis could sit down. 'I'd like to visit the Lakes, and I also want to see Cornwall. That's not too much to ask, is it, Francis?'

Francis held up his hands in laughing submission. 'Don't embroil me in your domestic arguments, I beg you.'

Richard sent a loving glance to his wife. 'Francis, you see before you a man who, it seems, will have to resign himself to travelling for quite some time.'

'Well, how are you, Francis? You're looking well,' said Emma approvingly.

Francis did look well. His face had lost the strained look, and the grey shadows under his eyes had disappeared.

'I'm very well, thank you, Emma.' Francis toyed with the cuff of his jacket. 'I've just come to let you know that I, too, will be leaving town shortly.'

Emma became all concern. 'Oh, what is the matter? Is it the duke? Has his health deteriorated?'

'No, in fact he is feeling much better, thank you. His Grace has decided that we will be removing to his estate in Warwickshire... London air seems to disagree with him.' Francis paused, his head bowed as a flush of colour rose up his neck. 'He, er, has asked me to convey his good wishes to you both and to thank you again most sincerely for your discretion and, er, for your understanding.' Francis looked up. 'And I thank you from the bottom of my heart too.'

Emma took his hand and gave it a squeeze.

Francis continued to speak, his fingers thrumming on his knees.

'Wheatley has also asked me to impress upon you most strongly that you're welcome at any of his houses whenever you wish. And if ever you should require his help or support, he'll be more than happy to oblige. His Grace begs your understanding at his not coming in person; he is still easily fatigued. He is looking forward to greeting you in person at the earliest opportunity.'

Richard spoke for them both.

'Please convey our sincere thanks to Wheatley for such a generous offer. We do what we do out of regard and love for you, Francis. You're part of our family now, and if the person you love happens to be Wheatley, we'll regard him as a friend also. Though we do understand that, as a duke, he may not wish to condescend too much.'

Francis smiled and swiped at his eye with the back of his hand.

'You don't know what your words mean to me,' he said at last. 'I thank you from the bottom of my heart.' His hands clenched in his lap. 'If you had any idea what it is to live in fear. Society is very cruel to people like Wheatley and me.'

'Shh, don't overset yourself,' Emma said, patting his shoulder. 'Perhaps someday society will change. Maybe not tomorrow, but someday. We can only hope.'

Francis bit his lip, and then, looking up, he sent her a lopsided grin.

'My apologies for getting emotional.' He cleared his throat. 'Well, I need to be off. I've promised to call on Grandmamma.

I'm quaking at the thought of telling her that I'll be leaving town. I think she had lots of plans for me.'

Emma chuckled. 'With luck, she'll be too preoccupied with plans for Jamie. He's going to stay with her while Richard and I are away. She'll need eyes in the back of her head.'

On cue, the drawing-room door swung open, and a small whirlwind burst in.

'Did I hear someone mention my name?' said Jamie. His eyes lit up at the sight of his cousin. 'Oh, it's you, Francis. Have you come to take me for a spin in your curricle as you promised? I'll just get my things.'

Without waiting for a reply, Jamie raced back out again.

Richard slapped Francis on the back and chuckled. 'Sorry about that, Francis. It's one of the penalties of being part of this family.'

The End

About the Author

PENNY HAMPSON WRITES MYSTERIES, and because she has a passion for history, you'll find her stories also reflect that. *A Gentleman's Promise*, a traditional Regency romance, was Penny's debut novel, which was shortly followed by more in the same genre. Penny also enjoys writing contemporary mysteries with a hint of the paranormal, because where do ghosts come from but the past? *The Unquiet Spirit*, a spooky mystery/romance set in Cornwall, was published by Darkstroke in 2020.

Penny lives with her family in Oxfordshire, and when she is not writing, she enjoys reading, walking, swimming, and the odd gin and tonic (not all at the same time).

For more on Penny's writing, visit her blog: https://pennyhampson.co.uk/blog/

Twitter: https://twitter.com/penny_hampson

Facebook: www.facebook.com/pennyhampsonauthor

If you have enjoyed this book, it would be great if you left a review on Amazon or Goodreads.

If you have enjoyed this book, please leave a review on Amazon or Goodreads.

Also by Penny Hampson:
The Gentlemen Series

(Regency Historical Mystery/Romances)

An Officer's Vow

A Bachelor's Pledge

The Unquiet Spirit

(A Contemporary Spooky Mystery/Romance)

Printed in Great Britain
by Amazon

83640395R00185